THE AMERICAN BOYS
Capone's Hitmen

"If history were taught in the form of stories, it would never be forgotten."
~ Rudyard Kipling

A Novel

by

Kevin Corley

HISTORICAL NOVELS BY KEVIN CORLEY

SIXTEEN TONS

THROW OUT THE WATER

SUNDOWN TOWN

13 STEPS FOR CHARLIE BIRGER

BOOTLEGGER HEAVEN: THE SHELTON GANG STORY

Also, one science fiction book he wrote for his grandchildren: *THE BEGOTTEN*

Also, special thanks to the following historians without whose research this book would not have been possible:

Helmer, William J. & Blick Arthur J. *The St. Valentine's Day Massacre*, Cumberland House.

Helmer, William J. *Al Capone and His American Boys*, Indiana University Press, 2011.

Waugh, Daniel *Egan Rats* Cumberland House, 2007.

Waugh, Daniel *Gangs of St. Louis*, History Press, 2010.

Angle, Paul M., *Bloody Williamson: A Chapter in American Lawlessness*, Prairie State Books, 1959.

Pensoneau, Taylor. *Brothers Notorious*, Downstate Publications, 1998.

Pensoneau, Taylor. *Dapper and Deadly: The True Story of Black Charlie Harris*, Downstate Publications, 2010.

AUTHOR'S NOTE

My goal in writing historical novels is to take the facts from history and weave them into a compelling story that will leave the reader wanting to know more about those characters and events.

To help the reader separate facts from fiction, I placed a few dates within the story and included a chronology of those actual events at the end of the book.

Whenever possible, I used the actual words said based on primary and secondary history records. Although fact-based, much of the presented personalities includes my perceptions of who these people likely were. Therefore, even the historical figures are still largely fictionalized characters.

Some readers may be surprised to learn that a few, such as Ma Barker, were not the flamboyant characters the media has falsely portrayed them to be. Also, some incidents, such as the Kansas City Massacre, did not go down as the media and FBI claimed.

THE AMERICAN BOYS
Capone's Hitmen

A Novel

by

Kevin Corley

MAJOR CHARACTERS

THE AMERICAN BOYS
Gus Winkler (born August Henry Winkeler)
Fred "Killer" Burke (born Thomas Camp)
Bob "Gimpy" Carey
Ray "Crane Neck" Nugent
Bryan Bolton
George Goetz - Fred Samuel Goetz,
        aka "Shotgun" George Ziegler

THE EGAN RATS
Dinty Colbeck – boss

THE PURPLE GANG
(Jewish hoodlums)
Abe Bernstein

THE CAPONE GANG
Alphonso "Scarface" Capone
Ralph "Bottles" Capone
Jack McGurn (born Vincenzo Antonio Gibaldi)
Verne Miller
"Tough" Tony Capezio
Claude "Screwy" Maddox
Tony Accardo
Jake "Greasy Thumb" Guzik
Frank Rio

THE MORAN GANG
(mostly Irish and German)
Joe Aiello
George "Bugs" Moran
Dean O'Banion
Hymie Weiss

**ST. VALENTINE'S DAY MASSACRE
VICTIMS**
Frank Gusenberg
Pete Gusenberg
Albert Weinshank
Adam Heyer
James Clark (born Albert Kachellek)
John May (Mechanic)
Reinhart Schwimmer (gang wanna be)

BARKER KARPIS GANG
Alvin "Creepy" Karpis - (born Albin Francis Karpavičius)
Fred Barker - Frederick George Barker
Dock Barker - Arthur Raymond "Doc" Barker
Verne Miller - Vernon C. Miller
Russell "Slim Gray" Gibson

GANGSTER WIVES AND MOLLS
Georgette – Gus Winkler, wife (maiden name Bence)
Irene – George Goetz, wife
Julia – Ray Nugent, wife
Rose – Bob Carey, girlfriend
Viola – Fred Burke, girlfriend
Bonnie – Fred Burke, wife
Vivian "Vi" Mathis - Verne Miller's girlfriend
Kate "Ma" Barker (born Arizona Donnie Clark), mother

Georgette Winkler never cared for the behavior of her husband's friends in the hours before they went out to kidnap, rob, or kill someone. Neither did her cat, Omerta, who leaped onto the Davenport and into Georgette's lap the moment the smell of alcohol and cigar smoke filled the apartment.

Omerta was more nervous than usual, burying her head so deeply between Georgette's thighs even her ears were hidden. Georgette considered the feline's behavior might have something to do with the fact that when her husband, Gus, and his friend, Fred Burke, entered the room, they were dressed in police uniforms.

Just the month before, a dozen blue-uniformed men had knocked the outside door off its hinges and swooped about the apartment breaking lamps and slicing open furniture with carpet cutters. The officers even cut open Omerta's fluffy bed cushion, as well as her toys. Finding nothing, they left as abruptly as they arrived.

Al Capone himself hand-delivered Omerta to Georgette six months before as a housewarming gift when the Winklers moved to Cicero, Illinois. "I hope you will do me the honor of allowing me to christen this little kitty," the man with the two long scars on the left side of his face whispered in her ear as he greeted Georgette. "Her name signifies the code of silence and loyalty within our organization."

The cat's name stuck and so too the chilling warning.

Now the uniformed Gus and Fred, each carrying a Thompson machine gun and shotgun, took seats on opposite ends of the dining table. Cigars in mouth, they disassembled and cleaned the weapons. A third man in the room, Bob Carey, limped toward the Davenport and flopped next to Georgette. He was dressed for the ladies in a dark suit jacket with matching vest and trousers, and a black fedora with a white silk band matching his tie. "Hey, pretty lady," the hoodlum said quietly, "Why don't you let me pet your pussy?"

"Stay away, Gimpy!" Georgette hissed. She rose so quickly Omerta also added a hiss, her claws flailing so wildly they couldn't get a grip on her mistress's skirt.

Beauty was not always a blessing when dealing with underworld types. Fortunately, Georgette had a powerful relationship with her husband even after nearly ten years together. She went directly to her sewing machine in the corner of the room while the feline escaped to the safety of the master bedroom.

"Take off that coat," she ordered her husband. "It still has a bullet hole in it. I got the blood out but didn't do anything about the hole."

Remaining seated, Gus removed the coat and tossed it over to his wife. He wasn't shocked by Bob the Gimp flaunting his crude sexual deviance right in front of him. A pervert in every sense, the man could not help himself. The gangsters tolerated his behavior because his gunplay made him handy to have around in a scrape. Still, they kept him in place by belittling him with the demeaning nickname, a constant reminder of Gimpy's leg wound from the Great War.

"Want me to shoot Gimpy for ya, Gus?" Fred Burke snapped a fifty-round ammo drum onto his Thompson machine gun. "He appears to be gettin' a mite fresh with your lady."

Fred's eyes were the color of coffee. His mustache was grown long before every illegal operation and then cut shorter afterward, short that is, so long as it was thick enough to help hide his hairlip and distract from his two missing front teeth.

"Nah, not today." Gus snapped a twenty-round box clip onto the gat. "But tomorrow, we might take him to the gun range with us. He'd make a mighty good target, I'd 'spect." He tossed the big weapon onto the Davenport next to Bob. Reaching down to the floor, Gus brought up a twelve-gauge pump-action shotgun and began working on it.

"I prefer a shotgun, Gus. You know that." Bob pushed the gat aside. "I like to see 'em bounce."

Finished with her sewing, Georgette stood and held the jacket up for a final inspection. Unlike Omerta, she was accustomed to her husband wearing a dick's uniform. He donned them often when he and his downstate gang did a job for Capone.

"Why can't Scarface have his Italian mafioso do his dirty work?" Georgette asked. She tossed the garment to her husband. "Why does he have to use you American boys?"

"Because," Gus said.

"Because ain't sufficient reason." Georgette put her hands on her hips.

"Because we American boys, as you call us, are virtually unknown to not only the cops but also to most other gangsters in Chicago."

Gus stood and slipped his arms into the jacket. Seeing his wife somewhat distressed, he pulled a nightstick from his belt, twirled it, then walked like a penguin in his best impression of a Keystone Kop. Georgette let life's problems drive her to the brink of desperation, a melancholy that brought about a constant weariness in her eyes. He'd learned long ago that humor was the best medicine for her.

Whooping, Fred leaped to his feet, pulled his own nightstick, and mimicking Gus, followed him around the room. When he passed Bob, he gave the thug a hard knock on the top of his head. Not to be outdone, Bob rolled off the Davenport into his best impression of a Chaplain-like criminal. With short steps, he raced from room to room to escape the clumsy Keystone Kops. Georgette laughed, as Gus knew she would, then sighed, as Gus knew she would.

Georgette walked into the bedroom to be with Omerta. Cuddled with her cat and worrying if the next time she saw Gus would be in a morgue was not the way she had anticipated spending St. Valentine's Day, 1929. She wished her husband was spending more of the romantic day talking about her and less about killing Bugs Moran.

Valentine's Day, 1920, was the most romantic day of Georgette Bence's life. It was the day Gus proposed to her. Never mind that he was still married to his first wife, a fact she later discovered.

When Gus knelt in front of her and produced a ring box, Georgette forgot to breathe. Gus was squirming around as if nervous, or maybe the back of his leg was cramping. Either way, she was going to need a minute.

She had only met him the month before and in a less than auspicious way. That fateful day she had answered a knock on the door to the boarding house she owned in downtown St. Louis.

"I'm here to see Isadore," Gus boldly announced.

"Well, aren't you dressed to the nines?" Georgette ran her eyes over his camel-haired coat and high-rise cuffed trousers.

"Yes, ma'am." Gus tipped his bowler hat. "And you cut a fine figure yourself, but this evening I'm here to see Isadore."

"I heard ya the first time. If I wanted an echo I'd be livin' in a cave."

"May I come in?"

"Oh, Gussie!" Isadore came running but stopping just short of embracing him, gave a slight curtsy. "Thank you, Georgette. I'll take it from here."

Isadore considered herself a flapper. She dressed as such, including the bust bodice that held her ample bosom tight against her chest, achieving a boyish look. Her straight, sleeveless, and low-cut dress was scandalously knee-length. Bobbed, chin-length hair and heavy cosmetics provided a bold, go-to-hell-if-you-don't-like-it appearance. The fact that Isadore was a prostitute didn't much bother Georgette. If not for the fortune of inheriting the boarding house, she might have been forced to walk the streets herself.

Isadore, though, liked to practice the art of lovemaking assiduously, much to the discomfort of everyone else in the house who was within hearing range. The truth behind the young whore's screams of delight was that they helped to bring the business to a speedy completion. Plus, it gave her customers a false sense of pride in their masculinity.

Isadore led Gus straight into the kitchen, opened the icebox, rummaged through the many items, and extracted a quart container. "Why don't me and you go lookin' for the bottom of this here jug of tanglefoot whiskey?"

"I do hope it's peach flavored." Gus's voice was a little high, almost boyish.

Liquor in one hand and her beaux in the other, Isadore left the icebox door wide open and led Gus quickly up the steps to her room.

Georgette liked all the jars' labels pointed forward and was more annoyed with Isadore for putting them back wrong than she was at her leaving the icebox door open. When the kitchen was to her satisfaction, Georgette returned to her guests in the parlor. Two tables had friendly games of mixed couple pinochle, the men in shirt sleeves and suspenders. Unlike Isadore and similar to their hostess, the ladies wore thick cotton stockings and union suits beneath dresses with long sleeves and high necklines befitting the January weather.

Seeing one of these customers pull a fur up over her shoulders, Georgette moved to the pot-bellied stove in a corner of the room. Using a poker, she pulled open the cast iron door, stirred the coals until she had a blue flame, and adjusted the damper and vents.

The three men standing near a table cluttered with liquor bottles had become silent when she approached the stove. The way they were huddled led Georgette to believe they were up to no good, probably planning an illegal activity. Activities she would abide, so long as they didn't bring trouble to her boarding house. Since the first day of prohibition, called "June thirsty first," fortunes were being made by moonshiners and bootleggers. These men were most likely looking to cash in on opportunities that came from the ridiculous legislation.

Georgette often told others, "Ever time the government tries to legislate morality, it opens the doors to even worse immorality." She herself had become quite adept at manufacturing and selling her own version of bathtub gin mixed with just a hint of her specially formulated rose water.

Noting her guests were comfortable, Georgette returned to the rocking chair and the crocheting she'd been enjoying before the arrival of Gus Winkler. Her fingers danced the needles and yarn in and out of various loops of the Dutchess lace stitch as the pink and white afghan grew.

Winkler seemed to be a strange character. Too handsome to be so shy, stuttering, and hee-hawing like a grade schoolboy, yet tall and powerful looking, qualities that should make him a leader of men. She surmised that his obvious shyness made him one who would follow those men with lesser abilities in pursuit of ill-begotten gains.

The next hour passed comfortably, as it usually did in her boarding house, for she would have it no other way. Then a shrill scream from upstairs brought instant quiet to the customers. It was not

the scream of fake lust that Isadore so often mim-
icked. All eyes looked toward the ceiling. Occasional pandemonium was not uncommon in the
Bence boarding house where men, alcohol, and
sex often coalesced to bring about unwanted behavior. Behavior that Georgette quickly nipped in
the bud with hurricane force.

A second scream sent Georgette running up
the steps, the men close behind. "Oh, God," she
shouted. "Screams like that usually mean someone is dead. I fear it."

The first thing she saw when she entered Isadore's room was Augustus Winkler passed out
drunk in the big portable bathtub in the center of
the room, his long legs bent knees upwards, pre-
venting his head from sinking below the water
line, which was suspiciously blue.

Isadore lay unconscious in the bed wearing
only a half-open uncorseted tea gown, her ample
snowy white breasts bare, nipples pointing toward
the ceiling.

"Hot dog, boys," one of the men shouted.
"How'd you like to be gatherin' eggs and find that
in the nest?"

Unexpectedly, Gus rolled sideways in the tub,
his head turning facedown into the blue liquid.
Georgette walked behind him, grabbed hunks of
hair with both hands, and pulled him half out of

the water until his weight nearly toppled the legs of the lion-clawed tub. His faded trouser legs were still in the water and his flat stomach was on the rim. She turned his head and forearms to kick-stand the entire washtub.

"Them cheap britches are what turned that water blue." Recognizing she still had a tight grip on Gus's hair, she let go, his forehead making a loud thump onto the wooden floor.

"I'll tote him for you, Miss Georgette," one of the men said.

"No need to be gentle with him, boys. Make sure to drag him downstairs by the feet so his head gets to meet every step. Then throw him and his clothes in the alley." As an afterthought, Georgette added. "But don't let that tub overturn or we'll have that blue-dyed water leakin' through the ceilin' onto your card game downstairs."

***

A few days later, Georgette again opened the front door to find Gus Winkler, now dressed in a spanking brown suit and holding a bouquet, standing there.

"Well, if it ain't the intrusion of the beast again." She put her hands on her hips. "What you wantin' this time? To see Isadore? Or to wash your britches in our washtub? If it's the latter, I'd appreciate it if you'd clean the ring when you're through. Last time it took us near an hour, and we used Bon Ami."

"I'm sure sorry about that, Georgette." With a desperate look in his eye and a quaver in his voice, Gus put his right hand deep in his pocket. He carried the same Indianhead nickel in that pocket every day. It had a buffalo on the back side. No matter how hungry he got, he refused to spend it because if he spent it, it would mean he was broke. Often, when he was nervous or upset, he would put his hand in his pocket and roll that nickel around between his fingers. He was furiously rolling it around now as he stared down at Georgette's slippers.

"Never apologize," Georgette advised. She looked down at her feet. *What is he looking at down there?* "We can't change what was, only what is to be."

"Actually, Georgette, I like your gumption, and you've got brains enough to go with your beauty. I'm here to see you, Georgette, if you don't mind, Georgette."

She blushed, so unexpected was the compliment. "Well, you're sure in a hurry to wear my name out." She sized him up by looking up and down his frame as he rocked his weight from one leg to the next. "You fixin' to dance a jig or state your business?"

For a moment, he couldn't speak. The hard had seized his throat again, so he forced his eyes to look at hers. There was kindness and beauty behind them. Eventually, his voice returned but it came low and gravelly. "I'm just a little nervous, I'd 'spect."

"Well, you should be. I've heard more complaints about you than I have about the weather."

"Sin is just a failure to choose goodness." Gus let his eyes drop to her slippers again. "You figure I'll be going to Hell, do ya?"

"I don't know, but if I was you, I'd be doing something holy before you wind up on the wrong side of the grass." Georgette studied her unexpected suitor. "Isadore sure surrounds herself with fine-looking men. Hell, her mechanic has to have dimples just to fill her gas tank. What am I sayin'? We stand here much longer, we'll turn into a vaudeville act."

Gus wasn't like the other gents who came calling. His chest was swelling and heaving like a storm-tossed sea. Finally, she shook her head and stepped aside. "Well, come on in, I suppose. It never fails. Soon as you get life figured out, something different happens."

***

For three weeks, Gus courted Georgette. He wasn't sure why. Her eyes fixed on him as hopefully each time he left as when he returned. Both circumstances always brought him a pang of heavy guilt. He'd never been the settling-down type. Each time he went away, he was determined to stop thinking about the feisty beauty, believing the feeling would pass with time. After all, there were plenty of steady men who could love her better, if not as much.

A few times he almost swayed. The opportunities were always there, tempting opportunities with ladies of every type. On those occasions, his instrument failed. The first time it happened, the whore he'd paid five dollars to demanded an extra five to maintain her silence concerning his ineptness. On the next two attempts with ladies of the evening, he checked how his manhood was doing before extracting it. Finding there was still a lack of interest, he found excuses to make a quick exit.

The perplexing thing was, there was never a lack of blood flow when copulating with Georgette. And her enthusiasm for him seemed equal to his for her. They could flail around the bedroom or even the front seat of his flivver with only brief intermissions between joinings. And their conversation was just as titillating. She was a giant compared to other women when it came to discussing business, politics, or even the weather.

Georgette was also perplexed. She was neither content nor bitterly discontent. She felt an aching sadness when she thought about Gus. He seemed to need her as much as she needed him. She felt guilty about falling in love with him, hopeless about it, but it was true. She wanted someone to say that everything was all right, that she could fix this. But no one could possibly know how she truly felt about Gus. Even if she could somehow explain it to another, she was certain they would just tell her to forget about him and move on.

Now, sitting in the parlor three weeks after they met, Augustus Winkler kneeling before her, Georgette was once again reflecting on matters of life. Theirs had been a whirlwind courtship. Sleigh rides along the riverfront drive and dinners at fine restaurants on The Hill. Where Gus got his money, Georgette didn't know. He'd shared with her how he'd lied about his age to get into the war and how he'd been an ambulance driver in France. She learned from a friend he'd only recently been released from a workhouse, an indication that he might have been involved in some shady dealings, though even vagrancy was currently a reason for six weeks in the work camp.

Now, with him kneeling before her, she pondered how much she really knew about Gus Winkler. "For near on a month, you've showed me the best sides of you, Gussie," Georgette finally said. "Before I say, 'I do', I want to see the worst side of ya. Will you do that?"

His face sagged. Gus rose slowly from his now sore knee and fell back into the loveseat next to her. "I fear you won't marry me if I show you the seedier side of my life."

"Well," Georgette answered directly. "I guarantee that if I say 'I do' now, I won't hesitate to say 'I'm done' if in a few weeks that seedy side shows up and don't suit me."

"Folks generally live the life they've been educated to live." Gus rolled the ring case around in the palms of his hands. "All I've known so far is ambulance-drivin' in the war. I've seen so much blood and death, I fear I've become immune. I got sent to the workhouse for vagrancy. There, I learned from the best how to plan a break-in, stage a getaway with multiple options, and then change identities so as not to get caught."

"You ain't too stupid to learn a straight life, are ya?" Georgette removed the ring case from his hands and put it on the side table. "I've not had the best influences myself. But we're both young. Can't we both learn a new and better way of livin'?"

"Yes, but 'til then we got to eat, don't we?" When Georgette didn't answer, Gus asked, "So, how exactly do I go about introducing you to the scoundrel in me?"

"I haven't met a one of your friends," Georgette said, despite knowing her best bet was to run. Her whole life, she'd relied on smarts. Now she had mislaid her smarts. Against her better judgment, she decided to give him a fair chance. "Take me to wherever you go when you hang out with them."

***

Later that night, after parking his flivver, Gus, hand-in-hand with Georgette, walked two blocks to a speakeasy called Jerry's Place. Her heart rate increased when they came to a decrepit building with no lights coming from any of the windows and started down a narrow stairwell beneath a pulldown fire escape. Gus gave the door a double, then a triple, tap with his knuckles. A small window slid open near the top of the door, and the sound of music playing came out of it.

"Gus Winkler and friend," Gus said quietly.

Georgette wasn't prepared for what she saw when they walked down another narrow, low-ceilinged stairwell into the establishment. Not because it wasn't the dirty place she had expected, but because it was hopping with movement and excitement. Loud music blared from a Negro band playing dance music. The man at the piano was the major attraction, his left hand leaping great distances along the keyboard, playing a four-beat pulse she'd never before heard.

Having a little training in classical piano, Georgette was mesmerized by the unique sound. Both the hands and feet of those dancing were synchronized to the swift rhythm.

"That's my friend Willie the Lion on the piano," Gus shouted to be heard above the music. "I met him in France during the war. I'll introduce you later."

Grasping her hand a little tighter, he led her in a zigzag pattern across the dance floor. They neared a vacant table and, as Gus was helping Georgette remove her cloak, Isadore Londe rushed toward them. With hands on hips, she shouted something that was drowned out by the gaiety in the room.

Just then, the band finished its set and, following a moment of applause, Willie the Lion announced a ten-minute break.

"I thought we were friends," Isadore hissed. "Why you stealin' one of my men?"

"If I wanted a friend like you—" Georgette met her angry gaze with her own. "I'd buy a dog."

"You callin' me a bitch?"

"I'm not fer sure, but I'll bet your mother had a loud bark."

"What cha mean by that?"

"No offense. That's just the way of talkin' back home." Georgette pulled her skirt up a little and sat. "If you're gonna be two-faced, at least make one of 'em purty"

Isadore drew a fist back and was starting it forward when it was stopped by the hand of a smiling Willie the Lion.

"Now don't be bustin' up that pretty little hand, girl," Willie said. "You'll be needin' it later to hold the microphone when you sing."

Isadore's eyes lit behind the blushing of her cheeks. "You want me to do a number? What shall I sing?"

"How about *I Wish I Could Shimmy Like My Sister Kate*?"

Isadore clapped her hands, squealed, and raced back to her friends at a table in the corner.

"Willie the Lion . . ." Gus shook his friend's hand. "I'd like you to meet my fiancé, Georgette Bence."

"Why do they call you the Lion?" Georgette held out her hand.

Willie took a seat at their table and leaned closer so she could hear his story above the chatter of the crowd. "When, during the war, they asked for volunteers to learn the rapid-fire artillery gun called the French 75s, I stepped forward. The French captain-in-charge told me, 'Well, I think it will take you a month to learn the mechanisms, and then we'll shoot you up to the front.' I learned that mechanism in six hours. They tabbed me as an A-1 gunner right off the bat. I shot those 75s at the Fritzies for forty-nine days straight without a break or any relief. Word got back, and the colonel came up and said, 'Smith, you're a lion with that gun.' That name stuck with me ever since."

"Well, you are also a rapid-fire lion of the keyboard," Georgette said. "I've never heard anything like it. And where did that dance come from?"

"Don't tell these other white folk," Willie said, leaning in even closer. "But that hambone dance came over from Africa with my people's ancestors. We call it Pattin' Juba. Want me to teach it to you?"

Georgette looked at Gus, who nodded. "Go ahead."

Willie the Lion stopped one of the band members as he walked by and whispered something in his ear. A few moments later, the band was playing robust jazz music. Willie led Georgette onto the dance floor to a place where they would be facing Gus at the table.

"The step starts off with a simple twisting of the feet to rhythm in a lazy sort of way." Willie rubbed the soles of his feet slowly back and forth. "Just like you stomping and squishing bugs. Okay, that's it, you got it, girl. Now a fast, kicking step, kick the feet forward and backward. That's great! Now let's do some stomping as well as slapping and patting the arms, legs, chest, and cheeks to keep time during a walkaround."

Making a small circle, Georgette followed Willie, both dancing steps to the rhythm of the band. Others, laughing and shouting, joined behind them to form a snake dance with everyone mimicking Willie's steps. She was having the time of her life. The big smile on Gus's face told her he was too.

In a second, everything changed. Gunshots. Screams. Band members, dancers, and everyone else ducked, fell to the ground, or ran for cover. Willie grabbed Georgette around the waist, pulling her beneath the bandstand. Staying low to the ground, Gus raced across the room to join them, and cloaked her with his arms and body. Just as quickly as it began, it was over. Blue gun smoke, its acrid smell overpowering, floated below the cloud of tobacco gray.

Two well-dressed men and one woman had collapsed in their chairs with bloodied heads and torsos. Another man lay face down at their table, a fountain of blood gushing in spasms from a neck wound forming a red tsunami that, reaching the end of the table, cascaded in a pink waterfall onto the floor.

The only ones standing in the room were two men with handguns. They turned, raced up the stairs and out the door. Gus wasted no time. He lifted Georgette by both arms and almost carried her to a back way out and down a hall, then exited into an alley on the opposite side of the building. Dozens of others followed. When the crowd reached the street, people fanned out in various directions. The sound of approaching police sirens grew steadily louder.

"Well, how about coffee and pancakes?" Gus asked, then wanted to kick himself. This was not the way he had expected the evening to go at the safest establishment on his long list of hangouts. Georgette's entire body was shaking. The gasps of cold air she inhaled through her mouth were uneven, forced. She shuffled her feet awkwardly, leaning sideways into Gus as if she were about to faint.

"It's okay, darling," Gus assured her. "No one but those Cuckoo Gang members who got shot were in danger."

"Cuckoo?" Georgette incredulous. "Cuckoo?"

Gus forced a smile. "No, dear. It's more like one cuckoo. One o'clock." He thought making light of the situation and a few jokes would calm her. "I just wanted to take you to the right kind of place. I didn't have any idea that would happen."

"Humph, Right kind of place, all right. For the wrong kind of people. Take me home! Now!"

***

Gus called on Georgette every day for a week. Each time, a tenant answered the knock on the door and Gus was sent away disappointed.

For Georgette, it took those seven days before the fright released its grip. She had taken to sleeping in her rocking chair in the parlor. Somehow, the crackling of the coal in the potbellied stove comforted her. Finally, one evening, she decided it was time to return to her bedroom. Before she could get up from the rocker, car lights made a sweep like a lighthouse across the walls of the room. A moment later came a knock on the door that she recognized as Gus's. She cursed herself for feeling excited. She cried and trembled—it was just more trouble and stress—this life. Still, she wiped her face with an apron and answered the door.

"Just give me a target to shoot for, and I'll hit it," Gus said quickly, then looked down at her bare feet. Even her toes were pretty. "Believe you me. I was as surprised as anyone when that shootin' started."

"I suppose you're also surprised when you look up at a flock of birds and get shit on your face." Georgette, arms crossed, still had not looked him in the eye.

"Left to my own devices, I'd probably never think about it." Gus raised his head. "Does this mean you aren't considering my proposal?"

"It has certainly given me pause." Georgette couldn't bring herself to send Gus away. She still had hope he might mend his ways. Leaving him standing in the doorway, she returned to the parlor and her rocker. Gus threw his fedora on the hat stand and sat on the loveseat next to her.

"Why won't you look for honest employment?" Georgette implored. "Or, would you rather have a big hole in your stomach?"

"No. I'm quite satisfied with the number of holes I was born with." Gus's eyes discovered a lamp that was less heated than Georgette's stare. His jaw ached from clenching his teeth. "Come on, Georgette. The only thing you get from straddlin' the fence is a sore backside."

"Stands to reason, I suppose." She turned toward the kitchen where a tenant was scrounging for leftovers. "Horatio, fetch Mr. Winkler's hat, would you, please? He'll be leavin'."

"I sure don't know what she sees in you," the man named Horatio told Gus as he handed over the fedora. Horatio was slender with the effeminate narrow shoulders of the theater crowd from which he came.

"It would scare me if you did." Gus tipped his hat. "I'll be back."

A week later, Gus and Georgette were married.

3

The first six months, Gus was everything Georgette had hoped he'd be. From sunup to sundown, he worked around the boarding house fixing the many damages done by rough customers who had little reason to care for their rooms. Nearly every wall had holes or scuff marks where angry male tenants proved their masculinity by punching or kicking, all the while hoping to strike only thin drywall instead of unforgiving studs.

Saturday nights, though, Gus still liked to spend time with the boys. On those occasions, Georgette had nerve storms until her husband staggered through the door. Dutifully, she helped him upstairs to their room, undressed him, and laid him in bed, a vomit bucket on the floor within reach.

The next day, Gus would wake around noon and return to the honey-dos Georgette assigned him. He was painting a wall one day when she surprised him by announcing she had to go visit her sister in the upper peninsula of Michigan.

"Blanche needs my help, Gussie. The bank is trying to claim possession of our parents' home they left to her. I'll take her the papers she needs to prove they're attempting to cheat us."

Seeing his wife disturbed, Gus put his paintbrush aside, wiped his shirt with a towel, and gave her a kiss and a squeeze. The couple had not been apart since their wedding day. If he'd been married to any other woman, Gus would have insisted on going with her to deal with the corrupt bankers. Georgette would never ask for help, and neither would she need it. It was the bankers who would need help.

***

Upon arriving in Marquette, it took Georgette a week before she was granted an audience with the bankers. Then, it only took her fifteen minutes to solve her sister's dilemma. She entered the bank conference room carrying a briefcase and wearing a matching skirt and jacket with a white blouse beneath. Her jacket was tailored with a buttoned-up sash around her slim waist, her skirt slightly flared below the knee, providing the three men in the room with a tantalizing view of her shapely ankle.

Georgette took a seat at the head of the table, opened her briefcase, extracted three folders of documentation, and placed them neatly before her. Without uttering a word, she responded to each of the bankers' inquiries by quickly retrieving the required papers and indifferently sliding them across the table. No sooner had the inquisition ended than Georgette retrieved her documents, flipped the bun of hair on the back of her head at the gentlemen, and exited the room.

The exultation she expected to receive from her sister the moment she walked into the family home never came. Instead, she was greeted at the door by a grim-faced Blanche holding a telegram that read: *Gus in St. Louis Hospital having surgery from bullet wound.*

All that night, the sisters took turns driving. When they reached St. Louis, Georgette dropped Blanche off at the boarding house before going to the hospital.

From his hospital bed, the dark pools of Gus's eyes searched Georgette's face for understanding. He thought it might've been fortunate that his wife had entered the room just as a nurse was changing the bandage on his chest, a painful, bloody experience that he used to his advantage by wincing and moaning. When the task was done and he saw his wife's broad smile, he pretended to force one of his own.

"Everyone can smile when things go wrong," the nurse said as if reading the unspoken emotions. "But it takes someone special to make others smile along with them."

"What happened?" Georgette asked when the philosophizing nurse was out of the room.

"I don't know, honey," Gus said, sounding more like a child faking sick to get out of school. "Fred and me was just arguin' with a taxi driver over our fare. The next thing I knew, lead bees were flying past my head. That's the last I remember 'til I woke up here."

"Did Fred get hurt?"

"He almost died, too." Fred was Gus's friend. He wanted his wife to sympathize with him too. After all, he was as solid a friend as a veteran of the war could expect.

"Almost wouldn't matter except it keeps us up nights." Georgette used that observation because she'd spent so many sleepless Saturday nights since Gus Winkler came into her life.

"Well." Her husband searched for an excuse. "Fred just don't know how to act 'cause he's spent most of his life behind bars. Hell, last time he got out, it took a month before he would go in any room that didn't have striped lighting."

"No, sir," Georgette wouldn't abide lies. "Now tell me what really happened."

"Okay, okay." Gus sat up as if he'd been stung. When a better fib didn't come to him, he opted for the truth. "We was runnin' away from a roadhouse with an old bartender chasin' us and shootin' at us, and, for some reason, the fella just dropped dead." Gus placed a hand over his upper lip and mumbled. "Must've had a heart attack or something."

"This day just keeps givin' me a fresh slap in the face every time I try to go in a different direction." Georgette wrung her hands. "What caused his heart attack?"

"I'd imagine it was Fred's bullet." Gus pulled his blanket up to his nose, his eyes begging for under-standing.

"I swear!" Georgette walked to the back of the room and let her forehead slam against the wall harder than she intended. "That Fred Burke's killed more people than the bubonic plague. So, why were you runnin' away from the roadhouse anyway?"

"Well, hon, Fred might of put some of the money from the cash register in his pocket when he thought nobody was lookin'."

"The problem is, all that Fred Burke wants is easy money." Georgette returned to the bedside. "That man would start a fire just to sell a bucket of water."

"Can't blame him for that," Gus moved a hand from beneath the blanket in case a slap was coming. He wished he had his lucky Indianhead nickel to rub, but it was in his trouser pockets, which were hanging up in the closet. "I'd like just once to have enough paper money to need a money clip."

"Then do it honest, Gussie." Georgette had made this plea many times. "I'm damned if I'll tolerate any guff from you. You are smart, handsome, and you'd be a natural-born leader if you'd quit following them Egan Rats thugs."

"How'd you know about them?" When she didn't answer, Gus launched into a rehearsed speech. "Them Egan Gang is the reason lots of folks have jobs around here. They keep order since the law fears them dago, kike, and nigger gangsters. Why, the Egan Rats are an absolute necessity to St. Louis."

"That which is necessary is not always that which is right," Georgette preached, her voice rising with each word. "You must find your true calling in life, Gussie."

"I *am* searching for myself, but that's a journey for a lifetime. In the meantime, folks gots to eat."

"I don't see you starvin'. What are you complainin' about? We're cookin' with gas, ain't we?"

Gus looked deep into his wife's eyes. Seeing no quarter, he humbled his tone. "I can be the person you want me to be. I just have to figure out how."

"Here's how. Put your mouth to God's ear."

"I'll try, Georgie girl. I really will try."

***

Georgette was in a foul mood that afternoon when she drove home from the hospital. It was a warm, cloudy day with a slight wind. She had a notion that if the sun would just come out, she might feel a little better. It had been a struggle not to give her husband a better tongue lashing, but his pouting like a schoolboy always left her feeling motherly. Keeping her anger inside had left her with such a sense of futility. She was resolute in her determination to keep Gus on the straight and narrow, a struggle that made her feel weak, totally without willpower.

The moment she turned her flivver onto her block, she knew something else was about to go terribly wrong. Three men jumped into a black sedan parked in front of her boarding house. Seconds later, it wagged its tail as it hit loose gravel, then executed a sideways skid at the corner and shot out of sight.

She parked the flivver and raced into her home shouting Blanche's name. The boarders were either at work or a local tavern. After several minutes of frantic searching, she stopped screaming her sister's name and listened. From upstairs came the dull sound of something thumping on the floor. The noise abated slightly, then when Georgette shouted Blanche's name again, it began louder than before.

Taking the stairsteps two at a time, Georgette found her sister bound and gagged in the first room she entered. Blanche's face was purple from hyperventilating through her nose. The dirty sock stuffed halfway down her throat and secured with a man's tie was slow to remove. When it finally was out, Blanche gagged and, with a loud belch, vomited a little.

"They said they were going to kill me if I didn't give them the loot Gus stole from Charlie Birger's roadhouse," Blanche finally was able to say.

"Birger?" Georgette finished untying the single rope that secured her sister's hands and legs. "Gus didn't say nothin' about it being Charlie Birger's joint they robbed."

"Who is this Birger fellow?"

"He's just the biggest bootlegger between Chicago and Cairo." Georgette rolled to the side and rested her back against the wall alongside Blanche, both still breathing heavily. "If Gussie has Charlie Birger's gang after him, he's not long for this Earth."

***

A few days after robbing the Birger roadhouse, Fred Burke drove like a madman to his home in Paducah, Kentucky. When traveling great distances, Fred liked to keep a flask in each pocket, four in all. Therefore, when he reached the state line, he was sauced to the gill.

His most recent wife was using her hand to masturbate the old landlord when Fred came in the door. Fred got a cold look in his eye, and the look in his eye wasn't very warm to begin with. He fired his pistol at the scrambling landlord's crotch until the bullets ran out, then leapt on top of the man and pistol-whipped him over and over again. Though only one of the bullets had grazed his groin area, the landlord's face was quickly unrecognizable—in fact, as mushy as a bowl full of smashed grapes, an ugly parity of humanness. Fred could no more stop hitting him than a blizzard could stop blowing. It took the combined strength of three neighbor men to stop the storm of rage in Fred.

That was the last Fred Burke saw of his wife or, for that matter, Paducah. By law, he was still married to several women, since he never bothered with divorces. His wives had done nothing but vex and disobey him once he married them. Life was much simpler when women were broken, when they didn't express their feelings, whether happy or sad.

Gus's wife Georgette always seemed stirred up about something and wasn't afraid to tell Gus what she thought. Still, Fred didn't think that Georgette would give their landlord or any other man a hand job. He knew, because he'd once asked her for one. Of course, Gus made sure he never asked again. It wasn't that Fred didn't respect Gus, for, in fact, he did, tremendously, it was just that he didn't respect women. Georgette had strength and she didn't neglect her duties; that he admired.

Fred told Gus that he believed that romantic love was a European invention started by William Shakespeare. Love was only lust that faded at the same rate as the woman's beauty. He considered himself a dog-in-heat romantic.

"Love making is simply mutual masturbation," Fred had been telling Gus just before they robbed Birger.

"Wrong," Gus argued, happy in the love of his wife. "Only sex without love is mutual masturbation. There is nothing more beautiful than love making between a married man and woman."

It bothered Fred that Gus and Georgette held hands so much. He had never in his life had a gal eager to hold hands with him. Gus was the closest thing he had to a friend, often giving him a double sawbuck when he asked for money. Fred always took the money and never thanked him, never thanked anyone, for nothing anyone did made him grateful. He had been born without sympathy and had resigned himself to believing he would leave the world the same.

As drunk and bloody as Fred was after beating the landlord, he was somehow able to drive back into Illinois and almost to the town of Herrin. When he felt himself losing consciousness, he pulled the flivver over into a stand of trees, got out, and tried to take in some fresh air. That was a mistake. He quickly recognized that if he leaned forward, he would vomit, and if he tried to stand straight, he would fall over backwards. The alternative was to drop back onto the car seat, there to sleep for the next twelve hours, his feet hanging out the open car door.

***

Gus was feeling vulnerable. The gunshot had not been the problem. Fred Burke had successfully used a razor blade to cut out the bullet, but infection set in that required hospitalization. The doctors were mandated by law to notify the police concerning any gunshots. With both Fred and Gus claiming the wound was the result of an accident, no charges were filed.

Two days of hallucinations and hellish dreams caused Gus to recognize his own mortality more clearly. That foreboding was intensified when, a few weeks after his release from the hospital, he and Fred were called before Dinty Colbeck, the head of the Egan Rats Gang.

Gus and Fred's robbing of the Birger roadhouse had gone against the code of the underworld. Such activities were supposed to be approved by the boss and, though it had simply been an unplanned opportunity, it caused repercussions that adversely affected the Rats. Charlie Birger had retaliated by having two Rats gunned down in broad daylight on a street in East St. Louis.

A talk with Colbeck could only mean one of two things. Either the gang boss was going to send them for a one-way ride, or he was going to offer them a job that was too dangerous for his more valuable hoodlums to perform. If it was the ride, Gus and Fred would more than likely be shot in the back of the head and their bodies dumped in a creek or behind the racetrack.

He and Fred were squeezed into the backseat of a big four-door sedan, large thugs on either side of them, both with one hand inside their overcoats. When the vehicle pulled in front of one of the Rats' roadhouses, Gus knew the second option awaited them. The question was, would he and Fred have what it took to survive whatever assignment Colbeck gave them?

4

November 1923

A few days later, Gus was driving the lead car toward Herrin, Illinois, for a caravan of six vehicles, each filled with Egan Rats gunmen. Uncomfortably unarmed, Fred sat in the front seat. Three of Dinty Colbeck's Rats rode in the backseat, their handguns holstered but available.

The task given to them was simple and direct. Hit both the Shelton and Birger gangs hard. Kill as many as possible. The only perk was that the hitmen could keep any loot they collected.

Much to Fred's dismay, Dinty Colbeck appointed Gus as the lead negotiator. The promotion was a shock to them both because Fred had been calling the shots since their return from the war. Most jobs involved Fred planning and committing the crime and Gus ensuring a swift and safe getaway, a talent that was often as complicated as the wrongdoing itself. Having been an ambulance driver in France during the Great War, Gus had experience behind the wheel while under fire.

"You're smart and cool-headed," The Rats boss explained to Gus. "But you can be cold-blooded and ruthless when needed. I've put together a team of red hots made up of both Egan and Hogan men to follow your orders. If any of them don't—well, you know what to do."

The Egan Rats had joined forces with another Irish mob with the unlikely name of the Hogan Jelly Rolls. The plan was to take over the southern Illinois roadhouses to payroll the recruitment of more hired guns. The Egan and Hogans could then go after the two Italian gangs, The Green Dagoes who had arrived recently from Sicily, and the American-born second-generation Italians who had been running their part of St. Louis for the past thirty years. Things seemed about ready to get very bloody in both St. Louis and southern Illinois.

Gus had to admire Fred's cool. Normally not very chatty, during the ride Fred had found topics—guns and skirts—the gunman sitting behind them could relate to. No one was certain how many Mrs. Burke's there were scattered around the country. Gus knew of three.

"The first date I had with the dame that became my second wife," Fred said, "began with her saying that she liked to be tied up in bed naked and beaten with sticks. I'll tell you, that may sound exciting, but it sure got tiresome, especially when her backside began gettin' callouses and looking like a white prune."

As the boys in back were laughing, Gus drove up behind a farmer on a tractor pulling a wagon of hay. The dirt road was narrow and winding with trees on both sides as far as the eyes could see. Gus couldn't get around him.

"Want us to shoot him?" One of the men in the back asked.

"No." Gus was practical in such matters. "We'd still have no way to get around the tractor and I doubt any of us city boys would even know how to drive a Fordson."

When there was a longer stretch in the road ahead, Gus pulled as far to the left as he could. A hundred yards away was a Ford sedan sitting sideways in the road with its hood up. A tall, smartly dressed man was inspecting the engine.

The moment the tractor puffed up and stopped, the old farmer wearing a straw hat shouted, "Get that damned motor car out of my way. If I shut off my machine, I'll never get it started again."

The man with the stalled car just smiled at the old timer and walked around the hay wagon to face the caravan of cars behind it.

"You fellas stay put and keep your weapons out of sight." Gus opened his car door, got out, and walked casually toward the man.

"Need a hand pushin' your motor car to the side of the road?" Gus asked when the stranded driver stepped forward to greet him. He was tall and handsome with the friendly demeanor often found in small town USA. His suit though appeared expensive and well tailored.

The old farmer didn't seem amused to be in the middle of a traffic jam on an isolated country road. He climbed off the tractor and drew himself up, clearly antagonistic. Glancing at the load of hay, he grabbed a hay hook that had been embedded in a bale and started beating at a snake that had poked its head out of the stack. The disturbance caused several of the men in the caravan to open their doors and emerge with drawn weapons.

The tractor backfired. Loudly. The explosive sound would have triggered a response from less seasoned men, but the gunfighters present didn't recognize the explosion as coming from any artillery they had ever heard.

A youngster hiding in the back of the stalled Ford was not seasoned. He rose from the back-seat and promptly emptied a shotgun into the old farmer's tractor. The machine gave one final loud puff before sputtering to its demise.

While the assassination of the tractor didn't bring about any other gunfire, it did cause dozens of men to step out from behind trees to see what was going on. Their emergence, in turn, caused Gus's men to move behind the open doors of their vehicles and prepare to do battle. The old farmer, not knowing what to do, dropped onto his belly and crawled under the hay wagon.

"What is this, an ambush?" Gus asked casually.

"Doesn't have to be," the smartly dressed man with the stalled car said calmly. He lit a cigar and handed another to Gus. The two stood smoking while their respective armies aimed weapons at one another from cover.

"Your boys are pretty disciplined," the man told Gus.

"So are yours. Except that young fella that kilt that tractor."

"He's a city boy. Probably thought he was shooting at an army tank."

"So, what do we do now?" Gus asked.

"Well, since my boys seem to have your boys surrounded—and, it would seem, better armed, why don't you fellas just get on back to the city and deal with them wops from Sicily?"

"You heard about that, huh?" Gus liked the man's confidence.

"Yes, I'd imagine that after you get done dealin' with the Green Dagoes, and after the Shelton and Birger gangs finish off them Klan fellas in white nightshirts, why, I suppose then we could continue this conversation if you're so willing."

"Which gang are you with?" Gus asked. "Shelton or Birger?"

The smiling motorist extended his hand. "Carl Shelton, at your service."

***

"So, you didn't do a thing I sent you to do?" Colbeck scolded Gus later that evening in his office. "Not one roadhouse shut down, not one Birger or Shelton dead?"

"That's right." Gus fought the urge to sit up on the front of his chair and bounce his leg. Instead, he reclined and lit a cigarette.

"Before I send you for a ride that you won't come back from," Colbeck said. "I'll give you one chance to explain."

"Southern Illinois is about to explode in a violence that the Egan and Hogans will want nothing to do with," Gus recited as rehearsed. "Birger and the Sheltons are fixin' to fight a bloody war against over ten thousand members of the Ku Klux Klan. The Klan are a bunch of Protestants who want to enforce prohibition. The Catholics enjoy alcohol and gambling, so they're on the side of the bootleggers. It makes sense to let the Klan and the gangs battle it out. Otherwise, it'll be us fightin' the KKK. If the Birgers and Sheltons should win, there'll almost certainly be a war between them for territory in Little Egypt. Especially if we help instigate one.

"Besides that, the Herrin coal mine is about to go on strike. If the owner brings in strikebreakers as he says he will, even more blood will spill. I say we stay out of southern Illinois until the smoke clears, then recruit or wipe out anyone left."

For several long moments, Colbeck sat quietly enjoying his cigar. Since the boss was watching his puffs of smoke rise and dissipate, Gus leaned back further in his chair, monitoring his body to avoid any sign of nervousness. Elbows on chair arms, he linked the fingers on his hands just in case they should begin trembling. Though the room wasn't warm, he avoided wiping the slight trickle of sweat forming on his brow.

Finally, Colbeck lowered his head and fixed his gaze on Gus. "I chose the right man. You acted wisely. We can now concentrate on securing St. Louis from the Green Dagoes. We'll leave East St. Louis to the Sheltons. I would have liked the capital gains from Little Egypt to finance our operations, but considering the merger of the brothers and Birger, it's no longer practical. We will allow a war of attrition to take place for as long as necessary, then we'll go in and wipe out whatever's left."

"Now I'm gonna ask you a favor as a fellow veteran." Gus used the burned-down blunt end of his cigarette to light another. "I need to find a way to gracefully depart from this life of crime."

"Why is that?"

"I married badly."

"How so?"

"She's a good girl. And I mean a good girl."

"Yes, I can see how that could be a problem. I'd hate to lose a heady fella like yourself." Colbeck's eyes returned to the spot on the ceiling from which his thoughts came, then said. "How would you like me to help you go semi-legit?"

"What does semi-legit mean?"

"Alcohol distribution." Colbeck leaned forward, stuffed a handful of cigars in Gus's breast pocket and patted them. "The only way to get in trouble from a job like that is by watering down the booze too much or squealing to the law."

Gus tried to look surprised. Through the grapevine he had heard that Colbeck was looking for someone to manage the distribution center. It was hardly a risky position since politicians and the law looked the other way. Prohibition was a noble but grossly unpopular experiment that was certain to eventually fail. But until it did, there was easy money to be had.

Then Colbeck added a caveat. "First, though, I have one more dirty job for you. We have a youngster in the hot car ring who knows too much. He's a puck, not a goodfellow."

"Who is he?"

"Smitty."

***

The very moment the death sentence was being handed down on him, the boy named Smitty was watering Georgette's flowers. She liked the young man. He was always polite, calling her Missus Georgette and bowing deeply as he entered and left her presence. Smitty was a simpleton. He slept on a small cot in the back of the downtown garage. His job there was to make certain no one broke in and stole the automobiles the Egan Rats had themselves carjacked. Many times, each night Smitty would hear a noise, jump from his cot, and start yelling, "Go away! Go away! Ain't nothin' to steal here!"

The problem was Smitty couldn't tell a lie to save his life, which made it a problem for the Egans. Fred Burke had even tried coaching him.

"Smitty, how old are you?" Fred asked one day.

"I'm twenty, Mr. Fred."

"Well, from now on, if anyone asks you how old you are, tell them you're eighteen. If you don't do that, I'll give you a beatin'. Do you understand that, Smitty?"

"Yes, Mr. Fred."

Later that day, Fred had one of the gang's police stooges test Smitty.

"Smitty, how old are you?" the cop asked.

"I'm twenty, but I'm supposed to tell you I'm eighteen or I'll get a beatin'."

Such sinister lessons were not allowed when Georgette was around. She cared for the young man despite his proclivities. And Smitty liked her, following her around the house trying to anticipate her every need.

"Let me put that water bucket in the shed for you, Missus Georgette."

"Thank you, my dear. Now you hurry on back to the garage and I'll see you in the morning." Georgette looked up from weeding her flowers in time to see the young man close the shed door and do a clumsy, one-leg-always-in-front-of-the-other trot down the block, careful not to step on any cracks in the sidewalk. She smiled.

Except for Smitty, the garage was empty later that night when Gus went to get him. The boy was under a car changing the oil. Gus could tell the car had just been brought in because it was still smoking a little from the exhaust.

"Smitty, would you come out here, please?"

Smitty had grease stains on his trousers and shirt, but it was the stocking cap on his head that Gus couldn't take his eyes off. The boy had got his head too close to the hot muffler and burnt a hole in the top. Little orange sparks dotted his exposed black hair, but the excessive pomade he had applied seemed to be extinguishing them into little whisps of smoke. His forehead was sweating profusely, but Smitty didn't seem concerned, and Gus saw no need to embarrass him.

After taking Smitty for a ride into a wooded area on the pretext of looking for snipes, Gus stayed behind the wheel of the car, his arms crossed on the steering wheel and his head on his forearms.

Fred walked while young Smitty skipped out into the trees to look for the imaginary creature called snipes. When the happy young man was turned away from him, Killer Burke coldly placed a gun to the back of the boy-who-could-not-lie's head and pulled the trigger.

5

Georgette was dismayed when her husband told her they were going to Carl Shelton's home in Fairfield, Illinois, to discuss business with the southern Illinois gang leader. Unlike their rival bootlegger, Charlie Birger, the Shelton brothers worked to keep a low profile, but they were still widely known as criminals throughout the area.

Birger was a little older and had been in the underworld community longer. He lived in Harrisburg, Illinois, and ran all of Saline County, including the sheriff's office. This unholy alliance with the law was accomplished by keeping his illegal activities confined to the rest of the downstate counties that were dubbed Little Egypt because Cairo, on the Ohio River, was one of its larger cities.

"Why does Shelton want to meet with you?" Georgette asked during the ride through the lower Kaskaskia River Valley.

Fred Burke sat in the backseat twirling his revolver. When Gus gave him an angry stare through the dash mirror, he holstered it quickly.

"It'll please you to know," Fred said, very aware of Georgette's bias against criminal behavior, "Carl has many legit businesses not just in southern Illinois but also in East St. Louis. Maybe he wants us to run one of them."

"Fred knows the Sheltons a little," Gus added, "since he ran bootleg whiskey for Charlie Birger for a while."

Georgette didn't much like having a pistolero sitting right behind her. Gus, though, was a great sponsor of Fred and most always stayed loyal to him. All the war veterans she had met seemed to share an affinity for one another, though it wasn't so deep that a girl or cash couldn't cause them to forget that bond.

"I wish Smitty could've come." Georgette sighed. "I love that boy like a June morning. When do you suppose he'll be back?"

"I don't know, hon," her husband said without taking his eyes off the road.

The secluded little country house where Gus parked was nothing like Georgette expected. It was quaint and homey, and the little old lady who came rushing out to meet them could've been anyone's grandmother.

"Oh, my goodness, you're as pretty as a picture," the lady said when Georgette opened the car door and stepped out. She came forward and gave her guest a big hug. "Now, why couldn't one of my dear boys have captured the heart of a classy dressin' lady like you? I'm Agnes, dear, but just call me Ma. Everyone does. Please come inside and meet the others."

The living room they walked into was clean despite being crowded with family members.

"That's Pa asleep in the rockin' chair," Ma said, still using her outside voice. Suddenly awake, Pa raised his head and looked around in a bleary way, then rolled his head back again and returned immediately to dreamland.

Ma pointed at the two young girls sitting on the Davenport. "Hazel's our oldest girl and can't quit twirling her hair and daydreaming about boys." Hazel glanced up and gave a little wave with the hand that wasn't in her brown locks. "And that's our youngest, Lula, who ain't gonna get much older if she don't get outside and take that wash down from the clothesline like I asked her an hour ago."

Lula had been reading a book, but she rolled her eyes and quickly put it down, then scampered through the kitchen and out the back door. She was rather a pretty girl—although her nose curved a little on one side and she had bruises from her face to her skinny ankles.

"That gal has no shortness of energy when you can get her nose out of books. Even the menfolk admit she can outwork most farmhands," Ma said, then asked. "Do you enjoy watching horseracing, dear?"

"Oh, yes, very much."

"Well, we'll have to take you and Gus to the race-track sometime."

"Ma! You got two more freeloaders," Lula's distant voice called through the kitchen's storm door. "Looks like one of 'em might be a gal. It's hard to tell through all that dirt."

Ma didn't stop talking as Georgette followed her into the kitchen and watched her put together two plates of beans and cornbread. "A lot of hoboes pass through this area," Ma told her. "I guess the word has got around that this house is good for a free meal."

"Do you know what your son wants to talk to my husband about?" Georgette had lost sight of Gus and Fred. Instead of following Ma into the home, they had disappeared around one side of the building.

"I stay out of my sons' business. They are all good God-fearing boys. Carl even teaches Sunday school and plays the organ in church. Even Bernie's a good boy, despite his propensity for fighting and carousing." The plates filled, Ma took them and two glasses of water out the back door.

While Ma conversed with the hoboes, Georgette looked out the back window in search of her husband. A half dozen men were actively loading a telegraph line repair truck to hide whiskey barrels. Fred Burke was talking to one of the hoboes and a dangerous-looking dark-skinned man. She heard her husband's voice in the living room and turned in that direction. Gus was shaking Carl's hand.

"We have a deal," Gus said. "I'll handle your beer distribution in East St. Louis."

"And I'll keep the rest of our interests on the Illinois side." Carl gave Georgette a glare when he saw her listening.

"My wife and I are the same person," Gus explained. "You can say anything in front of her that you can say to me."

Carl nodded, turned, and exited through the kitchen door.

***

"Go on in the washhouse and clean up." Fred Burke pointed toward a small shed attached to the side of the barn. He handed the hobo man a silver dollar, then said to the girl, "I'll see you directly."

"Clean your insides extra special," added the hobo. "You hear me, gal?"

"Abusing a woman simply don't sit right with me," a tough called Black Charlie said.

"Listen to you talk." Fred scoffed. "What about that bank teller you kilt? You ever think about his family?"

"Well, that's true." Black Charlie Harris shrugged. "I suppose that when we associate with outlaws long enough, we tend to forget about the other side. But, in my defense, I did shoot him in the leg to prevent his attack. Unfortunately, he bled to death."

Carl Shelton strutted out of the house in time to catch a glimpse of the hobo women's bare legs emerging from the washroom. The heel of her foot ran slowly and seductively up the door frame. A bare arm came next, the index finger of her hand motioning to come to her.

Fred thought he had first dibs. He was stepping forward when the eldest Shelton removed his work gloves and walked boldly toward the shed. Fred extended a hand in front of Carl, who stopped and glared at him.

Carl's brother Bernie quickly retrieved a Tommy gun from behind a chair and stared coldly at the St. Louis gangster. Since Fred had run with Charlie Birger's gang for a while, he wasn't fully trusted by the Sheltons.

"Give me that weapon, Bernie," Carl ordered.

Bernie tossed the gun to his big brother and grinned a goodbye to Fred. His smile turned to dismay when Carl flipped the gun. Holding it by the barrel he offered it to Fred Burke. Bernie just shook his head and went through the kitchen door into the house.

"This thing works?" Fred accepted the gat and began checking it for balance. "I've heard these weapons tend to jam."

"Occasionally, but they usually spout out enough chaos to make folks duck before they jam up. I've found it adequate time to draw and fire my sidearm."

Fred caressed the weapon.

"Make up your mind," Carl said. "You want this gun or are you just here to kick the tires on the Shelton gang?"

Fred nodded to Carl, who took that as consent they had a deal. Flipping a suspender from his shoulder, the Shelton boss continued toward the shed and entered.

Fred was so excited about the weapon he forgot to get his dollar back from the hobo for the poke he never got.

6

Fred liked the misty feeling that came with whiskey. He struggled to keep that feeling from the moment he awoke in the morning until evening when he could finally drink his way into unconsciousness. He had been told more than once that he would likely wind up hanging. Now that he had fallen in love with the Thompson machine gun Carl Shelton had given him, he felt assured of hanging—or a bloody blaze-of-glory death.

Fred was an inch shy of six foot and built like a prizefighter. Once, in France soon after the war ended, Fred fired a Thompson machine gun with sad consequences. His friend, Bob Carey, being an infantryman, had been provided one of the first submachine guns that came out of the factory too late to be used in combat.

Fred should've known mischief was afoot when Bob handed him the weapon and then moved quickly to stand behind a concrete bunker. No sooner than Fred had his finger on the trigger, the gun leaped like a bucking bronc and was ripped from his hands. He had fired every type of rifle and shotgun and thought he had a firm grip on it, but the instrument of war seemed to have a life of its own. Bob was laughing when he came out from behind the bunker.

"You did better than Crane Neck Nugent," Bob chuckled. "He didn't let go and plowed up a whole circle around him before he figured out to let go of the trigger."

"Yes." Fred had met Crane Neck and quickly formed an unflattering opinion. "Well, Ray's elevator don't quite reach the top floor, does it?"

After the war, it was Bob who introduced Fred to Dinty Colbeck and the Egan Rats. Bob was from St. Louis and had been with the Rats since he was fourteen years old.

With Gus trying to go semi-legit, Fred needed accomplices if he was going to continue pursuing his career as a criminal.

"It's always better to commit crimes in pairs," Fred told Bob one day over drinks. "One to watch the front and one to watch the back. But we also need a good getaway driver."

"How about Ray Nugent?" Bob suggested.

"You think he's smart enough?"

"Well, he handled explosives during the war and he's still alive, ain't he?" Bob liked Ray, despite his lack of smarts. Ray Nugent was often flighty in his actions but steady and loyal. Besides, those who had been to war together and survived had a special bond.

Bob looked forward to forming a new gang. He didn't think he could survive without the companionship of being in a gang. The gangs had been his salvation since he ran away from home to get away from his father's beatings. Besides that, he had to make a living and had few marketable skills. Why work an eight- or ten-hour day when he could make enough in a thirty-second robbery to eat for a year?

The first job Fred, Bob, and Ray took on was to heist a shipment of whiskey from the Hogan Gang in St. Louis. It was Bob's idea for Fred to wear the police uniform they had taken off a state trooper when he dared to stop them for speeding. The officer was unharmed except for several slight bumps on the head that rendered him unconscious. The best thing about this caper was the trooper was too embarrassed over being stripped naked to file a report.

The whiskey heist was almost as imaginative as stealing the uniform. The shipment warehouse on the west shore of the Mississippi River was easy to find, what with all the gun-toting guards around the premises.

Ray was heavily built, with a strong jaw, a long neck, and a dangerous gaze. He was nicknamed Crane Neck because his throat housed a larger-than-usual Adam's apple. He, his wife Julia, and their two small children simply drove by the warehouse occasionally until they spotted a truck with its load covered in tarp and followed it to see which roads it took.

As expected, the truck eventually noticed they were being tailed, pulled over and two thugs walked back to question Ray about his business.

"We're lost and thought if we followed you, we'd get back to a major highway," Ray explained as only a father with two young brats and a wife screaming for him to ask directions can do.

"Mommy, I'm gonna throw up," the little boy in the back shouted, followed by a gagging sound.

"Oh, God," the daughter yelled. "He's got the flu!"

A moment later the gunmen were back in their truck and driving on, with the Nugent crime family following, Little Ray and Julia happily nibbling on their rewards—Baby Ruth candy bars, named after President Cleveland's long-dead daughter.

April 25, 1923

The heist itself simply involved Fred in his policeman uniform standing in the middle of the narrow country road with his car parked sideways, an idea he got from the Shelton-Birger Gang.

Before the driver and passenger riding shotgun could get out, Bob and Ray leaped onto the running boards, pistols aimed at them.

Finding a buyer for the heisted whiskey was not as easy as Fred had anticipated. The stolen booze turned out to be Potcheen, an Irish moonshine that could be easily traced to the Hogan Gang. Plus, rumors, likely started by Italian competitors, spread that the hooch could cause blindness.

Fred, Bob, and Ray showed up in the hijacked truck at the Shelton farm just as Earl was in the middle of dehorning calves. He had one at that moment tied into a gate, the animal's head restrained on a dehorning table. Standing two feet away, Earl worked his hands back and forth with a Gigli saw, letting the sharp wires around the horn do the cutting.

"Doesn't that hurt 'em?" Ray asked, a hand over his mouth. He had a weak stomach for such amputations.

"Once in a while, we hit a bleeder," Earl said without stopping the sawing. "That don't make 'em very happy."

Ray wanted to grind his teeth. He remembered war surgeons in France using saws to remove arms and legs. He had many friends who returned to the States without one or more limbs. The idea of having an appendage severed in such a brutal way seemed the most horrible thing he could imagine. He decided he'd rather be shot in the head than lose a limb that way.

The three smoked while they waited patiently for Earl to tie up and dehorn three more calves. When he was finished, the farmer gangster put his tools away and followed them to the truck. Bob removed a case for him to sample. Earl inspected the bottle's label then opened it, took a short swig, and spit it out.

"To sell these paddies hooch, we'll have to rebottle it and relabel it," Earl Shelton told them. "Even if we cut it by watering it in half, you're lookin' at a fifty percent drop in its value for time and labor."

"We figured the entire truckload at eighty K." Ray struggled to do the math in his head. "So, you'll give us fifty thousand for it?"

"I'd say you're using Bernie Shelton math." Earl laughed. "My little brother didn't even make it out of the fifth grade. You're gonna have to let my boys unload and get started on the process. I'll give you a fair deal. But if you'd rather go try your luck with Charlie Birger, go right ahead. He just kilt three men in two days. Maybe he's not feeling as bloody now."

7

Georgette had never met anyone who took prohibition seriously. Not politicians, policemen, bankers, lawyers, nor average citizens. Therefore, the idea that her husband ran an alcohol distribution center didn't bother her much. From her point of view, Gus was a legitimate businessman.

For the next several months, she not only kept the books but helped by finding common folks who made much of their income by making moonshine whiskey, bathtub gin, and especially the fine wines the French and Italians specialized in. These homebrews were the most profitable for the Winklers, since they were not the Canadian and European blends that had to be expensively smuggled in from other countries. Locally made alcohol not only helped the St. Louis area's economy, but it also made the Winklers celebrities in a sense.

The only concern Georgette had was that her boarding house became an even greater gathering place for underworld figures such as Fred Burke, who rarely went anywhere without the Tommy gun Carl Shelton had given him in exchange for a poke with a hobo whore.

It was this problem that prompted Georgette to sell the boarding house and move her and her husband to a private residential community where the neighbors were well-established people of what she considered the upper-middle class.

The first thing she did after getting her new home in order was to throw a big to-do for this new, improved society of friends. She had made her husband promise to never tell his gangster buddies where they were now living. It was an oath she was confident her husband would keep, though the expectation that their secret would remain for long was hollow.

March 28, 1923

The party began at six o'clock, and, for the better part of the evening, was a huge success. Georgette made her homebrew and aged it for weeks before the event. A big canvas was laid across the yard to serve as a dance floor. She hired their friend Willie the Lion Smith and his band to entertain. Tables surrounded the dance floor, and beautiful Japanese lanterns hung from the trees. She and her sister prepared all the food, but she hired waiters in clean white uniforms to serve the guests.

"That's what I call puttin' on the Ritz." Gus linked his arm to his wife when he saw the spread.

"Oh, Gussie, I hope you don't think I'm being uppity, but it's so nice to have a few friends that aren't hoopin' and hollerin' like a bunch of Comanches."

"I understand, sweetie. And it's nice for me to be able to not worry about whether I'm better armed than the fellow dancin' next to me."

Well-dressed guests began arriving in expensive and well-maintained cars. Valets greeted each guest, opened the doors for the ladies, and drove the vehicles to parking spots along the streets. Gus and Georgette stood in a receiving line beneath a canopy at the end of the driveway. Each guest shook hands, some even after a bow or curtsy.

Willie the Lion's band played beautiful ballads that Georgette had chosen. When darkness arrived, the Japanese lanterns were lit and the band changed the tempo of the music, moving first to waltzes, then to the more popular jazz pieces.

That was when Georgette's dream evening ended. With loud honks and shouting from already drunk revelers, a long row of rickety old flivvers entered the far end of the street. They stopped right in the road in front of the Winkler home, double parking many cars in. Without even greeting the hosts, Fred Burke and his band of Egan

Rats misfits poured out of the vehicles. They were red hots of all kinds—safe crackers, pickpockets, and bank robbers, along with their flapper-dressing molls. They raced straight for the kegs of beer.

A few of Georgette's guests who had been invited began sneaking away toward their cars, leaving their drinks to be quickly snatched up and guzzled away by the newly arrived partyers. When the abandoned glasses ran out, some of the gangsters' molls invited themselves into the Winkler home. A few moments later, they came running out with any containers they could find, including pots, bowls, and even flower vases, anything that would hold Georgette's good homebrew.

"My party, oh, my party." Georgette dropped her forehead on her husband's shoulder.

"Never mind, honey." Gus patted his wife's back. "You're too good for their filth. It won't happen again. I made you a promise and I'll keep it."

Willie the Lion's band played a slower melody that was the waiters' signal to bring out the food. Instead of the elegant sit-down dinner Georgette had dreamed about, both thugs and molls rushed, using their hands to lift food from the serving trays before they even made it to the tables. They ate standing up until both food and drink were exhausted.

"Let's go where there's some excitement, gang," Fred Burke shouted when the food and drinks were finished.

The flivvers were loaded and gone as quickly as they had arrived.

***

Georgette cried herself to sleep that evening and stayed in bed the entire next day. Her glorious celebration was a fiasco. Gus hired some young boys to clean up, though he had to watch them carefully. On several occasions, he caught the youths drinking leftover booze and puffing half-smoked cigars.

The second evening, Georgette allowed Gus to cuddle her in his arms all night and half the morning. When she finally managed to crawl out of bed, she made breakfast with what pots and pans she could find that had not been filled with hootch and hauled away during the party.

The couple ate the meal without conversation. Together, they washed, dried, and put away the dishes. When finished, Georgette finally broke the awkwardness. Wrapping her arms around her husband's waist, she buried her head against the dampness of his shirt. That made her giggle. Gus had always been a sloppy dishwasher, a skill he had not practiced until he married Georgette.

"You're my man, Augustus Winkler." Georgette squeezed in tighter. "I know you want to provide me with an honest and stable life. It's easy for people with talent and natural abilities to succeed. My hat goes off to those who succeed despite all their flaws and handicaps. Like Smitty has done, but also like you and even me. Sometimes living among the underworld as we do is like being a passenger in your own life."

Uneasiness returned to Gus's body. This was not the talk of a woman about to announce she was leaving. Somehow, he felt her heart whispering something else.

"When you're called a mobster," she continued. "People you've never met already have a fifty percent judgment of what you're like. Now you have to convince them you're nothing like how they perceive you. That will be the greatest challenge to our marriage. But married we are, and married we'll stay, for better or worse. There, I've said my piece."

Gus wiped his eyes before the love of his life broke the embrace to face him.

"But if you go all bad, Gus Winkler, I'll get after you like thunder after lightning."

8

When Fred was feeling bloody, he spent his time cleaning his gun and seldom spoke. Other times, when the stiffness came to his pants, he sent Bob into Herrin to find him a woman.

"She don't need to be a whore," Fred told him. "Just a willin' gal will do."

The farmhouse the Sheltons found for Fred and Bob to use as a hideaway between their bank robberies was suitable for the two of them, but when Bob brought his girlfriend, Rose, to stay with them, Fred felt a little crowded, despite the place becoming cleaner.

Rose was the perfect woman for any man who enjoyed ménage à trois. She appreciated a pretty lady as much as Bob, though when she tried to bring a man into the picture for a foursome, Bob threw a fit and smacked her around as much as he thought he could without her leaving him.

What he didn't tell her was that the idea did titillate him. It was just that he needed a little more imagining before he would be ready to commit to living out the fantasy.

Rose was patient, actually enjoying the beatings more than she wanted Bob to know. She understood how some sins took longer to come to fruition than others. She didn't have to wait long. One day Bob brought a handsome young carpenter to the farmhouse to help him fix the roof.

She suspected he had sent the beautiful young man to tempt her, to wet her loins so she would moan louder, thinking about the carpenter's handsome face when Bob mounted her. Knowing it best she not appear too anxious, she didn't make any suggestions though. That would have to wait until it came from Bob himself.

Between sexual liaisons with the local cuisine, Bob and Fred took long trips to Detroit, St. Louis, Chicago, St. Paul, Cincinnati, and Kansas City, sometimes with Ray Nugent and sometimes with members of the Shelton Gang. The robberies were always quick and efficient with little gunplay involved. They did try one robbery with a couple of members of the Birger Gang, but they were too quick to get bloody and not as discreet and methodical as the Sheltons.

Fred wanted to stay out of the bootlegging business since a Ku Klux Klan leader named Glenn Young was fighting a violent battle with the Shelton and Birger gangs in his attempt to shut their bootleg enterprises down.

The Fred Burke Gang played it plenty safe during their robberies. Each heist and getaway was methodically planned and executed. It was afterwards, when they were celebrating with the money, that they often became drunk and careless.

April 10, 1924

It was this indiscretion that got Fred in his biggest trouble with the law. They had just taken John Kay's store in Detroit for seven thousand dollars' worth of jewels, a modest heist by their standards. A few days later, Fred, never a careful driver sober, even worse when drunk, and worse than that when being chased by cops, got caught and jailed. The loot from Kay's Jewelry was found in the side pockets of the car.

Fred spent until October in the Michigan State Prison learning from his fellow inmates dozens of new ways to make easy money.

***

"They tried to send the Ku Klux Klan leader, Glenn Young, to St. Louis to go after bootleggers," Gus told Georgette one day during breakfast, the one time of day they could talk since Gus got in so late from running the distribution center.

"Why do you say tried?"

"The Shelton brothers ambushed Young and his wife as they were driving along the Kaskaskia River Valley. He's in the hospital expecting to recover. She'll also recover from a shotgun blast to her face, but may be blinded for life."

"Oh, that poor dear." Georgette had often imagined a similar fate for herself.

"The bad thing for us is that to appease the voters, the law's cracking down on the distribution centers. I don't want you to be worryin', but ours did get hit yesterday. The cops found the safe with most of our money. We have enough to hold us over for a while, but I'm afraid our semi-legit business is out of business, at least for now. I think we should leave town and lay low."

"Where will we go?"

"Carl Shelton asked me to make some Canadian alcohol purchases up north. Get out your minks," Gus said tentatively. "We're goin' to Detroit."

***

Fred smiled at the girl, but she didn't acknowledge his smile. He knew she was just there to pick him up at the prison gate and take him to the gang hideaway, but he suspected his buddies wouldn't send just any female to drive him.

"Where's the boys staying now?" Fred asked.

"Johnny Reid has a bar," she said, her hands on the steering wheel and her eyes on the road. "I mean soda shop, they hang out at in Detroit."

"Right." Fred took a good hard look at her face then let his imagination undress her. "On to more important matters," he said bluntly. "How 'bout I try to weasel a blowjob out of ya?"

"Hot to trot?" The girl finally smiled.

"Blue ball will do that to you." Fred sighed. "Seven months on saltpeter, you know? So, how much would it cost me to get my little boy some relief?"

"One Benjamin."

"One hundred bucks? That's highway robbery."

"I'm better at highway robbery than you obviously are. I'm not the one who got six months in the slammer. But believe me, I'm worth every bit of one hundred bucks and you get me for the entire week."

"Sold! I'll drive."

The second thing Fred needed when he got out of prison was some quick money to pay his legal expenses. His first attempt on a gambling den in Detroit went badly, mainly because he used a rookie to help him. Fred hoped the youngster would be happy with a flat wage and would not demand part of the cut.

Robbing from fellow gangsters was tougher than banks where the guards don't feel like losing their lives for some rich guy's money. When it came to a shootout, the rookie froze long enough to get himself killed. Fred plugged the owner, but then had to dive through a closed glass window to make his escape—without the money.

As his cuts from the window escape healed, he drove down to Louisville, Kentucky, and made a quick withdrawal of thirty thousand with very little protest from the tellers or security guards. His debts now paid, he was ready to focus on bigger money, a cut from which he would have to share with his more experienced gangster friends.

9

Fred Burke was the devil's favorite demon. At least that's how Georgette saw him. He seldom went anywhere without the gat that Carl Shelton had given him, carrying it casually over his shoulder, holding it by the barrel. Gus knew of a few other gangsters somehow getting Thompson machine guns, though the weapon had not been widely used anywhere for illegal purposes, yet. He did hear the West Virginia State Police used them against striking coalminers at what had become known as the Battle of Blair Mountain in '21. The coal companies and the corrupt State government must have wanted badly to win because, besides gats, they also used airplanes to drop bombs on the ten thousand striking United Mine Workers.

He guessed that Carl had given the fifty-round magazine Tommy gun to Fred because models that fired twenty rounds from a rectangular box were easier to reload and less likely to jam. The Ku Klux Klan leader Glenn Young, who was put in charge of enforcing prohibition in southern Illinois, was known for carrying one.

Fred couldn't wait to find someone to use his beautiful gat on. The reason came in the form of a friendly poker game and a bottle of Scotch in Detroit.

It was a long, uncomfortable evening for Georgette when she and Gus accompanied Fred Burke and Bob Carey to their meeting in the Motor City. Besides being Henry Ford's car manufacturing location, Detroit was also the main entry port for whiskey and wine being smuggled in from Canada. The plan for the evening was to arrange the sale and transportation of Canadian whiskey to southern Illinois.

Following a half day of what Georgette thought was silly chest-thumping machismo by both sides, a deal was made.

Later that evening, the southern Illinois contingent retired to the apartment of two Purple Gang members for a friendly game of poker. James Ellis and Leroy "Doggy" Snyder were part of the Little Jewish Navy, as they were called, that owned several boats and participated in rum-running and hijacking throughout the Great Lakes.

The Purple Gang amazed Georgette. Made up of mostly Jewish hoodlums, they ran Detroit. Based on what she observed during the negotiations, they were more structured and focused than the St. Louis gangs. The Rats often worked independently without the approval of their leader, Dinty Colbeck. Everything the Purple Gang did was well planned and had to be approved by mobster boss, Abe Bernstein.

"Why are they called the Purple Gang?" Georgette whispered to her husband as he took her coat and laid it across the apartment bed alongside others.

"They're rotten," he whispered back. "Purple like the color of bad meat."

The two Purples, Ellis and Snyder, sat across from Fred, Bob, and local soda shop owner Johnny Reid, who was himself a former Egan Rat. Johnny was the reason his friends came to Detroit when things got hot for them in St. Louis. He was popular with thugs from several gangs. Normally happy and affable, Johnny had a much better grasp of the art of larceny. To him, the goal of crime was not to party after every successful caper, but to invest his ill-gotten gains in what might someday be a legitimate retirement venture. Selling soda and juices laced with alcohol seemed to satisfy both the customers and the cops, the latter of which stopped at his establishment several times a day for refreshment.

Johnny prided himself on fastidiousness, a trademark ignored by the thugs around him. He wore a striped dress shirt with white detachable pointed collars. Cufflinks matched his gold watch as well as the big ring he wore on his left pinky finger. Unlike the others, he used an ashtray and always tossed his beer bottle into the trashcan when emptied.

Despite Johnny's efforts, the apartment floor was still wall-to-wall with cigarette butts, as well as whiskey and beer bottles. Gus and Georgette sat at a small end table playing gin rummy. Georgette hoped her husband would pick up some tips from Johnny Reid that would allow them to return to live the halfway-legal life they had known in St. Louis.

From a stool in the back of the room was a makeshift bar, from which Black Charlie Harris watched the game. With legs crossed in the sophisticated style of a nobleman, he held a high ball in one hand and a cigarette in the other.

"That man scares me to death," Georgette whispered to her husband. She refrained from adding that she suspected Black Charlie was signaling one of the Purples what cards the Rats were holding.

"He's a lone wolf," Gus told her. "A man without allegiance to anyone. That's what makes him dangerous—and loyal only to the highest bidder. I'd imagine that gold tooth in the front of his mouth is the last thing many of his victims ever see."

"I raise you two Cs," Ellis's voice boomed from the card table. Black Charlie had just uncrossed his legs.

"You know I ain't got that kinda cash on me." Burke's face turned as flush as the five diamonds in his hand.

"How 'bout bettin' that gat you've been strokin' under the table all night?" Ellis suggested, followed by a hiccup that might have exploded had a match been held in front of it. His neck seemed unable to hold his head in an upright position for more than a second at a time.

Burke raised the Thompson machine gun onto one knee. He looked back down at his jack-high flush. "You're on," he said, placing the gun on the table, its muzzle pointed between Ellis and Snyder. "Call."

Ellis looked again at his own cards and laughed, enjoying the moment. "You must of broke a lot of rocks in prison. I spent two years there myself. That's where I learned to play the guitar."

"I was in a jailhouse band once." Fred again caressed his gat. "The whole rhythm section was the Purple Gang. Now, you wanna sing a song, play cards, or break rock? If it's the latter, maybe we could break 'em with artillery."

"Well, let's rock then." Perturbed by the insult, Ellis slowly stood, weaved in an alcoholic stupor, and cleared his jacket from the side, his gun tucked under his belt.

"Let's see now," Bob said. "You're gonna try to outdraw us with a gun that's tucked under your belt. Now, unless you are just stupid and want to blow away your manhood, that weapon either has the safety set or is on an empty chamber." He lifted his sawed-off shotgun from his lap. "Meanwhile, my twelve gauge is cocked and ready."

"Just a friendly little game here, boys." Drunk as he was, Ellis could see his folly. "No need to get rude." He tossed four kings on the table.

A wide-eyed Charlie jumped up, opened the door, and hopped into the hallway. The loud spitting of Fred's gat and the explosion of Bob's twelve gauge raised the stakes in the game to a completely new level. Gus threw his body over his wife's. There was no need though. The firing ended before he had a chance to drag her to the floor. Both shooters' accuracy was without error.

With their weapons smoking, Fred and Bob stood over the two bodies. Johnny walked up, squatted over Ellis, and examined a .45 caliber-sized hole in the center of his forehead.

"Should we take the bodies out in the country and dump 'em in the creek?" Bob asked.

"Hell, there's so many bodies already in that creek you could walk across it without gettin' your feet wet." Johnny Reid slipped a playing card into the sleeve of one of the dead men. "Just leave 'em. Ain't no law gonna care to find out who kilt a couple of card cheats."

The next morning, when the landlady opened the door to the room to change the towels, she saw the bodies of Ellis and Snyder, screamed, and called the police. The lawmen found the queen of spades in the shirt sleeve of James Ellis. As Johnny predicted, they ruled the killing as justifiable homicide.

10

Georgette couldn't eat or sleep for two days. She couldn't get out of her head the image of the two Purples being hurdled across the room by the combined power of the shotgun and Tommy gun. Her home in St. Louis beckoned.

When they had moved into their apartment on the western end of Detroit, it was filthy. The walls were covered with thrown food and drink, and the floors were stained with vomit and urine from drunken men sleeping wherever they fell. Cleaning it gave her mind a chance to reflect on her situation. Since meeting Gus Winkler, her home had been broken into, her sister tied up, and, including the shooting in St. Louis, a total of six people were slain right before her eyes. If only Gus was not so loving and understanding, she might be able to back out on her til-death-do-we-part promise.

Except for being a gangster, Gus was the perfect husband. Somehow, cleaning the apartment made her think that maybe she could clean up her husband's bad habits too.

It was cold enough in St. Louis, but that cold was nothing to the cold in Michigan. She had not ceased or abated shivering since arriving in Detroit. Overhead, the sky was thick with ducks and geese going in the direction Georgette wanted to go. It seemed their honks mocked her for not following them. The thought of wintering in Detroit filled her with dread, such dread as she had not felt in years. It was snowing but she knew that the worst cold didn't come with snow. It would come with the freezing wind blowing through the Great Lake area.

When her husband came home, she gave him an empty gaze. "My heart is here with you, but my body wants to be someplace warmer," Georgette said as she rushed into his arms.

Gus didn't understand what his wife was saying until he saw the look in her eyes. Desperation. She had complained about the weather before, but there was something intense this time. He had to admit that cold seemed to take the humor out of folks. There was only cold and work to be had in Detroit.

The fact was, his mind was on work at that moment. Johnny Reid was being blamed for a Sicilian mobster's brother being killed. Despite his fear that things were about to get bloody again, he struggled to forget these matters and concentrate on Georgette.

Maybe she was just having a fancy of some kind. He'd been told that females often developed fancies that would stay in their brains for weeks, maybe even months. Once, Georgette had caught him looking at a pretty waitress named Sally. She didn't say anything about it, but when she got mad at him three months later, she scolded him and shouted that maybe he should just go live with that hussy waitress, Sally.

"Well, honey." Gus had a sudden realization that if things were about to go bad, getting Georgette away might be a good thing. "We're nearly done here in Detroit. Why don't you take the train home, and I'll be there directly when business is done?"

Georgette was shocked. She had never expected Gus to offer her an option to stay or return to St. Louis ahead of him. She leaped at the opportunity to get to an even slightly warmer climate.

Gus hid that he was annoyed at his wife's decision to accept his offer so quickly, but he forced a comforting smile when he took her to the train station.

"You will stay out of trouble, won't you, Gussie?" The gray, snowy sky didn't seem quite so bleak knowing she was going south. "You're honor bound, you know."

"Bet on it." Gus kissed her hard. "See ya in the funny papers."

He stood, watching until the train disappeared around a bend, then turned and, with slumping shoulders, went back to work.

***

"The Sicilian mob is tryin' to extort protection money from me," Johnny Reid told the other Rats a few evenings later during a few after-hour drinks at his soda shop bar.

Gus wasn't in the mood to talk shop, especially if it involved mob activity. He never imagined he would miss Georgette so much. She had become his conscience concerning such matters. Sleepless nights resulted the next morning in long-distance telephone conversations with them both talking in loud enough voices to be heard across the hundreds of miles of wire. Unfortunately, the calls usually resulted in the lines being lost before enough I love yous could be said.

The Winklers had come to the city simply to organize the transportation of Canadian alcohol into the country and then on to East St. Louis. After several meetings with Canadian smugglers, Gus was looking forward to getting home to Georgette. Now, Johnny seemed determined to drag all the former Rats into underworld activities in Detroit.

"Why don't you let the Purples take care of the wops for you?" Gus suggested. Carl Shelton had made a positive impression on Gus. The Shelton brothers kept a low profile. They hired out their assassinations to the Cuckoo Gang whenever possible. Unlike Charlie Birger, who often surrounded himself with dozens of gunmen, Carl kept the number that he trusted low.

"We don't need those kikes." Reid shook his head. "Mike Dipisa is the Sicilian boss. I just got a report that at this very moment, he's at a blind pig down on Hunt Street. I say we do a drive-by and end this."

"Damned right." Fred hefted his Tommy gun with one hand and pointed it toward the ceiling.

Fearing the gangster might fire a few rounds through the roof, Gus slid his chair back. Fred preferred the Birger approach. He was most happy when surrounded by guns, gangsters, molls, and stolen money.

Since Johnny Reid had few allies in Detroit, Gus feared he might be attempting to recruit them to form his own gang. What would Georgette say if her husband told her they were moving to Detroit?

Black Charlie Harris was also unhappy to be getting involved in Johnny's fight with the Italian mob. Shaking his head, he stood, walked to the window, and stared out into the street. The "lone gangster," as Georgette called him, was still tired and edgy from transporting a truckload of booze hundreds of miles, then turning around and driving back to Detroit. Still, both he and Gus remained silent. It might be more dangerous to not go along with the others.

At the sedan, Gus assumed his customary position as the wheel man with Johnny riding shotgun beside him. Gat in hand, Fred Burke climbed into the backseat. Bob and Black Charlie joined him on either side, and both propped a pump action shotgun next to their knee.

More than a little traffic filled the well-lit streets. The many factories in the industrial area were changing over to the two a.m. shift. Both workers who were late for work and those hurrying home made for somewhat hazardous driving.

After ten minutes of directing Gus, Johnny pointed between two buildings. "Turn down this alley and stop just before the next street."

Gus parked next to a big trash bin.

"Dipisa wears a straw hat," Reid told Gus. He relaxed back in the seat, his head against the window, and shut his eyes. "You take the first watch for a couple of hours, then wake me."

Gus yawned, a habit he often did when nervous. Sicilians, even the ones under Dipisa, were nothing to scoff at. The ones in Chicago were terrorizing not only their own city but mobs in New York, Kansas City, and a dozen other metropolitan areas in the United States. For Reid and Burke to want to hit a Sicilian boss in Detroit seemed a good way to bring the entire Italian mafioso down on top of them.

"I've got the misery in my back," Black Charlie moaned. He opened the back passenger door and stepped out next to the trash bin. Fred and Bob were already snoring.

The sound of urine flowing slowly and weakly was followed by the smell of cigarette smoke, then the trumpet of a nose being blown. A moment later, Black Charlie appeared next to the driver's side door. Gus rolled down the window.

"Pissing hurts like cold water on a toothache." Black Charlie offered Gus a cigarette.

"You been with the Blonde Bombshell?" Gus laughed.

"Come sunup, I might be in the mood to tell you." Black Charlie's *damn you* didn't have to be muttered.

"Don't be a piker." Gus laughed. "Hell, Blondie's gave half of Little Egypt the clap. You thinkin' of livin' down there?"

"I might be tempted to hang my hat in Herrin for a while."

The two smoked in silence for several minutes. Finally, Black Charlie walked around the car to the passenger side, opened the back door, and got in. The three men sleeping didn't even budge when he slammed the car door harder than needed.

Three hours later, during Johnny's watch, he yelled, "There he is!"

Gus awoke from a half-sleep and started the engine. Bob and Charlie lowered the glass in their windows. Fred Burke sat up straight. He needed to prepare himself to lean out whichever window offered the best opportunity. All five men in the vehicle placed plugs in their ears.

The sun peeked above the buildings in the east as Gus floored the accelerator and pulled the sedan into the early morning traffic. Dipisa and two bodyguards stood smoking on the sidewalk to their right. Fred leaned across Black Charlie as if he weren't there, his Tommy gun in position.

Black Charlie just had time to pump a load into his shotgun when Fred let loose a hail of bullets. The flashes from the guns reflected off the windshield, temporarily obscuring Gus's view of the traffic in front of him. He jerked the steering wheel to avoid a swerving vehicle, then sped them from the scene. His flivver hurtled through the streets, hissed up a long hill, then took a corner so fast it left the ugly graffiti of black skid marks on the pavement.

"Damn!" Fred smacked a palm on the back of Gus's head. "You drove too fast. We missed him completely."

"I might've got one of the guards," Johnny said from the front seat. He was hastily reloading his revolver. "But I only got four shots off myself."

"Fine bunch of assassins you guys are," Bob yelled. "Get 'em on my side next time. I won't miss!"

"Hell, Bob," Johnny bellowed over his shoulder. "If you'd had any guts, you'd have stood outside the car on the runnin' board and fired."

"Stop by that hotel!" Fred ordered. "I need a shot of whiskey."

"It's morning, Fred." Johnny tucked his still smoking revolver back in his shoulder holster. "You need to cut back on your boozin'."

After enjoying a leisurely breakfast washed down with Bloody Marys all around, the five gunmen returned to the car. No sooner were they back on the four-lane than a Cadillac sped up next to them. Gus was the first to spot the danger. He floored the accelerator and whipped the steering wheel hard to the left just as bullets began bouncing off his sedan. With the enemy on his side of the car, Bob Carey now had the opportunity he'd longed for—only the rapid fire of pistols from Dipisa's car drove all of Johnny's gang to duck low in their seats.

Gus often bragged about driving while under fire during the war, but never with quite as many bullets finding their mark on his sedan. He too ducked below the dash, even as he pushed the brake to the floor so hard their vehicle slid sideways into a parked police car. The two policemen in the patrol car also ducked and stayed that way until Gus had time to rise back up and give chase to Dipisa and his thugs.

Fred Burke was incensed. He rolled across Bob Carey, who was still on the floorboard, opened the back door, and leaped onto the running board. As Gus sped within firing distance, Fred let loose a long volley of .45 caliber bullets until his ammunition drum ran dry.

"Give me the shotgun!" Fred yelled as he tossed the empty gat onto Bob's lap. Bob tried to reload the Tommy gun with a new drum, but the barrel was so hot he burned his trousers.

Gus used the traffic to his advantage. Seeing a bus blocking the Cadillac's lane, he swerved into oncoming traffic and then slowed just enough so Johnny and Black Charlie could unleash a blizzard of lead into Dipisa's car.

Dipisa himself was driving with one hand and shooting with a revolver in the other. He pulled the steering wheel hard to the left and rammed the back side of Gus's sedan. Sparks flew from the metal against metal, but also from the lead being fired from the rival gangs.

Gus again floored the accelerator. With little control of his damaged back end, he was forced to drive up on the sidewalk. Pedestrians screamed and leaped for safety into buildings and even into the street. One heavyset man was too slow. His body rolled over the hood and crashed through the windshield where he stuck, his butt inches from Gus's steering wheel.

Despite the lack of visibility, Gus managed to get the sedan back on the road. He quickly motored a few blocks before making a hard right turn that sent the fat man rolling into a fruit vendor's stand.

The vehicle looked like Swiss cheese. It coughed and sputtered, but eventually made it back to Johnny's speakeasy. Fred said nothing as he entered the saloon ahead of the others. He went straight to the bar where he grabbed a full bottle of Irish Whiskey, downed half of it without taking a breath, then fell sideways onto the floor.

"Is he hurt?" Bob asked.

"I doubt he sank to his knees to pray." Black Charlie shook his head.

Johnny rolled him onto his side. A bullet had found its way through Fred's shoulder and out his back.

11

When Fred awoke, he found himself in a room above Johnny's soda shop bar. Soft music from a Victrola floated into his ears from another room. He didn't know why the music made him sad or even what the sadness was for. His prospects were meager, but his luck seemed boundless. Proof of that was the bullet that passed clean through him without hitting anything vital. Luck was better than wisdom, at least while you were alive. Dying a quick and easy death was a lucky thing few could count on. Fred wasn't scared of dying if it came with little pain.

He preferred to be shot by a rifle so long as the bullet went clean through as this one had. Once, he had caught a rifle bullet in his shoulder, but the shot had come from so far away the bullet was spent. It lodged in a muscle and hurt like the dickens. Now that he had been shot again, he couldn't get a notion out of his head, the notion being that his luck might be running out. He tried to remind himself that he knew of men who had survived six or more bullets. Still, life was an uncertain business.

The next night, Fred Burke marched into Johnny's, Tommy gun in hand, wearing a bulletproof vest over his bandaged wound. Black Charlie wanted to laugh but didn't. No gangster he'd ever seen would stoop to wearing a flak jacket.

"Dipisa loves that dago food at Papa Leo Giorlando's Restaurant," Fred said. "It's in the basement of a sandstone. Even if he ain't there, I intend to ruin his appetite."

Johnny was out of his chair with Bob steps behind. Black Charlie moved slower but followed. He cursed himself for not leaving town after yesterday's fiasco. *But how could I know these idiots would be right back on the street twenty-four hours later?*

Again, Gus drove. After parking the car down the street from Leo's, he turned to Fred. "Listen, Fred. Leave the gat. This is a small place. Four pistols should do the job this time."

Burke looked down at his Tommy gun like he was saying goodbye to a beloved pet. He tucked it down on the floorboard, got out of the car, and led the way into the building. Gus remained in the sedan with it running in case a quick getaway was needed.

Inside, the four gunmen took just a moment to adjust their eyes to the candlelight glowing from each table, the ambiance of the room a perfect setting for romance. A half dozen couples sat at individual tables; the ladies dressed in low-cut gowns that left just enough to their dates' imagination to ensure an evening of attempted seductions.

At the cash register, Papa Leo conferred with his business partner and their master chef. The chef waved his arms as he argued something in Italian. A waitress with "Marion" on her name tag approached the four gangsters.

"You may sit anywhere you want. I'll be with you in a moment."

As she walked away, Fred pulled two pistols and unloaded them in the direction of the three men at the register.

Couples ducked and ran for the back door. Two of the men abandoned their high-heeled dates to fend for themselves. Johnny, Bob, and Black Charlie followed Fred's lead but aimed at mirrors, bottles of alcohol, and then at two men who had blown out the candle on their table so they could snuggle without notice.

Fred managed to cut down two of the men at the cash register, but somehow Papa Leo made it to the back door unscathed. He darted away into the darkness of an alley, even as a last fusillade of bullets flew all around him. The firing stopped.

Papa Leo's shouts faded as he ran down the street screaming in Italian, *"Dai! Qualcuno mi ha appena sparato!"*

***

Once they were back at Johnny's speakeasy, Gus worried the shooting at Papa Leo's would incite the ire of the Italian Mafia that was rapidly infiltrating every major city in America. They were arriving in the country from Sicily, driven out of Italy by the ruthless dictatorship of Benito Mussolini.

Gus was not alone in his worrying. Black Charlie slipped away that afternoon on the pretext of needing to help one of his sisters.

Johnny Reid, Fred Burke, and Bob Carey seemed unconcerned. Still, they put a closed sign on the door and took turns watching the streets from an upstairs apartment. They also laid out on the tables a vast armory of weapons and ammunition, enough for a siege that could last at least until the Detroit police arrived to save them.

Gus found a table away from the others and worked on a letter to Georgette. Lying came easy to Gus, but composing a fictional account of his activities that would not alarm his wife was tricky. He tried to replace the shootouts with a fib about going to a baseball game. He tore that page up when he realized it was getting too full of untruths. He would never be able to remember them all later if interrogated. Starting the letter again, he decided to stick to mush he knew Georgette would appreciate. This went fine until he realized the love letter had evolved into more truth than intended. His words evoked how much he truly missed his wife. When a tear dropped onto the paper causing a smudge in the wet ink, he leaned back in his chair and focused his attention on his fellow gang members.

Johnny was coming down the stairs from watch duty. Except for the sound of evening traffic and pedestrians on the sidewalk, the room was unusually silent. Then the telephone on the wall sounded one long and two short rings.

"Not my ring," Johnny said. He rapped a half-dozing Fred on the head with his knuckles, but the killer was so intoxicated he didn't even open his eyes. "Looks like you're up, Gimpy. And leave those Penny Dreadfuls here. You can't read and stand watch at the same time."

With a disgusted spit toward Fred, Bob tossed the magazines on the table, picked up a shotgun, and, with slumped shoulders, sulked his way up the staircase. Gus didn't blame Bob for being upset with Fred's drunkenness. His only worry was that Bob would spend his watch looking through girly pictures while his hand shook like a banjo player inside his trousers. The man's mind was seldom on anything except women. Fearing his obsession would be a distraction and put them all in danger, Gus decided to relieve him as soon as he finished the letter.

Johnny walked behind the bar, retrieved a bottle of his best Scotch, and waved the bottom of it toward Gus, who accepted the invitation with a nod of his head.

The store owner held up a pinch of ice. "Slow it down?"

"No." Gus folded his letter to finish later. "As it comes."

Johnny brought the bottle and two glasses to the table.

"One drink." Gus pulled a chair out for his friend to sit. "Then I'll relieve Bob."

"Probably a good idea." Johnny chuckled. He gave each glass two fingers of Scotch. "I'd 'spect that right about now, Gimpy's hand is busier than a cow's tail swooshin' flies in a hot barn."

"His mind does only travel in that one direction."

"So, what direction does your mind run?"

"Similar as yours, but with a mite less violence." Gus saw this as an opportunity to pick Johnny's brain about running a business.

"You want to go legit?" Johnny asked.

"As legit as I can and still provide for Georgette and any rugrats that come along."

"That's a narrow ledge to tread."

"Some folks seem to accomplish it." Gus sipped his drink. "Ownin' a home with a white picket fence and such."

"Yes, and they're usually one paycheck away from losin; it all."

"I plan on givin' it a try. Georgette is worth the effort."

The phone on the wall sounded two longs and a short.

"That's me." Johnny glanced at the window. "Would you get it?"

Answering it would mean putting himself in a direct line with the big store window. With one eye looking out onto the street, Gus got up, walked behind the bar, took the earpiece off the hook, and leaned forward to say hello into the speaker.

"Mike Dipisa has a message for you, Johnny," Gus announced after a full minute of listening. "He says that two of his men went rogue and blames them for making the extortion demand without his consent."

"Tell him to deliver them to us and I'll accept his truce."

Gus relayed the message and then returned to the table. He needed another drink.

An hour later a black sedan pulled up in front of Johnny's place. Wearing shirt sleeves, the unarmed driver got out, walked across the street, then down the boardwalk and out of sight.

"Fred." Johnny shook the drunken man's shoulder hard, then delivered an opportunity he knew would wake Fred. "There's a case of whiskey in the trunk of that car. Go get it and you can keep a bottle."

Fred tipped his chair over getting to his feet. Like a walking Leaning Tower of Pisa, he staggered outside and opened the trunk. He immediately slammed it shut, tripped over the curb, and struggled to make his way back inside.

"There ain't no hooch in that car," Fred slurred. "Just a couple of red hots, bound and gagged."

***

That night Gus drove the sedan cautiously north out of Detroit. He feared that if he got stopped by a cop the muffled screams of the men in the trunk could cause problems. Neither Johnny nor Bob seemed worried that using the same vehicle the two extortionists were delivered in could be a setup. Fred was asleep on the backseat floorboard with Bob's gimpy leg resting on his back.

"Take the dirt road that goes to the Lake Huron rendezvous," Johnny said. "I wanna leave one final message for these Detroit thugs to stay away from us."

Gus thought the gesture foolish. The lake shore rendezvous was a common location for several gangs to transfer Canadian alcohol into the United States. Bringing attention to this spot would be damaging to more than just Mike Dipisa. An action like this just cemented Gus's belief that the southern Illinois hoods were amateurs compared to the big-time city gangsters.

The dirt road was empty except for deer and other wildlife. With the glow of a nearly full moon, Gus was able to navigate with his headlights off. When they reached the lake shore, he did a tight U-turn so the vehicle was facing back in the direction they had come.

Perhaps sensing the excitement of a murder, Fred Burke awoke and was the first to exit the vehicle. By the time Gus joined the others, Fred and Bob had the two terrified extortionists out of the trunk and kneeling at the water's edge. One of the thugs was crying so hard, Fred had to grasp the hair on the top of his head to prevent him from falling forward onto the ground. The other doomed man seemed to accept his fate. With a smirk on his face and eyes blazing, he stared up at the moon and Venus. Gus admired his courage.

Johnny Reid pumped one bullet each into the back of their skulls. The cowering man was blasted forward with such intensity Fred was left holding a handful of hair. The body fell forward into the water.

Gus walked over and stood looking down at the gangster who had died so bravely. He was stone dead, eyes wide open, the smirk still on his face. He lay without quivering.

12

Gus didn't trust gangsters, much less Mike Dipisa. The deal Johnny made with the Sicilians was only as good as their sweaty handshake. The mostly Jewish Purple Gang were the ones most hurt by the car chase gun battle. Law enforcement was now coming down hard on organized crime, and the Purples, being the largest organization in Detroit, had the most to lose.

A month after dispatching the two extortionists, Gus, Black Charlie, and Fred Burke were on their way to pick up Johnny Reid at his home.

"Pass me a smoke, Gus."

"Tarnation, Fred." Without taking his eyes off the road, Gus reached into his breast coat pocket, extracted a cigarette, and flicked it over his shoulder into the backseat of the sedan. "I've never known a time since I met you that you've carried your own tobacco."

"But he never forgets his flask," Black Charlie reminded them both. He was already regretting not hiding out any longer at his sister's house. His brief relationship with the St. Louis boys had already gotten him in two shootouts—without any monetary gains. If his sister and her husband had not been such wet blankets, he might not have returned to the gang's headquarters at Johnny's. But they were teetotalers and crazy religious to boot, traits Charlie Harris couldn't abide.

Fred sank into the backseat, took a deep swallow from his flask, and then settled back to enjoy his smoke and wait. Perhaps it was the full moon that shone above Gus's side of the windshield that made Fred feel so bloody. It had been a month since the gang killed the two would-be extortionists by the light of that same moon hovering above and reflecting off the waters of Lake Huron. Fred had kept for a souvenir the handful of bloody hair that he had been holding when Johnny put the bullet in the thug's head. The blast from the .44 was powerful enough to litter the water in the lake with bits of skull and brain matter.

"I want a beer, and I wanna kill someone," Fred muttered.

Gus and Charlie looked at one another.

"Hell, Fred," Black Charlie chuckled. "Johnny Reid's got more enemies than a dog's got hairs on his back. I'm sure he can come up with someone for you to kill."

"Sounds like Fred's ready to go all Sherman scorched earth." Gus looked into the mirror at the killer in the backseat. "Ain't you startin' to itch before you git bit, old boy?

"Ol' Fred can't see past the brim of his hat." Charlie lowered himself in his seat as a police vehicle came toward them. No sooner than it passed, another squad car arrived at an intersection in front of them. It ran the stop sign and accelerated to catch the first one.

"Something's up, Gus." Black Charlie looked into the backseat to make certain their arsenal was hidden from view under a dark blanket. Neither Fred nor he could afford any more trouble with the law. They were both becoming well-known to local, state, and even federal officials.

"Let's just drive by Johnny's house in case he's outside waitin' for us," Fred suggested.

The lane leading up to the Reid home was dark, with a front lawn filled with trees and bushes. When they got close, a shadow moved behind one of the evergreens.

"There he is." Fred rolled down his window to signal Johnny.

"Don't!" Gus shouted when he saw much of the vegetation come to life with movement. "There's thugs behind every bush. He's treed like a coon."

Just as Johnny waved and stepped out from behind the tree, a shotgun blast struck at just the right spot on the back of his neck that his head was blown completely off his shoulders.

"Ambush!" Charlie ducked beneath the dash. "Floor it!"

At least one bullet ricocheted off their car as they sped away. They were in no position to make it a fight.

***

The following morning, the Egan Rats were mourning Johnny's murder by drinking up his liquor, which they now considered to be free.

"The medical examiner gave Johnny's death a creative cause." Bob Carey looked up from the newspaper. "He called it 'traumatic cerebral hemorrhage.'"

"They're trying to hide the gang war from the public," Gus suggested. He prided himself on public relations, having already negotiated protection for his St. Louis friends by paying off several cops and government officials in Detroit.

"I found out it's Frankie Wright that blew Johnny's head off." Fred's assertion surprised no one. Wright was a newbie in the underworld of Detroit. His gambling debts were building up to where he could easily be bought. "The Purple Gang boss, Abe Bernstein, also has a hit out on Wright for knockin' off one of their kikes. Bernstein said he'd pay—but good—to fix Wright."

"You gonna do it?" Charlie asked. He didn't like getting mixed up in gang wars.

"*We're* gonna do it," Burke corrected. He glared at Charlie as if seeing him for the first time. "You know, for a fella that's supposed to be such a tough guy, you seem mighty hesitant to get bloody."

Black Charlie glared back but knew better than to argue. Since Bernie Shelton had just sent him a telegram calling him back to Little Egypt, he had an excuse if he wanted out. Still, being labeled a coward was not something he could tolerate. The Sheltons could wait. "What's the plan?" he asked Fred.

Gus also was toying with various acceptable ways of saying that he wanted out. As hard as he thought about it, no honorable reason came to mind.

"The Purple Gang'll snatch Wright's friend," Fred explained. "Wright pays the ransom, and Bernstein tells him to pick up his friend at the Milaflores Apartments. We'll have rented out the entire floor. When he goes to get him, we're waiting."

Charlie found the plan workable. The following week, he, Fred, and Bob waited on a fire escape until Wright showed up with two of his heavies. When Wright knocked on the door where he was told his friend was being held, Fred threw open the fire door and began blasting with his Tommy gun. Charlie and Bob stepped in next to him and unloaded their .38 caliber revolvers. After just a few moments, the gun smoke became so thick the assassins couldn't see their victims lying on the floor. One of the dying men moaned.

"Get him!" Bob yelled. With shaking hands, he struggled to reload his .38. "Get him again!"

Fred didn't need encouragement. He unloaded a torrent of lead into the bodies until his ammunition drum ran dry. The three hitmen turned and raced down the fire escape. Gus had the motor running and, as the last car door slammed shut, he raced the vehicle out of the alley.

13

Georgette didn't tell Gus when cash began running low. She was afraid he'd succumb to temptation and do something to get himself in trouble. Instead, she took a job as a waitress working twelve-hour shifts and accepting all the overtime offered. She was on her feet so much her ankles swelled. Each night when she got home, she lay on the edge of the bed with her feet dangling into a bucket on the floor filled with ice water and Epsom salts.

Then one night, three boys, barely in their teens, walked into the café ten minutes before closing. They were dressed in letterman sweaters and dress pants. Georgette looked to Cookie's window. He owned the joint and since it had been a slow day, he gave her a nod. A few extra bucks in the till would help make the weekly goal.

Young men were the product of their parents, of that Georgette was certain. Either they had been taught good manners or they had not. Her first hint that these boys may not be the wholesome youth they appeared came when one of them smiled at her. It wasn't the courteous smile that should have come from innocence. Instead, it was a braggy smile, bristling with a confidence and worldliness that one so young should never have. The boy whispered something to his friends. Laughing, they turned and looked over their shoulders at her.

Georgette's beauty gave her a power she no longer appreciated. It was both a blessing and a curse. It meant nice tips, especially from elderly gentlemen of means who were still young enough to appreciate being served by a friendly beauty with a pretty smile. It also meant putting up with unwanted sexual suggestions, butt grabs, and sometimes even death threats when she refused the advances.

Georgette tolerated most brushes along her backside, but when the brash teen with the braggy smile pulled her blouse down and grabbed a handful of breast, she instinctively poured a pot of hot coffee into his lap. The fist that connected a few inches below her sternum knocked all the air out of her lungs. She fell forward onto the table, sending the salt and pepper shakers flying across the room.

Cookie hurried around the counter but stopped when one of the thugs stuck a pistol under his nose. The gun was twice the size as the youth's hand.

When she was pulled back off the table, Georgette's blouse was nearly ripped completely off. A hard backhand knocked her to the floor, the back of her head hitting the linoleum with such force she nearly lost consciousness. Next came several kicks to her side and one to her head. There was nothing she could do but curl up as tight as possible.

As much as the beating hurt, she knew the worst was yet to come—rape. Though she fought and scratched, she could not break free. His breath was like that of a possum, foul and dirty. She tried shitting her pants. One of her friends had successfully used that technique to discourage her attacker, but for Georgette, no shit would come. So, instead, she crossed her feet and squeezed her legs together as tightly as she could. The boy tried to wedge a knee between her thighs, but she was way too determined to budge.

Then, as suddenly as it was there, his weight was off her. Through glassy eyes, she saw the boy's body being hurdled across the room and landing cross-bodied onto one of his friends. The boy with the gun ran for the door, quickly followed by the other two.

A tall man knelt over her. Cookie appeared with a bowl of water, dipped a rag into it, and began rinsing her face.

"Not the dirty dishwater, Cookie!" Georgette turned her head to the side as bits of pulled pork, the day's specialty, stuck to her mouth and forehead.

Cookie raced back to the kitchen to try and find a clean bowl.

"You're Gus Winkler's wife," the tall man said.

Georgette took a good look at him. "Mr. Carl Shelton." Grimacing, she sat up, then kicked the bowl filled with dishwater away from her, though the odor of the foul liquid was as good as any smelling salt.

With great pain in her ribs and with the help of Carl, Georgette stood and walked over to a mirror behind the counter. Blood dripped from her lip and a yellowing bruise colored her cheek. She'd tended enough of her friends with similar damage to know the marks from the beating would not last more than two or three weeks.

"I'm obligated to report this night's events to your husband," Carl Shelton said. "I'd be sore at any man who wouldn't do the same for me."

"I don't mind you tellin' him you saved me. I suppose it's only fair you get credit that you'll surely use to gain favor on your next alcohol transaction. But would you mind not tellin' him I was waitressin' at the time of your gallantry?"

"Well, I suppose I'll leave the details to you," Carl said slowly.

Georgette couldn't control her head. The floor was rising to meet the ceiling. She clutched Carl Shelton's shoulders as if she were about to fall. He smiled at her in a way that made her think about death.

Then she lost consciousness.

***

Georgette dreamed that time had reverted to before she'd agreed to let Gus be an alcohol distributor. The ribs below her heart felt tingly like bubbles expanding, then contracting again between the bones. A voice came to her as if from a great distance away.

"Georgette. Georgy girl. It's me, Gus."

When she opened her eyes, Georgette remembered it was the third night in a row she'd been sleeping propped up in the hospital bed, a pillow over her chest that she squeezed against when she had to cough, which occurred often.

"Does it hurt, honey?" He was alarmed at his wife's despondency. Then, she looked at him, and it were as if a light turned on behind her pretty brown eyes.

"Worse than chiggers but not as bad as bedbugs." Georgette tried to laugh but it turned into a cough, causing her to pull the pillow tighter against her chest.

"Don't joke, Georgy girl." Gus laid his head gently on her shoulder. "When Carl Shelton called me, I got here quick as I could. What were you doin' in that dive so late at night, anyway?"

Gus's big head tilted her body just enough to bring pain to her cracked ribs. She tried to sit up a little straighter. Her husband clumsily tried to help but only made the discomfort worse. Accepting that the discomfort was not as painful as his help, she held up a hand.

"I'm fine now. Thank you, Gussie," Georgette grimaced. "You'll find out later, so I might as well tell you now. I took a job at the café to pay a few bills. I just didn't want to bother you with them."

Gus pulled back, then stood and paced. "If you had told me, I could have fixed it."

"To a man with a hammer, every problem is a nail." Georgette reached for his hand, which he gave her. "I have some skin in the game on this one, and I want to have my views heard. I didn't want you to do somethin' stupid to get the money. There's enough folks been killed for easy cash."

"You are just the most stubborn female I've ever known."

"If that's how you feel, I prefer you insult me." Georgette clutched her pillow as another bubble formed between her ribs. "At least I'll know what you're really thinkin'."

"Why couldn't you have just trusted me to take care of this without believin' I'd turn into a monster?"

"The world is full of monsters." Georgette suppressed a cough. "When we become desperate, the monster in all of us emerges."

"Well, I oughtn't to." Gus resumed his pacing. He searched for and found the lucky nickel in his pocket and began jiggling it. "There's just certain things my vanity won't abide."

***

Gus spent three months helping his wife get back on her feet and even longer before her full energy returned. She had been suffering from exhaustion even before the attack. Finally, her swollen ankles returned to their normal size. The ribs, however, healed more slowly.

Her long convalescence gave Gus time to learn the identities of the three youths involved in the attack. He didn't kill them, but he made sure their injuries would still be causing them pain long after his wife recovered.

Gus loved yardwork and gardening, but, when one rainy day Georgette tried to coerce him into helping her paint a room, he figured she was healed enough and made up an excuse to go away on business for a couple of weeks. The true reason for his exodus, though, was he had spent all the money he'd made on the Milaflores apartment assassination, a killing he'd hid from her, though its investigation was front page news for weeks, mostly because it was the first time a Tommy gun had been used in Michigan to kill someone.

Gus was troubled by the sorrow in Georgette's eyes. He'd never been meant for criminal life. Of that he was certain. He loved best the days in spring when they could work together in the garden. At night, she always held him in her arms, putting her legs over his. She wanted him to know that life with her would always be more rewarding than life on the lam.

She could change her husband's habits but not his history, and it was with this history the problem laid. The legal system and the newsmakers were beginning to label him an outlaw. Georgette had watched him go away before, always with irritation, and often, as now, with trepidation. Death always seemed a phone call or a knock on the door away.

On the next sunny day, Georgette was back in the garden. She had always teased Gus by how perfectly straight he sowed the seeds in the garden, even removing certain ones if they snaked their way through the soil and came in wrong. But this day, she sowed them carefully and slowly, as if her sanity or even Gus's life depended upon keeping the seeds in a perfect line. By the time her husband returned, the plants would be blooming. She didn't want Gus wasting valuable moments pruning the garden when he could be loving her instead.

14

"The paper says we got fourteen bullets into Frankie Wright," Fred told Gus. "But that son-of-a-bitch lived long enough to tell the cops, 'The machine gun worked. That's all I can remember.' Then he croaked. I hope that cop wasn't hankerin' for no long conversation."

"Well, I swear." It was all Gus could think of saying. Listening to Fred ramble for nearly two hours was getting on his nerves. There was no need to chatter just to please Fred. The Illinois country began to flatten out as Gus drove north along dirt country roads. He found he could drive anywhere in Illinois by the backroads since they were cut up into square miles. All he had to do was keep heading north. Most fields were barren with occasional deer scrounging for leftovers. Since Gus wasn't talky, Fred amused himself by sticking his pistol out the window to take shots at them. In his inebriated state, the wildlife was pretty safe.

The dust and pollen from the freshly harvested fields made Gus keep wiping his eyes with his fingers. His vision was swimming again, as it had when he was drunk. Lately, he felt he was going crazy from all the strain. Georgette's taking a job and her run-in with the three youths had been a rude awakening, making him tense with anger. In such a mood, Gus was apt to make tart remarks so he forced himself to not talk. The trick to not talking was the ability to not hear.

Luckily, Fred was getting rambling drunk. The beer ran out the corners of his mouth and into his dirty, tobacco-stained beard. Because of the facial hair, Gus knew Killer Burke was preparing for something unlawful.

Fred had shown little fidelity as of late, ranging from one gang alliance to another with hardly a look back at old friends. He couldn't fairly be blamed. Freelance work was where the money was. It wouldn't matter so much to Gus, but if Fred continued to burn bridges that connected to the St. Louis Irish mobsters, things could go south in a hurry. This day's meeting with a representative of the Cuckoo Gang would be an opportunity to mend one of those alliances. The Cuckoos pleaded urgent business in St. Louis and were willing to pay extremely well.

From atop a roll of the prairie, Gus spotted the rendezvous spot. They arrived early to scout out any possible ambush. A brick grain bin and a windmill next to a burnt-to-the-ground home were quickly investigated and found to be safe. They returned to the vehicle for a smoke. A couple of cows stood behind a barbed wire fence watching them, looking like they would be grateful if someone would cut the fence for them. To his credit and Gus's amazement, Fred stopped drinking. They sat quietly for an hour.

Finally, to pass the time, Fred got out of the flivver and relieved himself. While he was cleaning the back tire with a long flow of beer piss, a sedan approached and parked about a hundred yards away. An old man got out on the passenger side. Using a white cane, he tapped his way to the front of his vehicle and then in a straight line toward Fred. The driver, who appeared not old enough to drive, stayed behind the steering wheel, which he could barely see over.

It seemed suspicious that a blind man had been sent by the Cuckoo Gang to negotiate a deal. Gus reached inside his jacket and unholstered his pistol, then got out and walked toward the blind man.

After he had gone halfway to them, the old man's shout came forced and raspy. "It would help if one of you fellas would say somethin' so I don't lose my sense of direction." He coughed hard.

"Just keep comin', old timer," Gus said. "You're doin' fine."

The man gave a strange, jerky laugh then slightly adjusted his course.

Gus relaxed a little when he saw the blind man's eyes were milky white. His brown face was nothing but wrinkles. A few tuffs of the white hair on his chest stuck out from the top of his Farmer Johns. He had a heavy, round face. The back of his head, though, was flat all the way up from his shoulders.

"Your mother must've let you sleep on your back too much," Fred said rather cruelly. "I could iron a shirt on the back of your head."

The blind man's half laugh, half cough was followed by several moments of silence except for his heavy breathing to get his wind back. Finally, he turned his face toward the warmth of the sun. "Where am I?"

"You're standin' on a dirt road." Gus sensed the man had grown old and lonely, forgetting who he had once been. "Somewhere in central Illinois."

"Oh, yeah. Makes sense, I suppose." The old man put his cane in front of him and rested the palms of both hands on it. "You fellas wanna come over to my place for some rotgut?"

"That's neighborly of you." Gus chuckled. "We're here because you're supposed to deliver a message."

"Oh, yeah. The message is—" The old man's voice became a feeble whisper as if a cow might hear and get him in trouble. "Rub out. The Submarine Bar basement. Thursday, September twenty-second. Gus Catanzaro and anyone with him."

"That's the night of the Dempsey-Tunney title fight." Fred started walking back to the car. "I can't give anyone a dirt nap that night. I've got too much money riding on Dempsey."

***

"I accepted the contract," Gus told Fred during the drive back to St. Louis. "Why you suppose the Cuckoos want Catanzaro dead?"

"Don't know, don't care." Fred was on his last beer. "Stop at the next town. I'm still thirsty."

"Just doesn't make sense they'd pay three times the going rate for this job." Gus glanced over to see how his friend reacted.

Fred threw his empty bottle out the window. "Three times?" He belched.

"Three times," Gus repeated, then remained quiet while Fred did the math on how much he'd get if Dempsey got a knockout against his cut of the blood money if he participated in the knockoff.

***

September 22, 1927

[Radio:]

As they begin the seventh round, neither fighter is cut or marked yet. Tunney shoots a hard left, then follows up with a right. Then Dempsey lands a hard right! And Tunney is down. Tunney is down from a left and a right to the face. There is confusion in the ring. The referee makes Dempsey return to his corner, then he starts the count. One, two, three, four, five, six, seven, eight, nine, and Tunney is up. And now they are at it again. Dempsey is following him around the ring. Tunney backing away. Dempsey doesn't stop. Tunney is trying to protect himself. But nothing can stop this Manassa Mauler. Dempsey stands in the middle of the ring, motioning for Tunney to fight. Tunney's face looks bad. His eye is cut. Now, Tunney is down again, but only for a moment.

"That's it," Fred said. "The fight's in the bag."

Gus turned off the radio and checked his pistols.

"What, Gus?" Ray craned his long neck forward. "You plannin' on joinin' us?"

"After watchin' you and Bob at target practice the other day, I figured I'd better."

"It's rare sport," Fred said. "Gettin' to kill bad men like in a shootin' gallery. Just like we did at Papa Leo Giorlando's Restaurant."

"What makes them any badder than us?" Bob asked. He was cautious about what he said, for in his present mood Fred could flare up in an instant.

As they approached the bar entrance, Gus waved his hand for silence. He cracked the door open and took a peep inside the big barroom. He counted seven members of the Green Ones in all, six standing in front of the bar and one serving drinks behind the counter. Two of the men appeared to be twins. They were discussing the fight and, as far as he could see, they were unarmed. Fred stood so close behind him that his chin brushed Gus's shoulder.

"That was a long count in the seventh round," the barkeep said.

"Yeah, but only because Dempsey forgot the new rule that he had to return to his own corner after a knockdown," another man said.

"Oh, hell." The barkeep shook his head. "It wouldn't have mattered. Tunney was just takin' an eight count. He could've got up quicker if he'd had to."

"Tunney won fair and square," the first man shouted. "It was a unanimous decision after all."

"Dempsey lost?" came a shout from behind the closed door. "Dempsey lost? Capone said he had the fight fixed. How could he have lost?"

Gus knew Fred's shouts had lost them the element of surprise. He kicked the door open, his guns blazing as he led his crew of assassins into the room. They fanned out, firing as they went.

An incensed Fred was often too high-strung to be reliable, but in this case, propelled by a spasm of fury, his accuracy with the pistols seemed elevated by his anger. Using just two bullets from each gun, he drilled one gangster through the leg, the chest, and both hands. Another was able to hide all but his one leg behind the piano, but Fred got him three times in the kneecap leaving only a thin string of cartilage dangling between the man's thigh and calf.

With Fred and the others filling the room with gun smoke, Gus located Gus Catanzaro, their primary target, running for the exit. He managed to hit him on the left hip and right thigh. One of the twins was limping toward the same exit, his brother hunkered down while leaning against him. When they reached Catanzaro, they each grabbed an arm and pulled him through the doorway. While Gus reloaded, bullets from Bob and Ray hit everything except the three escaping men. Bottles and mirrors were shattered making the flying glass more dangerous than the two gunmen's bullets.

With their primary target gone from the scene, Gus signaled the others to beat it back to the car.

"Fred, I don't know why you were in such a hurry to kill those fellas unless you had a powerful taste for whiskey," Ray said when they were several blocks away. "I suppose that would be as good a reason as any for a quick dispatch."

"I don't think he would've been so reckless if Dempsey had won the fight." Gus couldn't bring himself to criticize Fred. His ability to cluster three bullets in a single kneecap seemed truly exceptional marksmanship. "I'm guessing that Fred's ire gave us the advantage we needed."

"Capone's men swore the referee would be a ringer," Fred fumed.

"They changed the referee just before the fight, Fred," Bob told him. "Someone must have leaked that the fix was in."

Following the shooting, Gus ordered the men to split up and meet back in Detroit. It was during his windshield time to Motor City that Gus came up with the idea for easy and relatively safer money—the snatch racket—not the kidnapping of innocent civilians. The Feds were threatening an organization that would have expanded powers in such matters, including crossing state lines in pursuit of suspects, but snatching mobsters that belonged to a gang. That, of course, would never be reported to law enforcement. As he drove the day-long trip, Gus began putting together a list of mobs that were large enough to pay but not so big as to seek revenge.

The next day, he showed the list to Fred Burke and Bob Carey at the late Johnny Reid's establishment.

"We'll need to identify gang members who are valuable enough for the gang to want back," Gus explained.

"That leaves you out, Bob," Fred quipped.

"I say we spread out our jobs," Gus went on. "Hittin' the gangs in Detroit, then New York, Philadelphia, St. Louis, and even Atlantic City. Then we circle back for seconds."

"Why not Chicago?" Fred asked.

"There's too much going on in Chicago right now, what with Johnny Torrio and Al Capone on the South Side duking it out with Joe Aiella and Bugs Moran on the North Side. That shooting at the Hawthorn Hotel has the whole town on pens and needles."

The attempted assassination of Capone at the Hawthorne Hotel had indeed rattled the city. A caravan of eight to ten cars filled with North Side gunmen led by Bugs Moran, Pete Gusenberg, and Hymie Weiss drove by the hotel and emptied dozens of guns into the building. Capone only lived because his bodyguard Frank Rio pulled him to the floor just before the shooting started.

"I heard Capone's got a contract out on Hymie Weiss for tryin' to kill him at the Hawthorne." Fred held up his gat. "Maybe we collect on that?"

"You go right ahead." Gus laughed. "Just don't come near me when the North Siders come gunnin' for you."

15

After six months, the snatch racket was proving too big for just Gus, Fred, Bob, and Ray. They needed a fifth man who could babysit the captive while the others worked to collect the ransom, a sometimes dangerous and complicated procedure.

"You fellas got anyone in mind?" Gus asked.

"Bryan Bolton, a thug from Thayer," Bob suggested. "Thounds like I'm Lithing, doethen't it?"

"What the hell's a Thayer?" Ray asked.

"It's a little town thouth of Thringfield, Illinoith," Bob said.

"Oh, can it, Bob," Fred said, seldom one for humor. "Have him come see us."

When Bryan Bolton walked into Johnny's soda shop a few days later, he was wearing jeans, a tee shirt, and a baseball cap. Gus thought he was there to interview for the dishwashing job.

"My name's Bryan Bolton," the young man said with a twang of country that made his statement sound more like a question.

Gus liked the boy as soon as he opened his mouth. He had a refreshing, not-a-gangster look, and Bryan immediately filled Gus in on his history, holding nothing back.

"I worked down south for a fellow named Hines, who contracted with Johnny Torrio and Al Capone to haul a truckload of liquor from Detroit to Chicago. What I didn't know was that Hines arranged for the booze to be delivered to Springfield instead. He told Capone's men the truck had been hijacked. The Chicago mobsters must not have believed him 'cause they came to Springfield and kilt ol' Mr. Hines. I heard that Scarface has my name, so you may hold that against me. I wouldn't want to bring my hardship down on you, Mr. Winkler."

Gus's only hesitation about hiring Bryan was that he was too nice and his pretty wife, Veva, even nicer. But they both assured him they knew what they were getting into.

His job was to watch over the snatched, and Bryan proved to be a most reliable addition to the gang, using his country charm and hospitality to make the victim feel unthreatened.

Fred, in particular, liked to bully and scare those he kidnapped, but when he would leave the room, Bryan would say, "Never you mind that old boy. He's just sore 'cause I beat him at cards last night. Say, would you like to play some gin rummy?" When the ransom was paid and the kidnapped were leaving, the only hand they shook was Bryan's.

Bryan's wife Veva was also an asset. She was a fine cook, an art even Georgette had never quite mastered. Veva set a fine table with more than plenty to fill everyone's stomach, even the kidnapped, to whom she often snuck an extra-large piece of her good cherry crisp pie.

One day as they were eating without snatch victims in the back room, Bryan's pal George Goetz showed up. Though Fred and Bob were a little leery of the handsome blond-haired visitor, Veva hugged him as if he were family and set an extra place at the big table. While she piled his plate with fried chicken and dumplings, Bryan introduced the men all around.

Unlike Bryan, George was more reserved and less prone to honesty. That didn't stop Bryan, though, from bragging about his friend.

"George graduated from the University of Illinois with a degree in engineering and three letters in football," Bryan told them, ignoring Fred's scoff. "But he turned away from it when he found he could make more money faster as an outlaw. He's been runnin' with the Moe Kleinman gang down Cleveland way."

That last comment brightened the eyes of Fred and Bob. They bombarded him with questions about working for the top bootlegger and most ruthless gangster in Cleveland.

"I was sellin' snake oil and pullin' cons with a confidence man named Joseph Weil," George said between bites of fried chicken. "When we came through Cleveland and tried a con on a bootlegger named Joseph Porello, he saw through it, but liked our style, so he brought me on to work under Kleinman."

Gus, too, had questions, mostly about how Kleinman was able to project a facade of respectability in his community.

"Easy," George said. "Like it says in the Bible. Give ten percent to charities, and folks will think you're a Christian. Look at Nucky Johnson over in Atlantic City. He's one of the most corrupt government officials in the country, pulling in a million or more a year off liquor sales, but he craps part of it out to charities and such, so Feds leave him alone."

"What's your weapon of choice?" Fred asked, more interested in killing than charity.

"Well, I like to play golf," George laughed. "So, I have a shotgun I favor that I call Twelve Iron."

***

George Goetz found that working Gus's snatch racket gave him a lot more time to play golf, hunt, and fish with his new buddies, though Bryan preferred time with his cute wife, Veva. At least, that was the excuse Bryan gave each time they asked him to join them. The truth was he feared Fred, Bob, and George when they got drunk, which was most any time after ten in the morning. He and Veva became good friends with Ray and Julia Nugent and their two young children, going on outings to parks and beaches when one was available. Bryan also enjoyed serving as a bodyguard for Gus, who was becoming increasingly careful in case one of the gangs they extorted ransom from got fed up with them.

Gus, too, began avoiding Fred, Bob, and George socially. The kidnap racket was going so well that he and Georgette moved to the Leland Hotel in Chicago. Money was coming in steady and easy. He began spending more evenings with Georgette, taking in movies, theater, and the finest restaurants. It irked him a little, though, that his beautiful wife refused to take on airs and dress like the dames in the picture shows.

"I dress for women. I undress for you," Georgette scolded when he brought her a lavish dress to wear to watch Billie Burke in the Ziegfield Follies at the

New Amsterdam Theater. "That's as much as you need to know about my attire."

She did, however, consent to the mink stoles, more out of the desire to stay warm in their softness than to stay fashionable. That evening after the Follies, Gus was looking forward to watching his wife undress down to her infamous birthday suit when a double knock, then a triple knock, followed by a single tap sounded on the door. Georgette had just swept her abundant hair up into an appealing bun, leaving her elegant neck and shoulders for Gus to appreciate.

"This had better be important." Pistol in hand, Gus stood to one side of the door. "Who is it?"

"It's Red."

Gus unbolted and then unlocked the door. Guards used nicknames to indicate the coast was clear. If young Bryan Bolton had said his name, Gus would've taken up his Tommy gun that was propped nearby and emptied it by blasting through the door.

Bryan's compressed lips and the nervous way he straightened his cufflinks gave Gus the impression that bad news was about to arrive.

"Capone wants to see us, you, us, I guess. Bob and Ray kidnapped a fellow named Mert Wertheimer, who is, I guess, a friend to Scarface."

16

The entire next day, Gus, Bob, and Ray sat in a corner of a roadhouse, drank hooch, and discussed their next move. Fred and George had gone out of state to collect on another kidnapping and wouldn't be back soon. That irked Gus a little, since George had done some previous work for Capone and might have been able to help smooth things.

Georgette and Veva took Bryan downtown to fit him into a proper suit, though he feared it might wind up being his funeral clothes.

That night Gus came to their room so drunk, Georgette had to go out in her robe and slippers to turn off the car lights.

The next evening, the four gangsters stayed in with Gus and stayed sober. Gus had convinced them it was better to pay the piper than try and run from him, especially since the piper was Scarface Capone.

"And don't call him Scarface. He don't like that," Gus instructed them. "This fellow Capone is a big shot. He's bigger than the dick's in this man's town, and that's something. Now, you guys act like gentlemen. One more thing. It's never a good idea to let a boss like this see you being indecisive."

"Oh, that won't be too hard," Bob said. "I'm pretty decisive that he's gonna kill us."

"I wouldn't wish this on a hottentot," Ray lamented, though it was just an expression he had heard, and he had no idea what a hottentot was.

"We'd best oblige him, then," Gus said.

Georgette had been listening in the hallway. She came into the room and wrapped her arms around her man.

"Never mind, honey," Gus said. "This was bound to happen, and I'm prepared for it."

***

The four drove Bryan's old jalopy to the meeting with Capone. Gus didn't think taking a better ride was necessary, since it would very likely be impounded if they were killed. Clouds, heavy and dark, began rolling in from the northwest. The thunder was so loud that people on the streets ran for shelter. Even the windows on the flivver shook, an ominous warning to the condemned.

For Gus, who was driving, memories, almost all involving Georgette, attacked him. Before they left, he had handed her all the cash he could get his hands on, enough to last her a couple of years if she were thrifty.

"They say Capone took a ball bat to a couple of men in his office once," Bob said. The rain that streaked the windshield matched the tears on his face. "They were found with their throats cut and castrated. Hopefully in that order. Anyway, the bodies looked like someone had poured a bucket of blood over them. Callin' for a thug to be killed is simply bookkeepin' to Capone."

As morbid as Bob's rantings were, no one could find their voice to shut him up.

May 20, 1927

Gus, Bob, Bryan, and Ray were searched three times from the time they arrived at the hotel until they reached Capone's outer office. A half dozen red hots were gathered in the foyer, all coatless, their pants held up with suspenders, crisscrossed by shoulder holsters. Gus took note of the weaponry. He had a theory that the better the marksman, the lower the caliber of gun they used.

If this were true, then Frank Nitti, who fancied a .32 caliber revolver, was almost certainly an expert marksman. Like the other Italians in the room, Nitti had made good use of pomade, slicking his hair in waves tightly against his head on either side of the part.

Nitti gazed at the three with such hateful anger, Gus wanted to move back a step or two. Yet, the situation they were in was so intense he was afraid to move a muscle, and the three partners with him seemed equally frozen. Gus had the conviction they were all going to die. He hadn't felt so sober since Johnny got his head blown off.

"Mr. Capone will see you now," one of Capone's thugs said.

Gus was relieved that no further delay was required. Bob had talked nonstop for over an hour on their way to Cicero, but now he was mute as a jug.

The office was plush, as Gus had expected. A record on a Victrola quietly played opera music. Large stuffed fish and animal heads hung on the walls. A golf bag with clubs sticking out rested against a gun rack filled with hunting rifles and shotguns. Capone's big mahogany desk covered one side of the room, with four leather chairs in front of it. Through an open archway going to another room was a very long table with over a dozen chairs around it. It seemed a minor victory that Gus spotted no baseball bats.

Al Capone stood by the window talking on the telephone when they entered his office. Gus's first impression was that he was taller than he'd appeared in the newspaper pictures. The Chicago mobster had a big, fat cigar sticking out of the right side of his mouth while he mumbled softly into the mouthpiece. He wore a checkered jacket, white flannel trousers, and fancy sport shoes.

Ray was stepping forward and was about ready to take a seat in one of the four big leather chairs in front of Capone's desk when Gus grabbed his arm and pulled him back. The four turned their heads toward the door they had entered and were surprised to see that none of the Chicago thugs had followed them into the room, even shutting the door behind them. They were alone with the most notorious mobster in gangland.

When Capone was finally finished with his call, he hung the receiver back on its hook, set the phone down on the table, took a deep breath, and gave a long sigh before turning to the four nervous men. His dark eyes seemed ill-fit for the round face and high forehead. Except for the two scars that ran down the left side of his face, he might have been a bank president. As stocky as he was, Capone moved across the room as quickly and gracefully as boxer Jack Dempsey.

"Gus Winkler." Capone's hand was small, stubby, and powerful, but also white and soft with perfectly manicured fingernails. He held onto Gus's hand long enough to ensure the message behind his steely eyes was well received.

"Please to meet you, sir," Gus said. "And these are my associates, Bob Carey, Ray Nugent, and Bryan Bolton."

"Wonderful to meet you boys." Capone shook hands with Bob and Ray first. His handshake with Bryan was a little longer, and his evil eye studied him more intensely than the others. "Have a seat."

Gus, Bob, and Bryan sat on the edge of their seats, holding their hats on their lap. Ray sank into the chair as if he were in his own house. He had a habit of crossing his legs and hanging his hat on his foot, which he promptly did. Gus hoped Capone would look away so he could quickly snatch the hat, but instead, the mobster boss gave the fedora a puzzled look followed by a nearly imperceptible snigger.

"We can give you back Mr. Wertheimer," Ray said, his forehead sweating profusely. He patted it with the back of his shirt sleeve. "Is that what you want?"

Gus resented that Ray had been so impertinent as to ask. Capone was probably thinking them to be rather bred down.

The Boss opened a drawer on his desk and reached for something. Inside Gus's head, he began reciting the Lord's Prayer. When Capone's hand came out it had four cigars in it which he held out to them. "Please, call me Al."

***

It was nearly four in the morning when Gus snuck quietly into his apartment to not wake his wife. He was shocked to see her sitting in her favorite armchair peeling spuds.

"Say, what are you doin' up?" Gus threw his overcoat and hat on the table. "You look like hell. You better start gettin' some sleep. You'll have gray hair if you keep carryin' on like this every time I go out."

"Capone," Georgette said, her voice weak from crying. "What did he say? What's he going to do?"

"You got him all wrong." Gus set on the arm of her chair and wrapped an arm around her. "Al Capone is a swell fellow. He didn't even get rough. He talked to us like a Dutch uncle tryin' to show us we were in the wrong racket and couldn't last long at it. He told us snatchin' was a rotten business and begged us to quit. Then he set up the drinks and took us to a swell feed.

"He told us, 'When you're famous in this business, people just naturally think you're badass. A gangster who puts one over on me will be fine if there might be a future use for him.' Then he laughs and jokes and makes us feel like part of his gang.

"But do you know what those two dirty bums of mine did? Bob and Ray got drunk—and after that preachin' I gave them. There I was tryin' to act like a gentleman crook, and those damn fools had their feet on Al's desk. I was ashamed for a big shot like Capone to see what kind of company I was in.

"Then he offered us some money, and I refused in a hurry, but wouldn't you know? Bob and Ray take the tip. Can you beat that? Both those monkeys took what he offered them."

"What about Bryan? Did he take the money?"

"Nah, Bryan barely ate or drank. Then, when we got to the door, Capone called me back and took my hand. 'Cut it out, Gus. If money is so hard to get that you have to go into a bum racket like the one you're in now, drop in and see me.'

"'That's Jake with me,' I says. I told him I would quit because he's the main spring around here and a regular fellow. He's makin' money and keepin' his nose clean, and so can I. Yes, sir, that Al Capone's a standup guy."

Fred Burke expected Gus and the others to be back in Detroit in a day or two. Maybe they'd have the ransom for the Wertheimer kidnapping or maybe they'd just gone ahead and killed him if none of his friends thought him valuable enough to pay for. Either way, Fred had his hands full in Detroit dealing with the Purple Gang. He and George Goetz were there to collect the ransom and release local Jewish merchant Abraham Fein.

"You sure the Purple Gang will pay this much money for a Jew?" George asked Fred while they waited in the car for the ransom to be delivered. There were no cars in front of the country store and the nearest building was over half a mile away. From the trunk of the car came a loud knocking. "And are you sure it's a good idea to bring the kidnapped to the rendezvous to get the money?"

"I know you've got plenty of experience robbin' and killin' and such," Fred admonished. "But you're still a rookie when it comes to the snatch racket."

"In the mind of the beginner, there are many possibilities for innovation," George lectured. "In the mind of an expert, there are few."

Blond-haired George was a seasoned criminal and the only gangster Fred had ever heard of who had a college degree. He had also trained as a pilot during the war, although he never made it overseas.

"Showin' off that education again, ain't ya?" Fred was already feeling a little envious of Gus for taking over leadership of the gang, and now he had to deal with a smart-ass college boy.

"The more educated you get, the more you understand how much you don't know." George sat back, pulled his gold cigarette case from his jacket pocket, and held it out to Fred. "Fag?"

Fred, never one to carry his own smokes, was about to accept the offer when the milk truck carrying the ransom pulled up in front of the store. The store owner walked out to help with the unloading as Fred had seen him do when he scouted out this exchange spot. Normally, they liked to have Ray Nugent drop off the kidnapped near Toledo, Ohio, after the ransom was paid, but none of the others were there, and Fred was feeling lazy. He would still wait for the money to be exchanged, then leave Abraham Fein on a country road on their way back to Detroit.

The milk delivery fellow did exactly as Fred had instructed. He and the owner carted the milk inside the store in three trips using a two-wheeled hand dolly. When the driver came out after the final trip, he returned the dolly to the back, shut the sliding back door, and walked around to the driver's side. Instead of getting in, he reached under his seat and extracted a quart milk bottle, the green of cash showing through the glass, placed it on the ground, hopped into his truck, and drove away.

While George got out of the car and walked over to retrieve the bottle, Fred also got out. He had an impulse. Going around to the back of the car he popped the trunk.

"What the hell are you doing?" George asked as he tossed the bottle on the front seat.

Fred didn't answer. Instead, he helped Fein crawl out of the back, untied him, and even handed him a couple of bucks.

"Go get yourself a soda pop, Abe," Fred smiled. "It was nice doin' business with you."

Abe took the money and raced into the store.

"He'll call the cops. Or worse, the Purples." George pulled his pistol.

"Relax. Put the rod away. There's no phone in there, and we'll be back in Detroit before Abe gets a chance to talk to anyone."

Fred let George drive so he could focus on counting the money and getting drunk. They were only a mile down the road when the first bullet hit the back window. Having been trained in elusive maneuvers as a pilot, George began weaving the big sedan from one side of the road to the other. Only one more bullet reached them, just glancing off the roof before they were out of range.

"You're something else, Fred!" George shouted. "Do you know that? You're really something else. I'm heading to Chicago. It'd be crazy to go back to Detroit now."

Fred moped all the way to Chicago. He lost count of the money each time he reached two thousand, so he finally gave up and announced it was all there. He didn't like being insulted by an arrogant college boy, especially since George was four years younger than he.

By the time they were cruising State Street, Fred was in the back seat feigning sleep. The thought of his mistake was a sore that throbbed every time his mind touched it. Unable to restrain himself in the face of George's insults, he cuddled his Tommy gun against his chest, caressing the stock. Then he rose to look at where they were.

"Hey, George, drive down Oakland Avenue past The Exchange, would you? There's a diner there, and I'd like to grab a bite. You want one?" He waved the ransom money next to the driver's ear. "I'll buy."

George shook his head and sniggered but did as requested, turning right when he came to the Oakland Avenue intersection. "Where's the diner?" he asked.

The explosion of the Tommy gun behind his head caused George to slam on the brakes. His ears rang as if the Liberty Bell was inside his head. He looked to his left and saw three men across the street doing a strange kind of dance as bullets tore holes in their tailored three-piece suits.

"Come on, you damn Purples," Fred screamed at the top of his lungs as he finished emptying his gat into the dying men. "You want some more of this? Huh? Do you want some more of this? Yeah, that's what I thought."

George floored the accelerator. When several blocks away, he stopped the car, turned, and looked into the backseat. Fred was passed out, his gat still smoking and a lit cigar burning a hole in his suit jacket. Still unable to hear a thing, George grabbed up the wad of money, his confidence in Killer Burke evaporated.

***

Fred was asleep in the Winkler apartment twelve hours later with Gus and George sitting at the dinner table exchanging adventures. George was more shocked at hearing of the meeting with Capone than Gus was to learn what an idiot Fred had been. George wanted to take him for a ride.

"I'll admit that Fred's poor company, but I'd hate to see him shot," Gus said. "He never was very good at thinkin' about two facts at once, much less two important facts. Still, he's the fella I'd want to be next to if I was in a trench in France again."

"Yeah? Well, you've never had that monkey firing off a gat six inches from your head." George turned his head sideways and stuck a finger in an ear. "My ears still feel stuffed with cotton balls." George was a team player, though, so he added. "What do we do about the war he got us into with the Purple Gang?"

"How about I get hold of Abe Bernstein and see what he suggests?"

***

Ray Nugent hadn't thought much about it when Gus suggested he be the one to go to Detroit and negotiate a peace treaty between the Purple Gang leader, Abe Bernstein, and their St. Louis Gang, as Gus's crew was being called in the newspapers. Since Ray's wife and two kids lived in Toledo, Ohio he figured he'd stop in and surprise them after the peace conference.

When he found out the encounter with Bernstein would take place at the Carlton Plaza Hotel, he was less enthusiastic. That was because the Carlton specialized in jazz music, and most jazz musicians and their audiences were Negroes. It wasn't that Ray hated colored people, but they did scare him a little. He found they tended to be louder and more likely to see themselves as equal to white folks when they were in the majority.

Ray was mighty glad to learn Willie the Lion was playing that night at the Carlton. Gus had introduced them once and, since they were all three veterans of the war, they had a lot of stories to share.

The minute he walked into the hotel lobby, Ray spotted Willie entering the restroom labeled COLORED. He never placed modesty very high among the virtues, but following a colored man into a room reserved for his kind was an intrusion that even Ray understood to be wrong. In the last days of the war, when the Spanish Flu was killing millions, it was believed that Black folk were immune to the disease. Therefore, White soldiers quit sharing canteens of water amongst their own kind. Like others during the pandemic, Ray often had drunk from the canteen of Black men, not only water but on occasion, when it could be located, hard liquor, though he was always careful to wipe the Negro's spittle from the rim first.

Ray sat in the hotel lobby waiting for Willie for a good thirty minutes. He saw several colored men enter the restroom, but few departed, and when they did, their eyes seemed red and glazed. Finally, The Lion emerged. Ray walked over and shook his hand like they were best friends. At first, Willie looked at Ray as if thinking, *how dare this strange White man be so familiar?*, but when Gus Winkler's name was mentioned, a little light showed in the Black man's glazed eyes.

"How's Gus and Georgette?" Willie asked. "That gal sure is a fine hoofer, that she is."

The two stood and talked until Ray saw he was going to be late for his appointment. He apologized to Willie for running and told him about his meeting with Bernstein.

"You be careful, friend," Willie said. "Them Purples be a bad lot. Watch your back."

For some reason he couldn't understand, Willie's advice shook Ray. While his confidence that the meeting would go okay was lacking, his resolution to complete the important assignment given to him was firm. After all, Gus was a straight shooter. Still, he put his hand in his big coat pocket and fondled his handgun.

A few moments later, Ray stepped off the elevator onto the eighth floor to find two men facing him at the end of the hallway. One was a squat man with a large, hairy mole beside his nose. The other fellow was tall with teeth the color of dark chocolate. The color of his teeth was evident because the man was smiling at him, evilly smiling at him. Both Hairy Mole and Dark Chocolate Teeth pulled their weapons at the same time.

Right away, Ray's face began to sag. He was glad he had the foresight to depart the elevator with one hand still in his coat pocket where he kept his snub-nosed revolver. There was another factor to consider, though—his deficiencies with a pistol. He had mastered the rifle during Army Basic Training, but a handgun bullet never seemed to wind up in the exact spot he wanted it to. Still, the distance between himself and the other two men was not so great.

Before he could overthink the situation any further, smoke and flame erupted from the weapons of the two men. Ray fell backwards and the ceiling above swirled. Still, he was somehow able to keep his finger on the trigger and empty it through his coat pocket in their general direction. The next thing Ray saw before he passed out was Willie the Lion tugging him by his coat collar and dragging him onto the elevator.

Sometime later, Ray awoke, slowly exploring his senses. He did a quick inventory of his wounds. Besides being shot in one hand and shoulder, he felt one of his ribs sticking through his skin, leaving his shirt bloody and wet. Weak, hysterical thoughts echoed through his brain. His mortality would most surely be cruel.

He seemed to be alone in a bedroom, but he wasn't lying in the bed that was next to him. Instead, he was on the floor looking up at the ceiling, a wall inches from him, a nightstand behind his head. Ray tried to sit up to see over the bed but groaned loudly and dropped back onto the carpet. Unexpectedly, the face of a pretty Black girl appeared.

"Youse just lay still and don't be makin' no mo' sound," the girl whispered. "Willie's fetchin' a doctor."

"What happened?"

"You kilt dem other two fellas. Willie says you must be a fine marksman, shootin' 'em both in the head and from your coat pocket no less. He say the Purple Jews be searchin' the hotel for you, but he don't tink dey be comin' in any Colored rooms. Anyways, you just sit tight, and Willie will get you back to Chicago shortly."

***

When Fred got the call that Ray had been ambushed by Bernstein's men, he decided it was time to quit using Detroit as his base of operations. A second reason to vamoose followed when he discovered the Purples had put a twenty-seven-thousand-dollar bounty on Fred's head, dead or deader. These seemed like good enough reasons to lay low by moving into the Winklers' new home in Chicago. Sponging meals off Georgette was a bonus.

***

The new hangout for Gus's St. Louis Gang was a joint in Chicago called the Circus Café. The Circus Café had a good cook named Gomez Lee Wolowitz. There was much discussion as to Gomez's race since he could cook Mexican and Chinese, as well as tasty bagels and a fine brisket. He ran off the morning after Christmas, almost certainly for fear of the trouble the St. Louis Gang would bring down on the soda shop bar. It was a great annoyance to lose such a good cook.

Since Johnny's demise, the cooking had been sporadic for the St. Louis Gang, each mobster trying their hand at cooking when there were no wives available. It was Gus's cooking in particular that riled the men. He liked to mix meat and vegetables in a big skillet. "They're all going to get mixed up in your stomach anyway," Gus would point out when the complaints rolled in.

Gus also missed Johnny Reid. He hated that his friend got his head blown off, though it was likely the quick and painless death everyone longed for. Still, decapitation was a hard way to lose one of the gang. He would have liked to have had more time to pick Johnny's brain on how to run a business and maintain financial records. Georgette was adept at such matters, but Gus was hoping to keep her busy putting out children and taking care of them and their new home.

There was considerable concern, though, as to why the couple had yet to conceive. It certainly wasn't for a lack of effort. They had even tried having Georgette stand on her head following copulation to let Gus's juices flow more easily to her eggs. She drew the line, though, when Gus wanted to stand on his head alongside her and do it that way to ensure a good hard squirt.

"Well, Gussie, why don't you just grab the turkey baster out of the kitchen," Georgette mused. "My pa used to try that with horses."

Her humor was one of the things Gus loved about his wife, even finding that it sometimes drove his lust to unparalleled heights. Still, even lust wasn't enough to conceive. Now, with Fred sleeping so often in the room that should've been a nursery by now, even the opportunities for making babies were limited.

Fred had his own reasons for not being happy with the living conditions during his hiding from the Purple Gang and the law. Intolerant of criticism and disdainful of most human opinion, Fred felt he had been meant to live and die in uninterrupted solace, but for short excursions to meet his most basic needs. Solitude was not a premium in the Winkler home. He already was in a shaky state due to the absence of spirits, a dryness which Georgette insisted upon when Fred, an avid lush, was present. An occasional fling with a whore might have helped, but the lady of the house also nixed that idea.

A perhaps minor problem was that the bathroom was just outside Gus and Georgette's boudoir and not far from the living room. Fred always had trouble taking a whiz with others close by. Of course, in small-town jails and even in prison, this was a major complication. Standing in front of the Winkler toilet one day, he came up with a peculiar way to get his stream flowing. He thought about film actress Bessie Love's legs. He didn't know why this worked, but it did. That solved at least one of his dilemmas.

Then one day in April, Ray Nugent, freshly emancipated after recovery of his gunshot wounds, showed up at the Winkler home with Bob Carey, George Goetz, and Bryan Bolton.

"There's a truck shipment in Toledo of American Express Securities that is just waitin' for the St. Louis Gang to take the money off their hands."

"How much we talkin'?" Gus asked.

"Two million."

18

Splitting two million dollars five ways was easy math and the easiest part of the planning for the Toledo heist, at least until they figured out they needed a sixth man, an expert safe cracker.

During Ray's convalescence, he'd learned about the two-million-dollar shipment through phone calls back to his family in Toledo. He, Bob, and George had worked out all the logistics, including the spot where the heist of the safe would take place, the getaway, the rendezvous place of the gang to blow the safe, and then the split of the loot before they went their separate ways.

It was one of the most foolproof plans Gus had ever seen. He couldn't believe the idiot Ray Nugent had helped originate it. Normally, two heads were better than one, but when one of those heads was Ray's, Gus usually preferred to do his own thinking.

They had mapped out all the streets they would use as well as how each bandit's stolen automobile would be utilized. Since Ray owned a home in Toledo, he would store and bring the nitro and fuses, and they would get an expert to blow the safe.

"We need a yegg," George said.

"What's a yegg?" Bryan, the farm boy, asked.

"An expert safecracker," Gus told him. He had already decided that Bryan was too green to take part in a heist of this kind, though he would get a small percentage for staying behind in case he was needed. "One who can blast the safe's drawer without destroyin' all the loot."

"Charlie Fitzgerald," Fred suggested.

"Ol' Charlie?" Gus had worked with him one other time. He was surprised he was still alive since he was in his late fifties, an old age for a gangster. "Is he out of the joint?"

"Yeah, and he's in Chicago," Fred said.

***

April 16, 1928

As dawn light spread over Toledo, the St. Louis Gang made their preparations for the heist, which included a backup plan—a shack located on the Ottawa River—for hiding if anything went wrong.

They departed for the heist from Ray's house, where his wife Julia and Bob's girlfriend, Rose, gave them a good going away feed. Ray's six-year-old daughter and five-year-old son kept the hardened criminals entertained, laughing as they swooped up and down the staircase and made silly faces.

Then, it was time to go to work. At 9:00 a.m., from a crowded street, a Chrysler with Bob and Ray watched from a block behind a security truck as three fairly small safes were loaded in the back followed by three guards carrying rifles.

In the Packard on the far end of the street, Gus was the wheelman, with Fred sitting in front with his gat between his knees. George was in the back, with his trusty Twelve Iron saw-off shotgun. Various other weaponry was also handy.

When the back door of the security truck was shut, Bob signaled the heist car by flashing his headlights on and off three times. Gus started the Packard and, weaving it in and out of the four-lane traffic, sped right up in front of the truck just as the driver was getting in. Fred leaped out of the car, jumped on the passenger side running board, and aimed his pistol through the window. The driver immediately put his hands in the air and Fred got into the truck beside him.

Meanwhile, Gus went past the truck, did a U-turn, and positioned his car right behind the security truck.

"Drive exactly where I tell you to and you won't get dead," Fred ordered. The heist had gone so perfectly the three guards in the back didn't even know they were being hijacked, a good thing for them, since if they had opened the back door, George, in the back of Gus's car, was prepared to blast them.

In twenty minutes, the truck was delivered to a wooded rendezvous spot not far from the University of Toledo. Once parked on a dirt road, Fred led the driver around to the rear of the truck and signaled him to open the back doors. The three guards inside thought they had arrived at their destination and exited the vehicle quietly until they saw six armed men pointing weapons at them. They made a show of raising their hands.

Ol' Charlie, who had been waiting in another Chrysler at the site, confiscated the officer's weapons and tossed them into the wooded area. Gus ordered the officers to lie down on the ground, and the others tied them up and covered their eyes with adhesive tape.

"Well, don't just stand around, let's get goin'," Gus said. "Who's got the explosives?"

"Nugent brought it," George said, turning to Ray.

Ray didn't move, his face a blank expression.

"Come on, come on," Gus snapped his fingers, "Don't stall around. Hand the stuff over."

"I, I, I forgot it," Ray stammered.

Fred and Bob were on top of Ray in an instant, pummeling him with hard blows. Ol' Charlie squatted and lit a cigarette, seemingly numb to the going-ons around him. He was agile enough in his youth and, though considerably angry with Ray, found that bones at his age were becoming somewhat brittle.

Gus shaved his own temper by sitting on the edge of the Packard hood, dangling his feet and watching the fistfight, such as it was. It gave him some satisfaction that Ray was getting the worst of the scuffle, but since Ray was still weak from being shot by the Purples, Gus finally stepped forward and broke it up.

"Knock it off, you guys," Gus shouted. "My ears get tired of listenin' to you fellas cuss."

"Let's bury it and scatter," George suggested. "We can send back after it when the heat cools off."

"Yeah," Fred said, untrusting as always in his fellow man. Especially since George had not helped them pummel Ray. "You mean *you* can come back and get it as soon as the rest of us are out of sight."

"Hell, we can't stand here and argue all night," Bob reasoned. "Let's get it back to town and force it open in Ray's garage. If we hurry maybe we can make it before the bulls get organized."

The most reasonable plan presented didn't prevent their situation from rankling each of them and rankling deeply. It was far beyond inconvenient.

Gus ordered the men to remove the safes from the truck and put them in the Packard. They then tossed the tied-up guards in the back of the truck and shut the doors. Since Gus was supervising, George jumped behind the seat of the Packard that carried the safes and started it up. Fearing he would take off with the loot, Bob leaped into the passenger seat beside him. The sedan's wheels were skidding in the grass fifty yards away by the time Gus was behind the wheel of the Chrysler with Fred next to him. Ol' Charlie followed in his car with a disenfranchised Ray still moaning from his beating.

It wasn't hard for Gus to wheel up quickly behind the Packard. George drove like an old lady, and the weight of the two safes seemed to add unbalanced ballast. Ten minutes away from Ray's house, George took a curve too fast and ran up a curb. When the wheels landed hard, one of the safes toppled over, breaking the rear window on the driver's side and sending glass flying onto the street.

Unfortunately, a police car was sitting nearby, with two officers in it sipping coffee and eating donuts. They immediately moved into traffic behind George's car. Gus fell in behind the police cruiser but was not terribly alarmed. The cops didn't turn on their red lights or sirens, seeming more curious than anything. They looked like they were preparing to turn off at a corner when Bob Carey spotted them. Panicking, Bob rolled over into the backseat next to the safes and knocked out the back window with the butt of a gat. When he aimed the weapon at the cops, the officer driving whipped the cruiser into the opposite lane and turned on his red light as well as the police siren.

George floored the accelerator and began weaving in and out of traffic, taking two wheels around corners and scraping up against any vehicle that got in his way. When Gus saw George turn onto a busy street followed by the cops, he saw an opportunity. He accelerated to an alley entrance half a block away and drove into it. His car barely fit in the narrow passage and sent garbage cans and one scared drunk up against the brick wall. At times, the sides of his vehicle scraped loudly against the walls, but he finally made it out.

He raced through the upcoming street and straight into the next alley, all the while ignoring the honking of horns as well as the screams of pedestrians. After doing this through two more alleyways and across another street, he whipped the car hard onto the next road and arrived at the following intersection just as George's car was crossing against a red light. Gus skidded his Chrysler to a stop just before the police cruiser arrived. The officer barely had time to swerve into a fire hydrant, where the cruiser came to a watery stop atop the broken main.

Gus calmly and slowly continued down the street. He arrived at Ray's house just after George. Ol' Charlie was already there standing outside the garage smoking as Ray raised the door. George pulled the sedan with the safes inside and Ray quickly closed the garage.

Gus's gang were resilient fellows all, not easily daunted, even though there presently were hardships. The opportunity at two million dollars somewhat inspired composure. Still, Gus was nervy in anticipation of another foul-up. He had lost his confidence in his colleagues. It was a lingering, troubling problem, and one that Gus knew he'd never get over. He had counted on Ray the Lummox to be able to do one simple task, and he couldn't even remember to bring the nitroglycerine and fuses needed to blow open the safes.

Ol' Charlie went right to work on one of the safes with various instruments while Bob tried his luck on the other. Ray went inside the house to have his wife help clean his many cuts and bruises from his beating. George followed him on the pretext of using the bathroom. Gus assigned Fred to guard one side of the garage while he took the other.

Now, all they could do was wait for the safes to be opened.

***

At that same time, Officers Zientara and Biskupski reported to headquarters on one of the many police call boxes located on corners around the city. After getting their orders, Zientara wished he had waited another fifteen minutes before checking in. He and Biskupski were assigned the very routine and boring task of going door to door at houses asking if anyone had seen a Packard that had been reported driving dangerously in the neighborhood.

Ray Nugent was exiting the front door of his house when he walked right into and was shocked to see Officer Zientara coming toward him. When Ray became bewildered his mouth always popped open and he began breathing shallowly through his mouth. In addition to this, he also immediately threw up his arms in surrender. Officer Zientara, equally bewildered, instinctively drew his revolver.

George was upstairs trying to talk Bob's wife into a quicky. Just as he made another of his sly attempts to steal a feel, he glanced out the window in time to see an officer with a gun trained on Ray. George grabbed up the rifle he had tossed on the bed and mowed the policeman down like a weed. Officer Zientara dropped to the ground bonelessly, the bullet entering his right eyebrow and exiting behind the right ear.

Seeing a government official fall by his hand greatly disturbed George. He had often put it out that he'd killed twenty-two men, one more than Billy Bonney had at his age. Now he had one more to add to his tally, though he wasn't thrilled about it. A dead cop would bring the Feds down on him, not to mention infuriate Al Capone, who expected his men to stay out of trouble unless he told them not to.

Zientara's partner, Officer Biskupski, heard the gunshot, drew his pistol, and ran around the corner of the garage and right toward a gunman who stood with a Thompson at his side.

Fred Burke's recent hiding out had taken away from his time to practice firing his Tommy gun. When he raised the weapon and pulled the trigger the gat moved with a bucking, twisting activity, more than he was accustomed to. It seemed to have a mind of its own, shooting itself like an out-of-control garden hose. Firing a gat was no exceptional feat once you learned where to grasp it firmly, but, for whatever reason, Fred didn't seem able to get a firm grasp on it.

The policeman dropped and Fred rushed over to take his service revolver from him. Had he checked, Killer Burke would have seen that Biskupski was playing possum with only a minor wound on his shoulder.

A moment later, the six members of the St. Louis Gang jumped into the police cruiser, this time with the expertise of Gus Winkler behind the wheel, and shot around the corner and out of sight, leaving the safe's safe from them and behind them.

Ol' Charlie watched them go, then took a walk until he found a car he liked, stole it, and drove on home, hoping he would never again see the Keystone Gang.

***

It wasn't until Gus pulled the car into the hideaway shack on the Ottawa River that George Goetz remembered he'd left his coat in the upstairs bedroom while he'd been wooing Bob's girlfriend. He tried to remember what was in the pockets that may give him away. And what would he tell Gus or Capone if he was identified as the cop killer? He could hardly claim to be ignorant when he was an engineering graduate from the University of Illinois.

Of course, he wasn't the only one silently weighing in on their mistakes. Ray Nugent was thinking about what his wife, Julia, and the children might tell the police. During the brief moments in the kitchen with his wife, before all hell broke loose, Ray, sporting a promising black eye from the beating the boys had given him, told her she had never looked lovelier. He knew he had paid his wife a fine compliment, so he was confused when she added a slap to his already bruised eye.

"What did you do?" Julia shouted at him.

In the same reasonable tone with which he had complimented her, he explained that he had just robbed the express truck for the benefit of her and the children. Then, in his best matrimonial spirit, Ray agreed to take the least objectional alternative, which was to vamoose with his gang and the money and send her his share of the two million dollars when he got it. So why was she still angry?

"I couldn't bear to see you go through a trial for robbery," Julia said, tears flooding her face.

"Would you rather see twelve men judging me or six men carrying me?" Ray asked, finally getting to use one of the expressions he'd heard a gangster in a picture show use.

"Away with you!" Julia bellowed. "You'll go now and leave us be."

Reflecting on that conversation, Ray could see that if she had not sent him away at that moment, he wouldn't have gone through the front door and straight into the arms of the police officer. He intended to scold Julia for that untimely indiscretion when he next saw her.

Bob Carey was pretty sure his girlfriend, Rose, would keep quiet, only because she knew what he would do to her if she didn't. He often gave her the back of his hand, though an occasional kick was what inspired her loyalty.

Fred Burke was contemplating his deficient use of the Tommy gun and hoping the cop he shot was good and dead so he couldn't later identify him. Such dire thoughts of consequences often followed Fred's actions, and he was kicking himself now for not putting a few more bullets in the cop while he was down. Forgetting his lack of practice of late, he blamed the damned gat.

Gus Winkler's only concern was his wife. He racked his brain to find a way to fix this atrocity so he could hurry back into her arms. To his growing vexation, no solution appeared. No matter how much he wanted to be nuzzling and kissing with Georgette, he had a responsibility to keep her safe until this fiasco blew over.

They had ditched the police car and stole a citizen's car at the first opportunity, so they were confident they would not be discovered as the inept robbers, at least long enough to smuggle themselves back to Chicago.

The gangsters spread out in the woods to sleep that night, each afraid of having their throat cut by any one of the others. Up until this point, they had been thick as thick, in war and crime, inured in bloodshed. Now each hoped the next blood would not be their own.

Just a few hours into his sleep, Ray developed a taste for his mother's flapjacks and homemade syrup. Never since he'd left home had he eaten such flapjacks, wonderfully light and fluffy as they were. He dreamed about those flapjacks and smiled across the dinner table at his mother when her eye exploded in a gush of blood.

"Ambush!" he screamed.

Fred heard the warning, and though completely inebriated, was instantly on his feet. Running and tripping through the thick brush, he raced through the dark toward the river. At least, he thought the river was in this direction, but his brain was cloudy from stress and booze.

At the water's edge sat a white bridge with a full moon hovering above it. His fuzzy mind thanked his luck for leading him to a dry crossing of the Ottawa River, which was still plenty cold in April.

With great enthusiasm, he leaped from the ground to the glow of the bridge. Discovering a moment later that his entire body was several feet underwater came as a shock. His first thought was that he had dreamed the warning scream of ambush. If that were the case, perhaps he wasn't underwater at all and a moment later he would be awake in his warm bed at the Winkler home. But then the cold of the water permeated his pores from head to feet and his arms moved weightlessly. When his feet touched down in squishy mud, he pushed with his legs and, reaching above him, pulled water downward with his hands. Just before reaching the surface, he reversed his paddling hands and stopped his assent.

The events of the previous day seemed to explode into his brain, making him certain the cops were waiting for him on the shore. His lungs needed air, but if his head broke the surface at the wrong moment, the law would either capture or shoot him.

Finally, he could hold his breath no more. He allowed his head to slowly rise out of the water into the night just long enough to let out the bad air and inhale the good. Curls of reddish water were breaking below his eye level.

"I think he's over here."

The shout from the woods sent Fred back under. The water was clear enough he could see a few shadows moving around the trees. He swam underwater as far away from that spot as he could before he needed another breath.

This time when he came up, he heard, "There he is. In the water."

Back under he went, but Fred couldn't survive the cold much longer. Again, he swam parallel to the shore rather than chance the middle of the river which, now that he was sobering, he remembered had dangerous currents and undertows. He was also prone to cramps in his hamstrings, calves, and the arch of his foot.

Finally, fatigue overtook him. Better to surrender to authorities than drown. This time when his head broke the surface, he found himself in shallow enough water that he could stand and raise his hands.

"There he is. Shoot him. Shoot him."

"No, I surrender!" Fred shouted.

The laughter that followed puzzled him until he recognized Gus, George, and Bob sitting along the shore pointing and rolling in laughter.

The history of those three men would have changed if Fred had been armed at that moment. As he climbed out of the water, he recognized that the bridge had been a mirage, a moonbeam of fairy light reflecting off the river.

Dragging himself from the freezing water, Fred hurried past the men he hated and back to his sleep area to warm up and get a beer. A lifetime accomplishment of one's reputation can be destroyed with one sixty-second mistake. Still, he believed that total despair might be two beers away, but after six beers, all would be forgotten.

19

The blues always struck Georgette when she least expected. Each night she missed Gus so much she had to sit up in her rocking chair in her warm, fuzzy robe and rock until she trusted herself to try to sleep.

She was just about ready to retire when she heard a cough coming from the bedroom. No purer bolt of joy had ever hit her than when she heard Gus's cough. His was the most recognizable cough she'd ever known, loudly coming up from deep down in the lungs.

Still, she couldn't let him see how happy she was that he was finally home. There was no need to let him think that extended absences without so much as a telephone call or a telegram would be tolerated. She walked demurely into the boudoir, stopped, and, with hands on hips, gave him a cold stare.

"I couldn't contact you for fear the Feds would be able to track me." Gus held up one hand as if that would be enough to stifle his wife's anger. "I know you're mad."

"Knowing and understanding are not the same." Raising her chin, Georgette turned her head away. "It's rotten behavior, if you ask me."

Such statements were served up for the sake of defiance; privately, she was enamored by Gus's charm. Her husband's presence provided her with some measure of reassurance. Just knowing he was near satisfied a need she couldn't define. She trusted him to keep her safe.

Gus couldn't decide what to do. On the one hand, he wanted to draw Georgette into his arms and smother her with kisses. Yet, he sensed that would be the wrong action. So, instead, he just stood, letting her fiery glare burn a hole in his defense.

He had either done something very wrong or had failed to do something right. Either way, it could be weeks or months before she educated him as to what it was. Probably after she had mulled it around several times with her girlfriends. In the meantime, it was best he just go ahead with life until the inopportune moment arose when she would ambush him with his long-forgotten mistake. Gus sat on the edge of the bed.

One result of his having to think all this through was that it gave her time to mellow a bit. Georgette knew her husband well enough to recognize when he was distressed. Gus had much on his mind and didn't need her attitude tonight. She found that lovemaking in the proper moment always cleared Gus's head and put him in the mood to do some serious reflection.

Dropping her robe from her shoulders and naked as Eve, she came to him.

***

The next day began hopefully. The blush of pleasure didn't usually stay on Georgette's cheeks for long after their romps in the bedroom, but as she served coffee to her husband that morning, her face was still aglow.

She allowed Gus a few moments of silence as he ate his breakfast while reading the newspaper headline, something about a failed robbery in Toledo. Afterward, Georgette accepted Gus's invitation to catch a matinee downtown.

Believing she was becoming an expert in the rank inclinations of men and not wanting Gus to think she had completely forgiven him, Georgette wore the black dress she wore to funerals during the war years and carried a good-sized black parasol.

The significance of the black dress was not lost on Gus. His wife's mood alternated between anger and amusement. In an effort to keep her focus on amusement, he decided to take her to the new Buster Keaton movie, knowing that to Georgette, Buster Keaton was the greatest man alive.

To her, Keaton was a fine-looking man with an athletic body and funny as all get out. Funny was a trait she believed all women most desired in a man. Gus often displayed a dry sense of humor similar to Keaton's deadpanning face, the difference being that Gus sometimes bordered on dark comedy, while Buster Keaton meant open-mouthed laughter.

To her disappointment, they arrived downtown to find the comedian's new movie, *The General,* was sold out.

"Well," Gus said. "We might as well go home. The other movie is *The Jazz Singer,* and why would anyone want to see a talky?"

"But it has Al Jolson," Georgette said, reminding Gus he was her second favorite entertainer.

"I suppose you'd rather kiss Al Jolson instead of me," Gus said, then wanted to kick himself as soon as the words were out of his mouth. Vanity had caused him to overmatch himself, a cynical fact he could not deny. Of course, his wife would rather kiss Jolson, just as he'd like to steal a kiss from Mary Pickford.

"Well, no, I'd say your kisses are quite satisfactory." Georgette noticed his blush. "In fact, I do not doubt that your smooches would put Al Jolson to shame."

Without further words, she marched off briskly toward the theater showing *The Jazz Singer*. Gus followed, resolving to take his mind off his woes and enjoy the picture.

The movie began like most silent films, with captions for dialogue. A woman on an organ near where the Winklers sat played background music as she followed the action on the screen. She not only played the music provided by the movie studio, but she also improvised her own sound effects with drums, cymbals, and a variety of other percussion instruments. Her flourishes heightened the drama, comedy, and romance in the film.

On the screen, the famous, black-faced singer, Al Jolson, played the jazz singer, a young man who defies his Jewish father and goes out into the world to become a cabaret singer. Fifteen minutes into the film, the organist sat back and became a spectator as the first sound came from a single speaker mounted on the wall. Jolson stood in front of a cabaret crowd and sang, "Dirty Hands, Dirty Face." Immediately following this song were the first words ever heard spoken in a film.

Jolson looked straight into the camera and said, "Wait a minute, wait a minute, you ain't heard nothin' yet. Wait a minute, I tell ya, you ain't heard nothin'. You wanna hear Toot, Toot, Tootsie? All right. Hold on. Hold on. Lou, listen. Play Toot, Toot, Tootsie—three choruses, you understand? In the third chorus, I whistle. Now give it to 'em hard and heavy. Go right ahead."

The music from the next song was completely drowned out as many of the men and women attending the film jumped out of their seats and began cheering and hugging.

Gus looked at his wife, who had tears streaming down her cheeks.

"I guess I was wrong. Maybe folks will like talkies."

***

"Don't be a fool," Gus told George before they entered the Boss's office. "Capone is square with his men. You tell him you're sorry, and that you won't do it again, and if you mean it, he'll know it."

Sitting behind his desk, Capone was rubbing his jaw, looking annoyed.

"Yes, he does appear disagreeable," Gus whispered to George. He felt more than a prickle of apprehension. It was the second time Capone had summoned him for a conference. The fact that he was to bring George Goetz made him more fearful than the first time, if that were possible.

"So, youse boys ran into a little trouble over in Toledo, I hear," Capone said without preliminary welcomes or handshakes. This time Capone was not alone in the room. His brother Ralph and a tough named Verne Miller stood on either side of him, stern faces and hands locked in front of their waists like church deacons just before collections.

Capone's eyes were not on Gus, however. They focused entirely on George who, unlike Gus, had a history of doing jobs for The Outfit.

"What can I say?" George met Capone's gaze. "I screwed up. I thought it was an easy mark. It wasn't."

"And that goes for me, too," Gus added.

"I don't need the mud of armed robbery and cop killing tracked back to The Outfit," Capone said.

Gus felt his face and body language being judged and was confident his sincerity was recognized. He hoped George was equally contrite. He had his doubts about that, though, when they were dismissed, but Gus was once again called back to meet privately with the Boss.

"You're a smart lad," Capone told Gus as he waved for his brother and Verne Miller to leave them. "You've got too many brains to be in the kind of rackets you've been in. I'm puttin' you on my payroll for two hundred dollars a week. From now on, you're my man, and you're quittin' that other stuff. You stick with me, and I'll stick with you, and everything will be okay, you understand?"

"I do. I want to tell you though, that Ray Nugent and Bob Carey are good boys," Gus said. "And they'll do whatever I tell them."

"I got no faith in them. They got no brains." Capone looked away for what seemed to Gus an eternity. Finally, he looked him straight in the eyes. "If it'll do you any good, and if they'll keep their noses clean, I'll have them put on the payroll too.

"And with that in mind, I do have a job for youse. One that my boys could never pull off and get away with. You American boys know of Frankie Yale, I'm sure. I want you to go to New York and knock him off."

Capone stood and offered his hand. His handshake had a firmness that exuded authority and, even without Gus's verbally accepting the assignment, sealed the deal.

***

"I can't tell you what it's about," Gus told Georgette while packing his grip that evening. "And don't expect to hear from me until I get back. Capone has given strict orders that we not communicate with Chicago. What I mean is, we're on our own."

"Who's going with you?" Georgette asked the question that concerned her the most. "I hope it's not those knuckleheads Bob and Ray. And Bryan Bolton is way too green for anything serious."

"I agree." Gus took his wife in his arms. "I'm taking Fred and George. We're meeting a friend of Capone's in New York. He's called Lefty Louie Campagna, and we're staying at his mother's house. So, if I come back twenty pounds heavier, you can blame it on her dago food. While we're gone, we want you and Irene to lay low. We picked up a nice apartment for you to share in Indiana."

The Winklers had been out socially with the Goetz couple on several occasions, even having dinner at each other's houses. Georgette knew better than to speak badly of the other women to her husband. If Gus ever let one of her comments slip and it got back to a gangster's moll, there could be blood spilled—and not necessarily from the men.

Irene Goetz would often, upon a selfish whim, demand that George buy her a new bracelet, watch, or mink stole. Her husband's expensive presents, it was true, had begun to have a corrupting influence. Irene spent more than any of the other wives with no concept of budgeting for rainy days.

Then when the husbands had been away to Toledo and Georgette caught Irene flirting with a thug named Fred Barker, she foresaw an unhappy future for the couple. Luckily for their marriage, Barker was arrested on a burglary charge and sent to prison to serve three years.

Now Georgette found herself once again leaving a home she had come to love and venturing out to live with a woman she privately scorned. To make matters worse, Lefty Louie Campagna's girlfriend, Mary, took a flat nearby. Mary admitted, during her first meeting with Georgette, that she was brought up to believe it was a wife's duty to keep her husband satisfied. A philosophy that Georgette only half agreed with.

20

Lefty Louie Campagna's mother lived in Brooklyn not a great distance from Frankie Yale's house. If ever a man looked like his boss, short, wiry, round-faced, and high hairline, even walking and talking like Capone, that was Lefty Louie. And he was without a doubt his mother's son, only she was barely five feet tall. "Mama," as she told the boys to call her, did indeed keep the American boys filled up on pasta as well as her homemade breads. Fred Burke, for whatever reason, was clearly her favorite, filling his plate every time the bottom of it became visible.

"Al took me right out of reform school and made me a bodyguard," Lefty said, talking through a mouth full of pasta. "I'd die for that man. Capone's like a father to me."

"God bless Al Capone," Mama said, crossing herself quickly, and then set more Italian garlic bread on the table. "Remind me to send him some of my good pasta sauce when you leave."

Each day for the next week, Lefty Louie directed Gus as they drove around Brooklyn hoping to spot

Frankie Yale at one of his businesses. They had each studied every photograph they could find of Yale, Gus more than the others. He wanted to be able to recognize their target at a distance with the same ease as he could recognize Georgette a block away on a crowded street.

The black Buick sedan they had paid cash for in Nashville was as inconspicuous a vehicle as they could find, but one with great horsepower. Yale's coffee-colored Lincoln Coup would be easily recognized since tan was a relatively new color in the automobile industry.

July 1, 1928

"If you had three wishes, what would they be?" Lefty Louie asked from the front seat as Gus drove.

"Money, sex, and liquor, in that order," Fred said quickly. He was half sprawled out in the backseat on the driver's side. He couldn't fully sprawl because between him and George there was a vast arsenal of two Tommy guns and assorted rifles, shotguns, and handguns.

"That would be a waste of two wishes," Lefty Louie said. "If you have money, then sex and liquor will follow for free."

Gus was not fool enough to think he knew everything about women, but he was certain he could teach these three hoodlums a thing or two. It was a struggle not to think about his wife as he drove, a dangerous reverie when so much was on the line.

"Take another jaunt past the Sunrise Café, Gus," George suggested. "Why's Al want him dead, anyway, Louie?"

"Yale got too big for his britches," Lefty Louie explained. "Frank was Al's first boss when he was getting started as a waiter and bouncer at the Harvard Club on Coney Island. In fact, that's where Al got his scars, over a skirt no less, probably 'cause he was also in charge of the sportin' gals.

"Anyhow, you fellas know the rest of the story. Al flees to Chicago to avoid a murder charge and gets in thick with Johnny Torrio. Then when Al takes over the operations in twenty-five, Yale starts buckin' his decisions. The final straw that brought youse boys here was when Frankie started letting Al's booze get highjacked to Nucky Johnson in Atlantic City."

Gus was only half listening to Lefty Louie's rambling. He wished the others would pay more attention to doing their jobs. The quicker they took care of knocking off Yale, the quicker he could get home to Georgette. It was just as his mind tried to imagine his wife in her birthday suit that Gus saw the tan-colored Lincoln coming straight toward them in the opposite lane.

"That's him," Gus said calmly.

The other three sat up quickly, Fred reaching for the one-hundred-magazine Thompson machine gun that Capone had acquired for them. He had been training with it by cutting down entire trees using just one magazine.

"Well, get after him then," George almost shouted.

"Calm down." Gus proceeded to the nearest corner for a legal and safe U-turn, then cooly moved the Buick around slower traffic to catch up with the Lincoln.

"Step on it, Gus," George protested. "You're going to lose him."

"I'm sure he's heading to the Sunrise Café," Gus said.

A few minutes later, his guess was confirmed. The coffee-colored Lincoln was in the parking lot in the back of the Sunrise Café. Gus drove a block away to a corner and pulled up next to a telephone booth. Getting out, he walked toward it and reached into his pocket where he kept change for just this reason, along with a scrap of paper with the phone numbers of all Yale's businesses. He recited to the operator the number for the Sunrise Café.

"Please inform Mr. Yale that his wife Lucy injured herself and we are taking her to the Coney Island Hospital," Gus said into the mouthpiece.

"Why did you say Coney Island Hospital?" Lefty Louie asked when Gus got back into the car and told the others what he had said.

"Because I don't know where his wife is at this moment, but all their activities seem to be between their home and the Coney Island Ferry. Plus, if I'm right, we can do the hit closer to the Staten Island Ferry and make our escape to Jersey."

"Smart," Lefty said. "Now I know why Al put youse in charge."

George Goetz made a slight scoffing noise that Gus heard and ignored. This was no time for egos. He drove the Buick to a corner where he could see the Lincoln if Yale took the bait. The traffic was heavy in all directions with pedestrians crossing at every corner.

The others readied their weapons. Just as Gus expected, Yale came around the building in the Lincoln, but had to wait on traffic before he could make a left turn onto the street.

"Go, Gus!" George shouted. "What are you waiting for? We got him."

"Yes, and the cops will have us if we do it now and can't make a getaway through this traffic." Gus looked over the seat at George and waved his hand palm down in front of him. "Just calm down, it's a long way to the hospital, and we'll get him."

Again, George scoffed.

Yale finally made his left turn and Gus a right so he'd have two cars between them. It seemed to take a long time to get out of the heavy traffic area of the city. When they finally did, the two cars between the Buick and Lincoln made right turns off the main road. Gus saw Yale reach up to his driver's mirror and adjust it, then sped up to the next intersection and took the corner on two wheels in a hard left.

"He spotted us," George hissed. "I told you we should have done him sooner."

"We've got him," Gus said, his voice still calm. "That Lincoln is heavy, probably bulletproof. Fred, fire that hundred mag through the back window. Let's see if the windows are bulletproof too."

Killer Burke didn't need to be asked twice. He raised the gat out the window while Gus and the others put in earplugs. When he was in position, Gus swerved the Buick as far to the right as possible to give him a good alignment.

A half dozen shots exploded from the gat followed by a misfire. It seemed unthinkable his weapon would jam so quickly, and yet the unthinkable had happened. Swearing, Fred tossed the gat on the backseat floor and swept up his trusty fifty magazine gat that Carl Shelton had given him.

"The windows aren't bulletproof," George pointed from the back seat. "Get alongside him and we'll let him have it."

Despite oncoming traffic, Gus pulled the Buick into the left lane. Cars careened out of their way, sometimes hitting other vehicles or running up on the sidewalk. Speeding along the four-lane street, Gus struggled to keep the Buick close to and parallel to the Lincoln.

George blasted with two handguns, while Lefty Louie let loose with a sawed-off shotgun from the front seat. Opening the door on his side, Fred climbed out onto the running board and shot over the hood of the Buick with his reliable fifty-round Tommy gun.

Whether hit or not, Yale was tucked down in the car seat beneath the armored siding on the Lincoln. With no driver at the wheel, the Lincoln ran off the road, over a sidewalk, and crashed against a brick bungalow. Gus slid the Buick sideways to a stop just past the wreck.

From the front door of the bungalow, a Jewish Rabbi and a dozen boys dressed for Bar Mitzvah came rushing out, followed by a group of men and women.

George Goetz grabbed a fresh pistol from their arsenal, opened the door, and leaped out. He ran up to the Lincoln, leaned halfway inside the window, and unloaded six shots into Frankie Yale.

The parents of the boys at the Bar Mitzvah rushed to cover their sons' eyes as they struggled to pull the open-mouthed boys from the scene of the murder.

When George was back in the Buick, Gus floored the accelerator and got them out of the Hollywood Brooklyn neighborhood as quickly as possible. When they neared the Staten Island Ferry dock, he drove a little distance past it, did a U-turn, then rapidly and expertly, reversed the car into an alley before braking to a stop behind a grove of trees.

"Take everything out of the car and dump it," Gus ordered. "Then split up and get on the ferry to Jersey. We'll meet back at Mama's house this evening."

As he tried to look nonchalant during his walk to the landing, Gus struggled to push dark thoughts from his mind. The slaying of Frankie Yale in front of the Bar Mitzvah boys would surely haunt them for the remainder of their lives. He hoped the parents had been able to restrain the youngsters from rushing to the Lincoln to look at the bloody scene.

Very shortly, the four killers were on the Brooklyn Ferry heading across the Hudson River to New Jersey, the Statue of Liberty standing proudly in the distance. Though each of their hearts were still racing with adrenalin, they spread out on the boat so as to not be seen together, each with their own thoughts.

Fred planted himself at the stern of the boat. He had learned not to dwell on gunfights; surviving them was enough. He lit a cigarette, then flicked it into the water. A cigar was more appropriate after such a successful assassination.

George was pacing in a state of high anxiety. When he saw a young couple staring at him, he grabbed the rail on the starboard side and forced his mind to slow. He had blown it again. In Toledo, he had left his coat behind, eventually leading the authorities to ask questions of Bryan Bolton because there was a cleaner's ticket in a pocket with his name on it. Now, he was kicking himself for leaving the one-hundred-magazine Tommy gun in the Buick. He left it because Gus had ordered them to dump everything, and he didn't appreciate Gus giving him orders. *Who put him in charge, anyway? Oh, well, Irene will be impressed when I describe to her how I was the one to finish off Frankie Yale.* The thought cheered him a little.

On the port side, Lefty Louie was hungry. He hoped Mama had a good meal ready for them when they got to the house.

The bow of the boat emitted a light mist that in the heat of the afternoon felt good on Gus's face. He stood in the mist for a long time, not trembling as he had been earlier, but thinking. Relief surged through him. He wasn't dead. Georgette would be waiting for him. Ready to love him and help get the vision of the horrified Jewish boys to leave his thoughts. He wondered if his wife would soon be reading the headline about Yale's murder in the newspaper, pausing occasionally to wonder if he was the killer.

Lefty Louie and George were wondering the same about their significant others, only in their cases, they couldn't wait to brag about the assassination. As soon as they arrived at Mama Campagna's, they hurried to the telephone to call their molls.

Late that night, Georgette rushed to answer her telephone when it rang. Would it be Gus?

"This is Irene. The boys will be home in three days."

"How do you know that?" Georgette asked.

"Read tomorrow's newspaper," Irene said and hung up.

21

The next day, as Georgette was dashing out to get The Chicago Tribune, a Bureau of Investigation official was going through telephone records of calls made by those suspected to be affiliated with the crime world. It was slow, monotonous work that was assigned to agents who got in bad standing with the Bureau's director, J. Edgar Hoover.

When he arrived at the phone records for the Campagna household in Brooklyn, he noted several long-distance calls to the Chicago area. He immediately picked up the phone. "Get me, Hoover."

***

George was so depressed, he gave his appearance no thought and was a little wobbly by the time he, Gus, and Lefty Louie had gone through the three routine searches, been escorted up the stairs to the seventh floor, and finally stood outside Capone's office.

It was a much-too-hot summer day for the elevator to be out of service. The gunmen in front and behind the three men were uncomfortably silent. Jake Guzik, one of the thugs of ugly demeanor, was sweating as a man his size might who had just walked down and now back up seven flights of stairs.

"That's quite a jaunt," Lefty Louie commented, himself breathing hard but seemingly unconcerned that in just a few moments he would be answering the questions of Al Capone.

Fred's absence was a little annoying to Gus. Killer Burke had gone into seclusion since their return to Chicago, most likely drunk in a whorehouse.

Jack McGurn, one of Capone's henchmen, opened the office door, followed them in, and stood stiffly at attention. McGurn scared Gus more than any of the others, including Verne Miller, who was scary enough. Both extremely proficient with Thompson sub-machine guns, he suspected the two of them could wipe out half the gangsters in Chicago if they put their minds to it.

Standing behind his desk, Capone had a hunched look as if he were a cat preparing to spring. In moments like this, he possessed a power that would brook no resistance.

Any comment had the potential to get Gus in trouble, but today it seemed silence also could get him in trouble. Still, he was determined to be res-olutely quiet. It was not he who had screwed up. Determined not to say a word, he nursed his sense of injustice, forcing the others to take the initia-tive to save themselves.

"So," Capone began. "The Feds traced several phone calls from Mama Campagna's house to the apartments of Louie and George. I thought I made my instructions clear that there was to be no con-tact with Chicago."

"You know how it is, Al," Lefty Louie said with some vehemence. "A fella about to do man-slaughter sometimes needs to talk to his skirt."

Once again, Gus recognized the belligerent air that Lefty Louie so often displayed in concert with his vanity. He and George shifted a little, wishing Louie would just be quiet.

"YOU HAD YOUR MOTHER TO TALK TO!" Capone's face turned red and a vein popped out on his nose. "Don't be a jabroni."

Louie shocked Gus by smiling and saying, "That reminds me, Mama sent some of her good pasta sauce that you like so much."

Capone's silence was unnerving, the scars on his face white against his red face. Finally, The Boss walked around the desk and stood in front of Lefty Louie. The two seemed to be trying to see who blinked first. Then Capone's face unexpectedly softened. He raised his hand and gave Louie's face a light, double pat on the cheek.

"So, what's your excuse?" Capone moved in front of George, but George's eyes were on the big Louisville slugger propped up behind The Boss's desk.

Lefty Louie had laid a clever, even fatal, trap for him. George didn't have Louie's history with Capone. He didn't know whether to joke or admit he'd screwed up like he'd done last time.

"I'm the one who killed Yale," George bragged, still hoping to gain the big man's good opinion. "He was still alive when I got to the car and pumped six bullets into him."

"Right," Capone sniggered. "Then he must have survived the shotgun blast to his head and the Tommy gun .45 through his brain, huh? We can't summon him from hell and ask him, can we?"

George colored, but he held himself in check. Capone stepped next in front of Gus.

"Did you talk to your wife too?" Capone asked.

"No." Gus felt a rush of admiration for Georgette's loyalty. It occurred to him that her good sense might save him.

"That's because you and Georgette are dependable and loyal," Capone said.

Gus felt a little awkward being the sole recipient of a compliment.

"Now," Capone went behind his desk and lifted the ball bat. "Get outta here before I change my mind."

George was the first one out the door, and he didn't wait for the others before he began descending the steps. When he reached the street, the July heat was nothing compared to that heat building up from his anger toward Gus Winkler. From feeling friendly toward Gus when they first met, George had begun to envy him, and, in his book, envy was akin to hate.

***

Shell shock from the war always came into Gus's mind when he least expected it. Soldiers dead with their heads or limbs blown off. Or, possibly worse, those still alive without their limbs.

"Reminiscing?" Georgette asked from her makeup mirror as she applied blush.

By her reflection in the mirror, Gus saw his wife looking at him. He had learned long ago not to hide any more from Georgette than necessary. Indeed, telling her his woes very often brought him relief.

"What I'd been through—over there, makin' the world safe for democracy. What a crock." Gus took a big swallow of bourbon. "Did I ever tell you the last ambulance runs I made with wounded came *after* the war was over? A few generals wanted to pad their resumes with one final victory, I guess. The war ended at eleven o'clock in the morning on November eleventh—eleven, eleven, eleven. We all knew it was comin', but those generals kept us fighting until ten fifty-nine that morning, one minute before the armistice."

"Maybe you'd like to try some brandy instead of whiskey." Georgette finished doing her makeup, walked to him in his armchair, and took his glass from him. "I find it to be cheerier."

"Why do you take so much time to get ready?" Gus asked. "You're just having lunch with the wives."

"A gangster's moll will clock every wrinkle." Georgette fitted her hat to her head with pins, kissed her husband on the forehead, and walked out the door.

***

Georgette liked Bryan and Veva Bolton. The other wives called Veva "Dumb Dora" because she often used words incorrectly. She and Bryan were country hicks to them, but Georgette found them refreshingly naïve about the world. They reminded her that life could be simpler and sometimes had its comic aspects.

"I have a mindgrain headache," Veva complained during lunch at The Garden of Italy restaurant.

Irene and Bob's girl, Rose, put their napkins to their mouths to hide their smiles. Georgette wanted to be patient with Veva, a hard thing since she was not a patient person by nature.

"That's migraine, dear," Georgette corrected as gently as she could.

"Your grain, what?" Veva asked.

"Never mind, dear. How's your salad?" Georgette asked while Irene and Rose giggled.

For too long, the wives had been crowded together, like sparrows all wanting to roost on the same tree branch. They had just ordered their food when Georgette spotted Al Capone in the back of the restaurant eating by himself, four burly guards standing watch nearby.

"Bob says he orders killing as calmly as the rest of us order drinks," Rose whispered.

"Maybe that's why he looks so blue," Veva said, seeking a rose in every thorn bush. "I feel sorry for him."

"Didn't you hear the news?" Rose leaned a little across the table. "His friend Tony Lombardo got accidentally murdered. Bob says it was retaliation by Joe Aeillo and Bugs Moran for Capone having Frankie Yale killed."

"Oh, shit!" Irene closed her eyes.

Georgette took a pen and paper from her purse, scribbled a note on it, folded the paper, and called the waitress to their table. "Please give this note to that gentleman sitting by himself in the back of the room."

Capone, finished with his meal, was enjoying a glass of wine when the waitress arrived to collect his dishes. She handed him the note and pointed toward the wives' table.

It was the first smile of the crime boss's day. He motioned his guards to hold their position, then stood and walked over to the wives' table.

"Thank you, Mrs. Winkler, for the kind note," Capone said with a slight bow. "Yes, our friend Antonio's death was quite tragic. If you'll have your husband send me some dark glasses, I'll go down to the funeral home and have a last look at him."

"I guess our boys will be going back to New York now," Irene said.

Georgette kicked Irene's leg under the table. George's wife instantly recognized her mistake and clamped a hand over her mouth. It was too late though. Capone gave Irene the evil eye.

The wives were all trying hard to not act nervous, but none of them succeeded. Fortunately, the food arrived just at that time. Capone touched his hand to the front of his fedora and left, his bodyguards closely behind.

"You've sure got a lot of moxie," Rose said to Irene. Rose had been looking rather cheerful until this moment. "Now your husband is in for another ass-chewing, if not worse."

Irene's face lost its color. To no one's surprise, it was Veva who reached across the table and placed her hand on hers.

Annoyed as she was at Irene's bad behavior, Georgette noted several heads at other tables turning their way. She wanted to make a graceful exit. The heads moving close together and the whispers were a sure indication, in her opinion, that they too had noticed aggravation on the famous gangster's face as he departed.

***

George knew of no men still above ground who had survived three tongue lashings from Scarface. Yet, here he was, walking out of the Boss's hotel unscathed. He blamed Gus and his wife. They thought they were so perfect. What kind of woman would have sent Capone a condolence note over the death of a putz like Tony Lombardo? She was just sucking up for her husband.

The way others talked about Georgette's beauty bothered him too. What caused men to look at her with such appetite? Even women gushed over her.

Still alive after meeting with Scarface, he just wanted to spend the rest of his day off in bed getting sloshed with the youngest sporting gal he could find. First, though, he needed to go home and give Irene what for. Her stupid mouth made her as guilty as Georgette. After that, he would gather the St. Louis Gang. Following the tongue-lashing for telling Irene that he had been in New York, Scarface had said, "I have another assignment for my American boys."

***

Vincenzo Antonio Gibaldi hated Capone's American Boys. Listening to George Goetz grovel in front of the Boss was embarrassing. No Italian would behave so badly. He hated much about America. It was because of Americans that when he went into professional boxing, he had to change his name to Jack McGurn. The fighting Irish ruled the boxing world, and unless he was prepared to take a dive when ordered to, he had to become one of them, thus the name change.

"You are just stupido." Capone had waved his hands in George's face. "You don't have the brains of Gus Winkler. I am telling you now. You either start listening to your superior or face the consequences. You understand my meaning?"

McGurn could have vomited seeing Goetz cower. A real man would have stood his ground and made eye contact with Capone. Take your punishment like a man, even if it means a bullet, a ball bat, or a knife across your throat.

Goetz was also a shotgun man, another weakness in McGurn's opinion. A weapon for women to protect their home. McGurn was proud to have earned his nickname Machine Gun Jack when Capone sent him to knock off Hymie Weiss for leading the assassination attempt on him at the Hawthorn Hotel shooting. McGurn had crossed himself and kissed his rosary before Tommy gunning Weiss as he stood in front of the Holy Name Cathedral in downtown Chicago.

For that favor, Capone gave him the names of the three men who had killed McGurn's stepfather. Within a month, Machine Gun Jack tracked each down and Tommy-gunned them in separate hits.

"Now, how can I be assured of your loyalty?" Capone had asked George Goetz.

"I would take a bullet for you," George promised weakly.

Capone laughed. He pointed at Jack McGurn. "That man took bullets for me. Pete and Frank Gusenberg cornered him while he was in a telephone booth and Tommy-gunned him. You think you could take bullets like that and not run for the hills?"

Goetz nodded, but when his eyes met those of Machine Gun Jack, they all knew he was lying.

22

The first time Bryan Bolton ever played golf was with Gus, Fred, and Al Capone at a golf course in Wisconsin. Ray and Bob played a foursome in the next flight along with Lefty Louie and Verne Miller.

Still lacking Capone's good graces, George Goetz was assigned bodyguard duty alongside Jack McGurn, who was still moving slowly after being shot by the Gusenberg brothers. Though not playing, George and McGurn both carried a golf bag containing enough weaponry to wipe out a large flock of geese if the golfers got tired of hitting a little ball into a hole.

Having been a pretty good baseball player, and with Capone and Fred Burke coaching him, Bryan picked up the drive swing pretty quickly. But he found putting nearly impossible. It didn't matter to Capone, Fred, and Gus, because by the time they reached the back nine, they were getting drunker with each hole.

There were plenty of side bets as well as cheating, expected activities since they did consider themselves, after all, some of the most notorious criminals in the world. The one side-bet the novice Bryan was not allowed to take a swing at was the game called "Blind Robin." That was because one golfer would lie down on the ground and balance a ball on his chin while his partner teed off.

On the first hole of the back nine, Fred, being the best long-ball hitter of the bunch, used Bryan's chin as his tee. Despite Bryan's trembling, Fred smashed the ball a good two hundred thirty yards.

When it came Gus's turn to tee off Capone's chin, there were plenty of oohs, awes, and laughs. The Boss didn't flinch though. Handing his thick cigar to McGurn, he lay flat on his back and balanced the ball on his confident chin.

Gus shook his head when Fred patted him on the back and chuckled. He then went to his golf bag, returned with his putter, and tapped the ball lightly. Capone and everyone were still laughing when Gus used his three-iron to drive the ball thirty yards short of where Fred's ball lay but with a much better view of the flag.

It was Bryan, however, who shocked everyone. For the first twelve holes, he kept up with the others off the tee as well as on fairway shots. It was only when he was trying to get out of the sand trap on the thirteenth hole that Gus saw him bend over, lift his ball out of the sand, and put a tee beneath it.

"Uh, Bryan, you can't tee up on every shot, you know?"

"I thought you were supposed to tee up on every shot except the putts."

Since Bryan had collected nearly fifty dollars in bets, Jack McGurn stepped toward Bryan and reached into the golf bag he carried. Fred stepped between Bryan and McGurn. Everyone looked at Capone to see how he would react. The silence that followed was chilling and seemed to last forever to Bryan, who looked like a puppy that had just been whipped for peeing on the carpet.

Then Capone began a slow, half-hearted snicker that erupted into a full-bellied laugh. Gus quickly joined in the laugh, followed by George, but McGurn and Fred continued their staring contest.

The following hole was a par four dog leg with a narrow fairway. Gus, Capone, and Bryan chose to drive the ball to the end of the fairway where they would have a straight second shot to the green. Fred, teetering a little from heavy drinking, thought he was strong enough to drive his tee ball over the trees and close to the green, a difficult but not unheard-of shot.

Bets were placed, the biggest by Jack McGurn.

"A nickel says you won't make par," McGurn growled, pulling fifty dollars from his jacket pocket.

"A dime says I birdie," Fred countered.

"You're on." McGurn agreed.

Bryan was nervous. Both Killer Burke and Machine Gun Jack were former boxers, and McGurn, being himself a scratch golfer, likely knew the difficulty of making such a shot.

But what really scared Bryan about McGurn was just last year, Machine Gun Jack had been assigned to convince the famous comedian and singer, Joe E. Lewis, to renew his contract with the syndicate establishments. McGurn owned a speakeasy jazz club called the Green Mill Cocktail Lounge. When Lewis refused the suggestion, McGurn cut his face and part of his tongue, then left him for dead. The singer barely survived but was now slowly recovering and hoping to perform again.

Fred teed his ball; no Blind Robin for this shot. He lined himself up and took three deliberate practice swings. There was no wind to consider, and the trees were in their fall foliage with few leaves near their tops. Even if it struck those smaller branches, the ball would have a chance of dropping onto the dog leg side of the fairway.

His backswing and follow-through were near perfection. The ball exploded off the tee, high and straight. It began its descent as it reached the back of the trees. Just when it appeared it would clear them, a small branch, barely visible to the naked eye, was clipped by the ball, causing it to lose momentum. Like a wing shot on a flying pigeon, it changed course ever so slightly, almost certainly ending Fred's hope for a fairway shot.

McGurn smirked loudly. Gus, with his driver still in his hand, moved between the two burly killers. George, disliking both Fred and McGurn, walked down the fairway.

"Do you think it made it?" Bryan asked hopefully.

"Doubt it," Capone said, showing little concern for the tension between Killer Burke and Machine Gun Jack. "Let's hit our second shots and we'll find out."

The foursome, along with their bodyguards, arrived at Bryan's ball first. Without the aid of the tee, he shanked his ball into the trees somewhere close to where Fred's had been headed. Both Capone and Gus reached the green, but a good thirty feet from the flag. Not seeing Fred's ball on the fairway, they all headed toward the trees to look for his and Bryan's balls.

"You're playing a Black Dunlop number two aren't you, Fred?" Capone asked. "What's yours, Bryan?"

"They have numbers?" Bryan asked.

Everyone laughed, and since no one had bothered to place a bet on his shot, they agreed to let Bryan play any ball they found.

"That's fine," McGurn said. "But if we don't find Fred's, he'll have to go back to the tee and he'll be hitting his third shot. Remember, this is for a hundred dollars."

Fred told Bryan to search in the high grass close to the fairway while he looked a little deeper into the trees. Bryan did as instructed, following a few yards behind. The six men had only searched a short time when Bryan shouted. "Here it is." He bent over toward the ball.

"Don't touch it!" McGurn bellowed and came running. He looked down at the ball and saw the Dunlop insignia with the number two above and below. He looked at Fred suspiciously. The ball was in direct line with and about twenty feet from the pin and in low grass.

"I'm not the one who found it." Fred smirked. He took out his jigger, lined up his shot, and chipped the ball to within three feet of the hole. Even Bryan could have made the putt for the birdie.

"You cheated," McGurn said.

"What makes you say that, Jack?" Capone seemed amused.

"Because," McGurn reached in his pocket and pulled out a black Dunlop number two ball. "I'd already found this."

Fred bloodied McGurn's face with two hard haymakers followed by a half dozen misses as his opponent began bobbing and weaving with Jack Demsey-type head movement. It only took a few punches to Fred's head before his thirty-five-year-old face turned red and he was breathing heavily. At twenty-six years old, McGurn was still in his boxing prime. When he opened up on Fred with left-hand leads followed by vicious undercuts, Capone finally called an end to the battle by swinging his putter down hard between the two combatants.

"Enough, you two *stronzo's*," Capone snarled. "I need you both alive and healthy. We have a *figlio di puttana* to kill."

That night, Capone, McGurn, and the American Boys stayed up late plotting the assassination of George "Bugs" Moran.

***

"Gussie," Georgette called to her husband from the kitchen. "Telephone for you. Jack McGurn."

Gus picked up the extension in the living room.

"Moran and Aiello just had Al's friend Pasqualino Lorordo killed," McGurn told Gus. "We need to step things up."

"Sounds good to me," Gus said. "How we gonna do that?"

"He wants me to get Abe Bernstein to call Moran and tell him he has a truckload of Canadian whiskey that he hijacked, and he would deliver it to the Clark Street garage for fifty bucks a case. Get your crew over to Screwy's place. Tell them to bring enough for a long stakeout."

23

"It's my birthday, you know," George Goetz said.

"No shit! You was born on Valentine's Day?" Fred asked. "How old is ya?"

"Thirty-two."

"Well, see to it you make it to thirty-three." Fred laughed.

Gus, Fred, George, Bob, and Ray sat at a round table in the Circus Café playing poker. Though the Café was co-owned by one of their friends, Claude "Screwy" Maddox, a former Egan Rat himself, none of the five trusted many of those known as the Circus Café Gang, particularly the Italians.

"It's been two weeks, Gus," George whispered, trying to push away the feeling the whole expedition was foolish.

Gus looked around. Jack McGurn was at the window as he had been almost every day. He glanced at the five gamblers from time to time but seldom spoke to them. Fred, in particular, was unnerved by McGurn's fleeting looks—such a thing was unnecessary, even unnatural. The five were there at the table as they had been every day for the past two weeks, waiting for the phone call.

Seeing nothing to provoke unease, Gus whispered, "Just stay the course." He himself was being cheerful and friendly in an effort to reduce the tension.

Fred ignored this simple suggestion. Since his fight with McGurn at the golf course, he had been itching for a rematch. With a grimace, he looked at the knuckle on his right hand. It still hurt from contact with Machine Gun Jack's tough jaw. The others treated McGurn fairly, but Fred didn't want to feel friendly toward anyone he might have to kill.

"If I get one more shot at him, I'll break that big-nosed dago," Fred muttered, the golf course fight weighing on him.

"Just drop it, Fred," Gus said sternly.

"Droppin' things is not what I'm good at," Fred growled.

"I trust Bryan Bolton and even Swede as look-outs," George sided in. "But those two wops, Accardo and Capezio, I don't know about them."

"They're just supposed to run interference if we get chased by cops," Gus said.

"Or they're supposed to block us in so we *can* get caught," George said. He and Fred had been taking sides against Gus quite often lately. In fact, it was their collaboration that morning that insisted George be the one dressed as a uniformed policeman to enter the garage rather than Gus, a change that Gus was not entirely opposed to, since it meant he wouldn't have to be one of the gunmen and could do what he did best—drive.

Ray was equally uneasy, since to him, Fred's was gloomy talk, for sure. Not only were the five of them going to have to kill Bugs Moran and any witnesses, but they would also have to watch their backs afterward in case McGurn or any of his goons tried to backstab them. It was not at all uncommon for hired assassins to be eliminated so that in case they were caught, they wouldn't take a plea bargain and tell who hired them, a concession to avoid the death penalty.

Bob had told Ray that the good thing about doing the killing in Chicago was that Illinois used hanging and not the gruesome electric chair, as some other states did. Neither Bob nor Ray liked the idea of their head being shaved, eyes popping out, and their flesh burning like a pig on a spit.

Bob himself wasn't really worried about being betrayed or even getting hung. His concern was that it had begun snowing during the night, and now the snow had turned to sleet. Though it was slightly warmer now, if the hit and escape came too late in the afternoon, there was always a chance of an icy accident or the roads getting blocked for travel.

***

Bryan and Jimmy "Swede" Morand had been staked out in the apartment across the street from the S.M.C. Cartage Company garage every day for going on two weeks. Their turns sitting in front of a window on watch duty were monotonous and as difficult a job as Bryan had ever had. Who would have thought that the whiteness of the snow on sunny days could be so treacherous on the eyeballs? He often found himself blinking through watery eyes even when he wore dark glasses.

When February fourteenth came around, Bryan was thinking of little else than the custom Veva had started for them three years ago. Each Valentine's Day, she would decorate their bed with as many flower petals as she could afford, and they would make love. He was thinking about her slim body when he glimpsed a man wearing a brown fedora walking toward the garage.

"Swede," Bryan said. "Get over here."

Swede was playing solitaire on the bed and had just unleashed all his aces and kings. Reluctantly, he abandoned the game.

"There's six others already went in the garage," Bryan told him. "One's dressed like a mechanic. The others are suits."

"It's hard to tell from here," Swede said, his eyes not being what they once were. "Might be Albert Weinshank. He's about Moran's size."

"Yeah, but he's wearin' the brown fedora and overcoat." Bryan was hoping it was Moran. Maybe he could get home to Veva in time for the bed of flowers celebration. "That's what we were told to watch for."

Neither lookout had ever seen Moran in person, only through photographs, and Bryan had never been very good at remembering names or faces to begin with. He sometimes thought it was a novel learning problem no one else had. He could literally be talking to someone and, five minutes later, see them as total strangers.

"Well," Swede said when the two men entered the garage. "I'm about half sure. But at least we know the Gusenberg brothers are in there. Those two shot up Jack McGurn and murdered Capone's friend Pasqualino Lolordo. He'd surely be happy to get them knocked off."

"I'm makin' the call." Bryan hurried out of the apartment to use the payphone at the end of the hall.

***

A half-hour before Albert Weinshank was spotted by Bryan, he received a message that Bugs and his boys would be unloading a stolen truckload of Canadian whisky at the Cartage Company garage. He told his wife he was going there to tell Moran he had a new job and was quitting as leader of the labor graft.

"It's so cold out," his wife said. "Why don't you just call him?"

"Moran's a face-to-face type of fella." Weinshank kissed her on the forehead and walked out the door.

At about that same time, failed optometrist Reinhart Schwimmer entered the Cartage Company garage and was happy the first person he saw was Adam Heyer. Heyer, a salaried man, wasn't doing very well as Bugs Moran's business manager and needed cash for an operation for his wife and needed it soon. Heyer was sitting with his feet up on a desk, going through the racing forms for the day. A mechanic worked beneath a car nearby.

"Any hot tips today?" Schwimmer asked.

"If I had any, you think I'd tell a piker like you?" Heyer sniggered.

Schwimmer liked hanging out with the North Side gang to get tips on horseraces. He kept up his fondness for gangsters even after their tips put him in hock. Luckily, he had a mother who couldn't say no when he came begging for handouts.

"Hey, Doc, come look at Myrtle," a thug named James Clark said. His rolled up sleeves revealed a tattoo of a nude woman on his left forearm.

Schwimmer, who the boys liked to call Doc, hurried over. He appreciated any positive attention he could get from the gang.

"What you callin' her Myrtle for?" Pete Gusenberg said. "That's my wife's name."

"Relax, brother," Frank Gusenberg said. "Your wife has a much better body than Clark's tattoo. I should know, I've enjoyed it enough when you're away."

Pete playfully slapped his brother on the head just as Albert Weinshank walked in. Not used to having the head of the labor racket in their presence, everyone turned to look at him.

"Is Moran coming?" Weinshank asked. "I need to discuss somethin' with him."

"He'll be along." Heyer shrugged, then went back to studying the racing forms. A long shot named Tommy looked good in the fifth.

***

When the wall phone rang at the Circus Café, Screwy Maddox answered. A moment later he looked at the five poker players who were staring at him.

"You're on, boys," Screwy said. He immediately picked up the phone again to call Tony Accardo and Tony Capezio on North Clark Street. One of the Tonys would run out to their black Cadilac to get it warmed up and ready to run interference for the assassins, should it be needed.

The Circus Café Gang was famous for driving black Cadillacs, so there was no shortage of them to convert to a police car with proper decals, sirens, and two red lights. The five hitmen followed Jack McGurn through a hallway and into a garage with a half dozen other Caddies as well as a less conspicuous '26 Peerless sedan stolen from a couple of Chicago detectives.

Quickly slipping into their police uniforms, Fred and George got into the Peerless with Screwy Maddox behind the wheel. Dressed as plainclothes detectives, Bob and Ray got in the Cadilac squad car. Gus, wearing a blue suit, matching fedora, and a chinchilla overcoat, got behind the wheel.

Once everyone was in position, McGurn opened the swinging garage door and Gus led the caravan of two cars onto the snowy street. Traffic was moving cautiously, which upset Bob, who sat in the backseat with the barrel of his Thompson machine gun sticking upwards between his legs.

"Come on, Gus," Bob chastised. "You act like you don't want to get there."

Gus ignored the backseat driver, but when a light in front of him turned yellow and he began braking, Bob shouted, "Take it!" Gus, uncharacteristically on edge, gave the Caddy some gas and proceeded around a car into the left lane to beat the light, which, by now, was turning red. A truck in that lane lightly smacked the Caddy and immediately stopped.

Gus's car slid sideways a little in the snow before he also came to a stop.

"What the hell are you doing?" Bob hissed.

Forcing himself to regain his calm, Gus got out of the car. The truck driver also got out, visibly upset that he had struck a police car. "I'm sorry, officer," the man said.

Gus smiled. Seeing little damage to either vehicle, he said, "No problem. Be more careful from now on."

The two returned to their vehicles and continued on their way.

Gus drove the Caddy another block to the S.M.C. Cartage garage and parked on the street just outside the alley. A moment later, the '26 Peerless sedan eased into the alley and proceeded fifty yards before stopping near a set of double doors. The two fake police officers, Fred and George, got out, cracked open the unlocked double doors, and walked in. Screwy Maddox then drove the Peerless to the end of the alley, exited onto that street, and headed back to the Circus Café.

***

A block away, Bugs Moran, walking with two bodyguards, Ted Newberry and Willie Marks, was approaching when the Cadillac police car pulled up next to the garage.

"What the hell's this?" Moran quickly ducked inside a spot where two buildings formed a little nook and huddled with the bodyguards on a step going into a coffee shop. They watched until two men who looked like they could be detectives emerged from the car and walked to the front door of the garage, waited just a moment until it opened, then walked inside.

"Let's have a cup of coffee until the dicks leave." Moran pointed at the coffee shop door, Newberry opened it, and they walked in.

***

Fred and George came into the garage with handguns drawn. The lighting was dim—a single bulb in the middle of the spacious room. A dozen cars, two on jacks, a mechanic on a pallet beneath one changing out a transmission filled the space.

230

A German Shepherd, tied on a chain leash nearby, stood and gave a low growl until George bent down and offered his hand. The dog accepted a few strokes, then lay back down.

Unaware that anyone had just entered, six men wearing fedoras, gloves, and heavy coats milled around a pot-bellied stove near the back wall drinking coffee and trying to stay warm in the eighteen-degree temperature of the garage.

The first one in the building who saw Fred and George was the mechanic, John May, who had just slid out from under a sedan to grab a different wrench. When May saw the two cops with their guns drawn, he wished he'd stayed home in a warm bed with his wife, but his family needed the money for food as well as clothing for the winter. Those necessities had brought him into the underworld of Bugs Moran and his henchmen.

Leading May at gunpoint, Fred and George stayed behind him as they approached the six men in the room. Adam Heyer looked up from his racing form and laughed. *Probably a couple of dicks who heard about the shipment of booze and are looking for a payout,* he thought. *No problem. We'll give 'em a few bucks and they'll be on their way.*

The Gusenberg brothers didn't laugh when the cops walked toward them. They were pissed.

"Hey, flatfeet," Frank said loudly. "This ain't the time or the place to shake us down. Youse boys must be new in town."

"Line up with your hands on that wall," Fred ordered. "All of you."

Some smiling and others scoffing, the men assumed the position they knew well, hands on the brick wall and feet spread.

"But I'm just a mechanic, officer," John May pleaded. "I don't know nothing what goes on here."

George shoved him in with the others and then began frisking and removing weapons while Fred held his gun on them. All but the mechanic and one other had a pistol in their shoulder holsters.

Carrying the confiscated guns, George walked back, threw the weapons onto the desk, unlocked the front door, and let Bob and Ray in. From beneath their topcoats, Ray produced a gat and Bob a shotgun like the one George was now drawing from beneath his own policeman's coat. Fred did the same, drawing his favorite Tommy gun.

Ten feet in front of the four gunmen, six of the seven were very relaxed. Three of them hadn't even extinguished their smokes. All had plenty of experience with shakedowns, plus they knew there were no illegal products in the building, since Bernstein's Canadian liquor had yet to arrive.

"That ain't Bugs Moran!" Fred whispered to George. He pointed his gat at the back of one of the seven men facing the wall. He'd been looking forward for two weeks to again using the Thompson machine gun.

"No shit!" George whispered back. He raised Twelve Iron, his twelve-gauge pump-action shotgun. "The lookouts must have been fooled by his brown fedora and that he's the right size."

Dressed in police uniforms, Fred and George both raised a hand and loosened their collars at the same time. This was not the way things were supposed to go down. Capone had made it very clear that Bugs Moran was the one he wanted dead. To George, the Gusenberg brothers and James Clark were successful assassins that Capone would be glad to be rid of. George clicked the safety catch off on Twelve Iron.

The mechanic, John May, very nervously shifted back and forth on his legs. Though it was very cold in the building, he was perspiring heavily. Vapor exited his mouth and skin. It was deathly silent. May recognized the click of a safety catch being flipped. He had a shotgun at home that made a similar sound. While the other men tensed and clenched their teeth, John May turned his head and looked back over his shoulder at the four men aiming the barrels of their guns at the Moran men.

A shotgun blast tore the left side of May's face off. He fell to the ground as the six men beside him began a jerking, spasmodic death dance. Bullets tore into them, sometimes exiting and carrying pieces of bone and brain matter that splattered on the wall.

May survived the hail of lead from the first barrage, though he was numb and bleeding from a dozen holes in his body. Laying partially beneath Reinhart Schwimmer, he saw with his good eye that the four men were reloading. The Tommy gunmen completed the task first, one reloading with a fifty-round ammo drum and the other a twenty-round box clip. The box clip man knelt to one knee and let loose with another volley. John May's last thought was *I should have stayed home today.*

The third man from the left, Albert Weinshank, took seven bullets to the back and four more below the waist. A bullet through his heart mercifully prevented him from dwelling on the fact that he should have done as his wife suggested and used the phone to tell Moran he was resigning.

The force from both Tommy guns hitting him at the same time bounced Adam Heyer against the brick wall and onto his back where he had just a few seconds to wonder if he had enough money in his cookie jar to get his sick wife the operation she needed. Two .45s from a Tommy gun blew his skull away, ending his worry.

James Clark, himself a hired assassin and now second in command to Moran, instinctively dove alongside the wall at the first gunshot and tried to use the bodies of the others to shield himself. For a moment he thought the pain in both legs and left forearm wouldn't be fatal, but when he felt two bullets pass through his chest and blood spurted out of his mouth, he knew it was over for him. His tattoo of a naked Myrtle barely survived mutilation, with one bullet above her head and another just below her feet.

When the shooting started, Rinehart Schwimmer was at the end of the lineup on the right. He had been standing straight with his knees locked, so while the other six victims ducked or collapsed from the first barrage, he remained upright longer, allowing him to absorb twenty-five hits. Of the sixteen bullet wounds in his back, twelve were grouped in a tight pattern with barely enough room for five pea-sized slugs he also received from a shotgun blast.

On the left-hand side of the lineup, Pete Gusenberg collapsed across a chair on his stomach, arms across its back, his legs sprawled behind him. Out of the eleven bullets that struck him, Fred and George made certain that several tore through his groin and ass, thereby tearing his trousers and exposing his rear end as well as private parts, which had only an hour ago been happily clapping against his wife Myrtle's shapely backside.

Next to him on his back was his brother Frank, his right leg bent as if he were relaxing and watching clouds float across the sky. Though riddled with fourteen bullets, he was still breathing so shallowly the shooters didn't notice. Seven of the bullets passed through his body and were now wedged into the brick wall.

The Gusenberg brothers' assassination attempt against Jack McGurn and their murders of Capone's friends Tony Lombardo and Pasqualino Lolordo was now avenged.

Citizens inside apartments who heard the fireworks-type gunshots looked out onto the street. Others assumed it was a jackhammer or similar electric tool being used in the garage. Those curious enough to investigate saw two police officers holding guns to the backs of two men in street clothes who had their hands raised high up in the air. They all got into a Cadillac police car which lurched away from the curb and with red lights flashing and sirens blaring moved into traffic behind a streetcar. The squad car then cut into the oncoming lane and zoomed around the trolley before swerving back into the right lane and speeding off.

Chicago citizen Charles McAllister walked hesitantly into the Cartage Company garage. A German Shepherd was whimpering as he strained at a chain fastened to his collar, trying to reach a man lying on his back on the floor. The entire left side of the man's face was gone, leaving a bloody half skeleton of cheekbone and teeth. Another man's body sprawled over his legs. Several others lay to the left, pools of blood spreading out across the floor toward the canine.

A man on his stomach crawled toward McAllister.

"Who is it?" Frank Gusenberg groaned.

"What happened?" Those were all the words McAllister could come up with.

"I won't talk," Frank gasped, then added. "Cops did it."

McAllister turned and ran out the door to call the police.

In the coffee shop down the street, Bugs Moran heard the police sirens and looked out the window as the squad car hurried past. He, Ted Newberry, and Willie Marks put their gloves back on, bundled their collars high on their neck, and stepped out onto the street. Dozens of people were already gathering in front of the Cartage Company garage talking excitedly. In the center of them, a woman without a coat stood screaming.

"Let's get outta here!" Moran said.

Frank Gusenberg survived the ambulance trip to Alexian Brother's Hospital, but it wasn't doctors standing over him when he regained consciousness, it was police officers.

"You're gonna die, Frank," the detective told him. "You might as well tell us who shot you."

"Nobody shot me," Frank whispered. He died at 1:30 that afternoon.

24

At the Winkler home, while Frank Gusenberg was dying, Georgette served coffee to Gus and Bob as they sat looking out the window discussing what went wrong. Her husband said nothing when she took a seat nearby to listen.

"Why did you guys open fire if you knew Moran wasn't there yet?" Georgette asked when she caught on to what happened. "He might have shown up."

"Right," Bob scoffed. "He'd have just walked right on in with your husband sittin' in a police car right outside the door."

"The plan was for me to park there," Gus said defensively. "So no other thugs showed up at your back."

A knock at the front door caused all three of them to freeze. Gus and Bob pulled their revolvers and took positions on either side of the door. Georgette opened up to find a man in a police uniform. It was George Goetz.

"Just funnin' ya," George laughed.

Gus reached out and grabbed him by the jacket, pulled, and then tossed George onto the floor. "What the hell is wrong with you? You screwy or somethin'? We could have shot you."

The scarlet in George's face said everything. Still, he tried to act jubilant. "Relax, everything's gonna be fine." Remaining on the floor as if being there was his idea, he rolled over on his back, put his hands behind his head, and smiled at the ceiling.

"Bryan's the one who made the call that Moran was there," Bob said, returning his weapon to his shoulder holster. "I'd hate to be in his shoes when Scarface finds out."

"I took care of that," George said, without moving. "I called Capone in Miami to tell him what happened before he heard it from someone else."

"How did he react?" Bob asked.

"How do you think he reacted? He put it over in spades. He wants us all to lie low until we see how the media and the public take it. It ain't the first hit Chicago's had, you know."

Georgette brought George a cup of coffee.

"To hell with coffee," he scoffed. Remaining on the floor where Gus had tossed him, he pulled a flask from his police jacket. "Let's open a keg of nails."

"I just hope they took the bodies out before the shutterbugs got pictures," Bob said.

"H-how many bodies?" Georgette asked.

"Seven," George said proudly.

Georgette was shaking when she turned and left the room.

"Why can't you keep your trap shut," Gus said to George.

"There you go again, tying yourself in knots dwelling on past mistakes," George chuckled, clearly delighted to see he was causing grief to the perfect little couple. "She'll read it in the papers anyway."

Gus got up and followed his wife into the bedroom. She was lying on the side of the bed facing the wall. He put his hand on her shoulder. She shrugged it away.

"Can't you tell when I don't want to be pawed?" Georgette wiped her tears. "How could you, Gus?"

"I just want you to live a life of comfort, honey."

"What good is it to be the richest person in the cemetery?" Georgette shouted. "Money never did the dead no good. My comfort was bought with the blood of others. Now, just leave me be."

"You'll need to get packed tonight." Gus rose and moved toward the door. "We leave in the morning for St. Joseph, Michigan."

"Just us?" Georgette asked.

"No," Gus was afraid to tell her the rest. "For our protection, we'll be stayin' in a cabin with Lefty Louie, Bob Carey—" He hesitated. "And George and Irene Goetz. I've got a few things to clean up, so the Goetz's will pick you up at the corner tomorrow at one o'clock."

***

"The newspaper says that over one-hundred-sixty machine gun casings were found in the garage," Irene Goetz told her husband as he packed a grip the next day. "Fred Burke is the only one with a warrant on suspicion of the massacre."

"Fred's on his way to Kansas City," George said over his shoulder. "Ray took off for Florida. He's become buddies with Al Capone's brother Ralph and plans to work with him."

"Ray and Julia always wanted to live in Florida," Irene said wistfully. "How is it that a dummy like Ray gets out of this cold weather and you and I are staying in the north?"

"Stop whining, woman."

"Are we still picking up Georgette as Gus asked?"

"Hell, no!" George smirked, remembering being tossed on the floor like a bag of potatoes. "Let Gus take care of his own dame."

***

Mindful that harsher weather was approaching Georgette grabbed her coat and earmuffs. Carrying her valise, she left the house for the long walk to the corner where she was to be picked up.

She stood with her luggage for four hours waiting for George and Irene to come get her. By the time it started raining, she was so cold she started crying. She couldn't go back to the house for fear the police would show up. Just then Bryan Bolton drove past, saw her, and backed his car up where she stood shivering.

"What's going on?" he asked, leaning across the seat to open the passenger side door.

"Oh, Bryan. Thank God." Georgette threw her valise in the back and got in. "Just drive, please."

As he drove, Georgette removed her wet coat and hung it on the back of the seat to dry. That was when she saw that Bryan's hands were bandaged. "What happened to you?"

Bryan gave her his country-boy blush. "Well, Tony Capezio and I decided we might get a few kudos from Capone if we got rid of the Cadilac we used for the hit. We were trying to take it apart so it could still be used for parts. Neither one of us knew much about doing something like that, and when Tony used a blowtorch, a gas canister exploded. I guess we should have moved it out of the way first."

"Oh, my! Was Tony hurt too?"

"His arms and legs got it worse than mine. I took him to a hospital, but when we got there, he was afraid they'd call the police, so I took him home. He went through a lot more pain than me, but he's doing better now. The only good thing that came out of it is he got a new nickname."

"What's that?"

"They're calling him Tough Tony."

***

The St. Valentine's Day Massacre, as the press was calling it, was causing Capone more problems than he'd ever imagined. The press, the public, and both state and federal officials were fed up with gang violence, and Capone took the brunt of the blame.

He was arrested three times in the next three months, once for violations of federal prohibition laws. Then for contempt of court for feigning illness to avoid a court appearance. Finally, in mid-May, Capone was arrested in Philadelphia, Pennsylvania, for carrying a concealed weapon.

Capone laughed at all these charges, but when the judge in Pennsylvania sentenced him to one year in prison, he had no choice but to find people he could trust to run the Outfit.

Gus knew when Frank Nitti got the top honor it would mean trouble for him. While Nitti was head of operations, Jake "Greasy Thumb" Guzik would be the head of administration, and Tony Accardo took over Nitti's job as head of enforcement.

None of these men cared much for Capone's American Boys. Still, when Jack McGurn and a thug named John Scalise were brought in for questioning on the massacre, they said nothing, though they could have thrown the American Boys under the bus.

Gus was still lying low, but he and Georgette, tired of putting up with George and Irene at the cabin in Michigan, moved to Gary, Indiana. It was while he was there that Gus was told that Capone wanted him to come to his Lexington Hotel office before Big Al reported to prison. It was to be a reconciliation party that he was throwing for his bodyguard Frank Rio, who had had a falling out with him the month before.

"You aren't going are you, Gussie?" Georgette asked when he told her of the invitation.

"With the Feds coming down hard on all mobsters across the nation, even Capone's own Sicilians are turning against him. Bugs Moran put a fifty-thousand-dollar bounty on Capone's head. People are choosing sides. I pledge my loyalty to Big Al."

Gus wore his best tuxedo to the party. He found it odd that he wasn't even frisked when he entered the Lexington and rode the elevator unescorted to the fifth floor. Jack McGurn was outside Capone's office handing out Louisville Sluggers to everyone as they got off the elevator. Gus noted that *everyone,* included some of Capone's top henchmen. The sandlot team included Frank Nitti, Jake Guzik, Verne Miller, Lefty Louie Campagna, Frank Rio, and Tough Tony Capezio.

Jack went to the door of Capone's conference room and, using the bat, gave it three light taps. "The team's all here, Boss."

From inside the room, a smiling Al Capone swung open the double doors, holding a baseball bat of his own. "Welcome, sluggers. I hope you're all pleased with the bats I selected for each of you. You'll note the signature on each of them autographed by some of my favorite players. I, of course, have the bat Babe Ruth gave me."

Gus glanced down at his bat, which was signed by Rogers Hornsby, who had only recently been traded to the Chicago Cubs. The men entered the conference room.

Tied to three chairs were the men known as the "Murder Twins," Albert Anselmi and John Scalise, two of the most feared and reputable hitmen the mafia had ever produced. In the third chair was the Unione Siciliana president, Joseph Guinta.

***

"The coroner wrote there wasn't an inch of their bodies left unbruised," Fred told Gus a week later when he came to visit the Winkler home in Gary, Indiana. "And it was hard to locate a bone that wasn't broken—everything from head to toe was shattered to pieces. The bullets that riddled their bodies came after the beatings, probably after they were put in the car in a sittin' position."

Gus hadn't told anyone he had participated in what Capone laughingly called a simple game of mobster pepper. In fact, Gus had stopped at his office to throw away the baseball bat as well as his bloody tuxedo before he put on fresh clothes and went home to Georgette.

He hated to go to sleep for fear of the nightmares that came every time he shut his eyes—nightmares of the savage look on the faces of Capone and the others as they took turns bashing the three men's bodies. So the victims would stay conscious for as long as possible, Capone had made them begin on hands and feet, then progress up the bodies, saving the heads for last. The most hardened of the killers tortured them patiently, wanting to keep the adrenal feeling for as long as they could maintain it. There was plenty of betting on who could knock out an eyeball or the most teeth in one vicious swing. It had lasted for over an hour until finally there were no more bones to break. Gus, too, had to take his licks at the three men, silently feigning glee each time he took a swing.

"I heard Frank Rio tricked the three into recruitin' him to help them kill Capone so they could split the fifty K reward from Aiello," Fred guessed correctly. "Rio reported everything they did to Capone. They threw the party to lure the three into the trap." Fred hooted. "I guess it was quite a bash in more ways than one."

"Well," Gus said. "Whatever the reason, I doubt there will be anyone else looking to end Big Al."

"I drove up here to see if you've heard anything about the pay for the Valentine's Day job," Fred said, himself ready for a subject change. "I'm runnin' a little low."

"Capone told Nitti to pay us, but with Al now in prison until next spring, Guzik is in charge of money, and he refuses to pay up."

"Gus, there's a ripe bank just down the road from here in Peru, Indiana. You and I hit it; we should be good until Capone gets out."

Gus looked at Georgette in the kitchen cleaning stains out of clothes by scrubbing them on a washboard. He sure would like to buy her one of those new washing machines. If not for the many business operations he was trying to get started in Chicago, he might take her away from the cold and windy city. But money was tight, what with those fledgling investments. How lucky Ray and Julia Nugent were to be living down in Florida.

25

Ray Nugent decided that women in Illinois and Michigan looked better wearing lots of clothing. He came to that conclusion when he arrived in Miami and saw beautiful, well-tanned ladies wearing practically nothing. His wife Julia, on the other hand, was light-skinned with winter fat covering much of her body.

He was having the time of his life in Florida. He opened a bar in Miami and went into business with Ralph Capone running rum from the Bahamas to the Outfit in Chicago. Ray and Julia even hung out a few times at Big Al's Miami home before he reported to prison, partying and swimming in his pool.

Ray especially enjoyed going to the beach during the dimming late afternoon sunlight. He found dark-skinned women looked better in this light. He got the shock of his life one such afternoon when he was admiring the way the skin of a group of shapely women shined, only to discover when they got closer, they were of the African persuasion. He was more careful after that, but it took weeks to get the guilt of that arousal out of his head.

Acting on his urges toward any woman besides Julia was out of the question, though. He had become adept at getting drunk, getting into bed with his hefty wife, turning off the lights, and thinking about some of the well-tanned young girls he had seen that day.

Through their business dealings, Ray and Julia became great friends with Al's older brother, Ralph "Bottles" Capone, and his wife Velma. Ralph wasn't as crazy fun as Scarface, but was still fun.

"How did you get the nickname 'Bottles'?" Julia asked Ralph the first time the couple went to dinner at a swanky new restaurant called Club Deuce.

"People think it's 'cause I run a legitimate bottling company for soda. But, really, my family gave me the nickname 'cause I drank some sour milk once and got so sick, I lobbied some of my buddies in the Illinois General Assembly to make a law that milk companies had to stamp the date the milk was bottled."

"So, you're the reason that labels are on the milk." Julia thought a second. "What does *lobby* mean?"

"It means to be a glad-hander," Ralph said. "Slap the good old boys on the back and tell 'em how glad you are to see them and how great they are, then slip 'em a few bucks to do what you want. That's how government works in Illinois."

"Oh." Julia laughed. "A kiss ass like Crane Neck here."

"Yours is the only ass I like to kiss." Ray blushed. His wife's use of his nickname made him feel ineffectual.

"Let's set the table over again," Ralph said, recognizing that the conversation was becoming uncomfortable. "We're gettin' some competition for the Jamaican rum from the Shelton brothers in Southern Illinois. Youse knows them, boys, don't ya, Crane Neck?"

"Well, yeah, I ran with them a little, back a few years ago."

"The one called Earl is runnin' rum out of St. Petersburg." Ralph leaned in. "I want you to convince him to take his business elsewhere. You know what I mean?"

***

Julia Nugent tried to think back over the years she and Ray had raised their children. Her husband never claimed the youngsters when they fouled themselves or needed to be rocked. The only time he touched the kids was to spank them for behaviors that riled him.

She had considered leaving him after the Toledo Express truck fiasco. "Our kids' bellies ain't never gonna be full with you as their father."

If it hadn't been for Georgette Winkler sending her money for a good lawyer, both she and Bob's girl, Rose, might have spent time in prison, since their men abandoned them after George murdered the police officer. Luckily, the one Fred shot lived.

Then, Ray got on the payroll of Ralph Capone's Outfit and things began looking up again. When her husband asked if she'd like to take a boat ride through the Everglades for his meeting with Earl Shelton, she thought it would be fun. She'd heard that such excursions were wonderful. Her only hesitation came when they arrived at the marina and she saw two of Ralph's bodyguards were their tour guides. It probably wouldn't have bothered her as much if they had not been dressed in suits with fedoras and dark glasses.

The beauty of the day, though, was extraordinary. Their motorboat left the docks and headed up the river with green and brown expanses of sawgrass. Great flocks with thousands of birds each swooped in synchronization as they waved back and forth across the sky. When they got deeper into the wilderness, Julia became a little uneasy as she spotted fewer people in boats and more and more alligators and snakes. Still, there were also colorful birds such as anhingas, ospreys, herons, and occasionally beautiful pink flamingos standing in shallow water.

Soon, however, the boat came up to a spooky little cove with trees so thick the sunlight was almost completely blocked. They pulled up to a crudely built dock. Ray said nothing as he held out his hand and helped his wife out of the boat and up a little hill where a quaint wooden shack had been built. Remaining in the boat, the two thugs extracted cigarettes and made themselves comfortable by leaning back in their seats.

"We will only be here a short time," Ray told her.

A moment later, another boat with three men in it came into the cove and docked. A tall, nice-looking man stepped out, walked up to Julia first, and shook her hand.

"My name is Earl Shelton." He hadn't even looked at Ray. Earl himself appeared to be dressed in the same jeans and shirt as he'd worn when he was dehorning cattle at the Shelton farm when Ray first met him.

"This is where you shake *my* hand," Ray finally said, sounding quite peeved.

Earl ignored him. "Shall we go inside and get your wife comfortable while we talk?" He extended his hand and let Julia lead, but before Ray could move, Earl stepped in behind her, opened the door, and followed her inside.

Inside the one-room shack was a small kitchen area, a couch, and a table with six wooden chairs around it. "Please make yourself at home while your husband and I go outside to discuss business. There are canned food and drinks if you like, but no ice, I'm afraid. Electricity has not made it out here yet."

Julia liked Earl. He was affable and funny, despite Ray pretending to be a Capone tough guy. She hadn't missed her husband's resentment from the lack of a handshake. The hideaway shack was nice for a shack in the middle of nowhere in a swamp. She did worry a little about alligators and snakes, which were plentiful. Alligators couldn't get into the house as long as the door stayed closed, but snakes in Florida seemed to find their way easily anywhere they wanted to go. The shack had everything in it except a toilet.

When the two men walked out toward the boat dock to discuss business, Julia decided she needed to make water but short of a squat there was no decent place to go. Since she was alone in the shack she found a bucket, made sure there were no snakes curled up in it, and made do.

The boat dock was close enough to the house that Ray and Earl heard the tinkling.

"I like that wife of yours," Earl laughed. "She's got spunk. Did she enjoy seein' the sites on her way over here?"

"The ceiling's the only thing I want my woman looking at," Ray repeated the words he had heard Fred Burke once utter. It had made Fred sound tough, so why not him?

"That's pretty crass, don't you think?" Earl didn't seem impressed. "Just exactly what's your wife's life worth to you anyway?"

"How's a plug nickel sound?" Ray wished he had not made that last comment, but he felt he was in too deep with the tough guy act to back down now.

The two boats sitting on either side of the dock each had two thugs waiting for their bosses to finish business. They sat smoking and passing a jug. Ray wasn't sure he liked that the roughnecks Ralph had sent with him were getting so familiar with Earl's rednecks. The Capone gunmen were dressed in typical gangster suits, but Earl's boys looked like Cajun fishermen out to collect gator skin to make boots.

"I did a few jobs with your gang in southern Illinois," Ray said, puffing his shoulders.

"Really? Can't remember." Earl didn't even give him a second glance. "Must not have made an impression."

Ray had never been made to feel so inconsequential so quickly.

"Say," Earl said. "Before we get to discussin' commerce, would you mind if I take care of a little business of my own?"

Ray again moved his shoulders, this time in a shrug.

Earl waved to the two men in his boat. They lifted a long gunny sack from the bottom of the craft and carried it onto shore. One of them opened a pocketknife and cut the sack from top to bottom, then rolled a tied and gagged man out of it. He cut the rope binding the captive and ripped the tape from his mouth. The man's eyes were opened wide, but he didn't utter a sound.

"The boys caught him after he took a shot at me from the swamp," Earl said.

"How did you find him in these Everglades?" Ray asked.

"We followed the smell of blood," one of the swamp rats said, his voice so deep it was more of a growl.

"Oh, you used hounds?" Ray asked.

"No," the growl said.

"So, are you ready to talk?" Earl asked.

"Nothin's going to change my mind," the man said.

Earl pulled his gun.

"What are you doing?" the doomed man asked, his eyes widening.

"Changin' your mind." Earl shot him in the kneecap. The man screamed and was still screaming as he reached down to his knees and began crying and breathing heavily. Earl then looked at Ray. "I learned from trial and error that kneecaps hurt worse than anyplace else."

"It was Charlie Birger's boys," the man squealed. "They sent me to kill you."

"Charlie got hanged over a year ago." Earl smiled. "I can't believe his boys still have a grudge against us."

He waved to his two henchmen. They grabbed the screaming man by the wrists and ankles, hauled him twenty yards to a tree at the edge of the water, used the ropes to bind him to it, and tied a long cloth around his mouth. The one with the knife gutted him, then reached inside his stomach, pulled out some intestines, and chummed the area nearby.

They returned to where their boss was standing. Ray's two men left their boat to come watch. Earl motioned them all to squat down and stay silent.

Within five minutes several alligators made little waves as they moved through the water toward the man who was now squirming against the ropes and making muffled screams. Ray wanted to stop watching and throw up, but he fought the urge. He couldn't show weakness. Despite the victim's screams, the chomping and ripping of his flesh and limbs began. By the time the alligators had retreated back into the water carrying their rewards, part of the torso where the ropes held him against the tree was the only thing left of the failed hitman.

"Not as clean a job as hungry sows can do," Earl observed casually. "But I suppose his leftovers will be prizes for ants and such." He looked at the wide-eyed Ray. "Now, what business would you like to discuss?"

26

December 14, 1929

Fred wondered why some women liked pretty boys with such feminine facial features. George Floyd would've been a pretty girl had he breasts. That's why they called him Pretty Boy, he supposed. Fred's new moll, Viola, was tripping the lights fantastic on the dance floor with Floyd, laughing and having a high old time. So, Fred just sat in the St. Joseph, Michigan, bar and sulked. He always resented his parents for bringing him into the world with a hair lip, a deficiency that made him the fighter he was. He was very happy when he was finally able to grow a mustache to hide the embarrassment. Still, he didn't let it define him. After all, it seemed to him that most people were disappointed with their lives.

Viola didn't want to put up with her boyfriend's glooms anymore. His glooms always came at a sad time, or a sad place, or both. They weren't really married, as they told everyone. Few of her friends knew that. She had told Georgette. "When it comes to marryin', that old dog won't hunt. At least he won't marry anyone close to his age, and I'm every bit as old as him."

When she finally came off the dance floor, her face was fiery red, and she flung him a look of contempt. "My God. Such a loser."

Fearless to the point of folly, her tongue was like a saw. He had never known such a devilish woman. Usually, Fred's go-to move at parties when the mood came on was to pretend he was unconscious. On this night, he felt like his hangover was starting before he even got fully sloshed, a wasted evening if ever he had one. He tried to recollect where he put the car key, but his memory was drunk too.

"Why do you sulk so much?" Viola asked.

"Would you like me to tell you?"

"I'm in for a penny."

"You are always on the move but goin' nowhere fast." Fred searched his memory for insults. "Why can't you just give me a hand job and shut your trap?"

"I'd rather go milk a cow." Viola's voice was more of a screech. "At least I'd get a good drink out of it. Besides we can't have sex tonight. I ran out of Dutch caps, and I don't want to get pregnant."

"Knock it off, doll, you're too old to get pregnant. So spread 'em or I'll go back to one of my wives.

It's time for you to start showin' me a return on my investment."

"Investment? Ha!" Viola knew which insults would hurt the most. "What have you got to invest? You drank away most of the money we had."

"You're a pip and a half." Fred waved his hand as he got to his feet. "I didn't come here for your vaudeville campaign. I'm going home. Give me the key. You can take a taxi."

"Here's your damned key." Viola tossed it to him. "Why don't you do everyone a favor and run your car into a tree?"

It wasn't a tree that Fred ran his Hudson into fifteen minutes after leaving the tavern, but the fender of another vehicle. He would've just driven on, but his car had died upon impact, and he was having trouble starting it back up. The next thing he knew, his door was opening and the irate driver was pulling him out.

"Here's five bucks," Fred said, holding out what he hoped to be a five.

"Forget it, Buster," the man shouted. "That's two hundred dollars of damage, for sure."

Fred pushed the man as hard as he could, got back in his car, and was relieved to be able to start it and speed away from the scene. Through his blurred eyes, he could barely see the road and felt the side of his car swipe another vehicle. Just when he thought he was in the clear, the first car he had hit raced up alongside him in the lane on his right. A crazy police officer was standing on the driver's side running board, waving a gun at him to pull over.

How Fred was able to cluster three bullets into the cop's chest, he would never know. The last thing Killer Burke would remember from that night was struggling to keep his car in the middle of a dirt road and knowing he wouldn't be going home. He was on the lam again.

When Viola got to the house early the next morning, she had no sooner put on her nightgown than the front door was knocked completely off its hinges and a flood of police officers rushed in. The next thing she knew, she was handcuffed and being taken downtown.

"Why are you taking me in?" Viola shouted.

"Your husband just killed Officer Charles Skelly."

In the spare room, the cops found stolen bonds, a bulletproof vest, pistols, shotguns, thousands of rounds of ammunition, and two submachine guns, one of which Carl Shelton had given Fred Burke for a two-minute fling with a scar-faced hobo woman.

Ray Nugent's biggest mistake in life was that he thought himself smarter than he was. He was so impressed by the alligator feeding that when Earl offered him a piece of the Shelton pie simply to tell him when Ralph Capone's rum shipments were coming in from the Bahamas, Ray couldn't think of any reason not to.

What Ray hadn't counted on was Earl not knowing how to swim. That deficiency got the middle Shelton brother caught by the Coast Guard when the sea dogs on his smuggling boat jumped overboard and swam to shore leaving Earl adrift with a load of illegal liquor and not enough time to drink it all or even throw it overboard.

Earl only got two years in a Georgia prison, but that was because he implicated Ray and a few other small-time thugs so he could get a reduced sentence. Earl was smart enough to not say anything about Ralph's business ventures, but that didn't stop the Capones from learning that Ray had burned both sides of the candles between the Capones and the Shelton's.

March 1930

Ralph may not have even learned that Earl had ratted on their mutual partner, but when Ray got stopped for running a stop sign and subsequently drunk driving, Ralph happened to be his passenger. The cops taking Ray downtown gleefully exposed his involvement with the Shelton smuggling enterprise.

It shouldn't have come as a surprise to Ray that after posting bail and getting his car at the impound, he was knocked in the head, trussed hand and foot, and tossed into the trunk of a car. All he could think about was that he was there because he had run a stupid stop sign. One stupid stop sign and his life wasn't just ruined, it was likely over.

Ray's sudden coming from the darkness of the trunk into the sunlight caused him to shade his eyes with what would have been a less than proper military salute, had he still been in the army.

"Olly, Olly, oxen free!" Ralph shouted, his cruelty for the first time eerily similar to his brother's.

Ray hit the ground so hard his teeth cracked. Ralph and two of his goons leered over him.

"I didn't mean to offend you," Ray pleaded through his bloody mouth.

"And yet you succeeded." Ralph laughed. "I just read a book called *The Most Dangerous Game.* Ever heard of it?"

"No." Ray wanted to get to his feet but knew better than to try. "I don't read so good."

"Well, here's the game. I'll give you a head start, let's say two hours. Then I come after you. If you get away, Say La Vie, or whatever them Francese say." Ralph looked at his pocket watch. "Starting now."

Ray stood. "Come on Ralph. This isn't right."

"Clock's tickin', Crane Neck. Time to take it on the lam."

All Ray had were poor excuses and half-measures that would never stop the syndicate. So, he raced into the swamp.

Possessed by boundless energies, Ray ran and walked all day and all night. His chance for an escape seemed gone. The chance wasn't much of a loss, so slim it was. If he could get to the hideout on the other side of the swampland, he could at least get some food and a decent night's sleep. Maybe then there would be some hope.

As he walked, he often heard dogs and sometimes saw campfires in the distance. He had done enough coon hunting in his day to recognize the howl of dogs on the scent as well as when they had a coon treed. Most hunters stayed close to the river bottom, so Ray was careful to travel well up the valley rim.

By the second day, there were cockleburs all over his pant legs. His blue, three-piece gabardine suit had been slept in for three days and had a tear in one shoulder, white fabric jutting from the rip. He suddenly stumbled and swore, but when he looked to see what had tripped him there was nothing. He was going to have to gamble and steal some food or kill for it if he had to. Each painful step signaled how weak he had become from lack of nourishment. He thought of drinking from the river or the swamp but knew that would be the beginning of the end for him.

When a light rain began, he immediately sought shelter under a thick canopy of bushes and relished the trickles of water that flowed off the branches into his mouth. Ray had stopped trying to get the cockleburs off his trouser legs and squatted quietly, catching his breath. In his condition he couldn't afford to get wet; his head and throat already causing him pain. The throat most likely was sore from stretching his tongue back to comfort a hole in a molar, probably from being knocked face down on the ground.

By mid-morning the rain stopped, and the sun shone brightly. Since his coat had absorbed a little mist that had leaked through the bushes, he found a comfortable spot on a hill facing the warmth of the sunlight. He lay for over an hour and would have enjoyed the moment longer except for the sound of an approaching airplane. He couldn't imagine Ralph Capone hiring an airplane, but since he couldn't be positive, he found cover in a dry area above the swampy ground and fell asleep.

He awoke to the sound of footsteps in the grass, somewhere back in a fog that was drifting low to the ground. The clouds were whittling at his sunlight. In the growing dark, he had to hurry. It was a still, windless night, and soon very dark so he commenced a ponderous jog. Above him, the fairy-like light of the stars made it seem that life was becoming even more abnormal. He felt he was having one of those dreams where you are running toward something but never quite get there.

Then he stumbled hard down a ravine, rolling and rolling, unable to stop his fall. A blow to his head as he crashed into a tree stopped his descent and brought dizziness. The lick had made a dull sound. Instantly, a stream of blood gushed across his face. He tried to get up but fell again. His left leg was sticking out at a right angle just above his ankle, severely damaged but not fatally.

There came no pain, just numbness, which was worrisome. That meant the bone was completely severed. Pain only comes when bone nerves are rubbing against bone nerves. That pain would come later and in abundance, when the bones were set back into place, that is, if he ever got to a place where they could be set. Ray lay down and cried, letting the tears flow. He had no idea how long he had been running or how far he might have traveled. The law of time and distance seemed reversed.

He sat there for hours, not even trying to wipe the blood off his face, though the bleeding had stopped. The smokey, foggy dawn came at last. Recognizing he was probably getting close to the hideaway, he found a downed tree limb to act as a crutch. He limped along off and on all day, wading through often waist-high murky swamps, snakes and alligators always nearby.

By evening, he felt a breeze. At the tops of the tallest trees, branches blew as the uncomfortable darkness returned. Then, when he came through a little clearing, he saw it—the hideout, the screen door hanging loosely by its top hinge, the front door wide open.

Inside, someone had done a number on all the furniture. Everything had been smashed to pieces and thrown into the middle of the room. They had even hammered open the freshly plastered wall that had recently been fixed. The rest of the shack was filthy with spider webs and there was rat shit everywhere on the floors.

"They found the money," a man's voice came from behind the closet door. "All of it, damn you to hell." The man's curse was so violent, even the tree rats stopped in their tracks. Silence spread like the swamp fog that was slowly creeping toward the hideaway.

"I sure enough made a bigger mess than a sow's bed," Ray groaned.

Ralph usually bubbled over his witticisms, but he was not bubbling at this moment. What with the bop on the head during his fall and the ache in his tooth, it was difficult for Ray to put his thoughts into words, so he said nothing more. Hoping to make his former friend feel sorry for him, he pointed down to his leg.

"I've known many a fine man laid in unmarked graves." Ralph raised a pistol. "But no. I'd rather let the alligators have you."

The bullet he fired was a perfect kneecap shot. Not his bad knee, the good one. Now, collapsing onto his back, the pain came so intensely that he barely felt Ralph wrap a rope around his neck and pull him out into the glade. The gangster dragged him screaming to the same tree Earl Shelton had used on the would-be assassin. With Ray's feet almost hanging into the water of the swamp, he wrapped him as tight as he could with knots high enough that he wouldn't be able to reach them on his busted limbs.

"The alligators will be along shortly," Ralph hissed. "You're the fourth man we've fed to them, so they consider this their dinner table. Their teeth will probably want your legs first, they usually do."

Ray was too weak to protest but he could beg.

"Please shoot me," he pleaded. Thoughts of the man he had seen eaten in this very spot flashed through his head.

Ralph just smiled, backed off almost to the shack, and watched.

Ray lay still, whimpering in short gasps, keeping his eyes on the water. The wait took longer this time, or at least it seemed to. Finally, Ray saw a pair of blackish-red bubbles surface, appearing angrier and crueler than any eyes he had ever seen. The closer the eyes floated through the water, the more still Ray became, too horrified to even breathe.

Then, with a powerful flip of its tail, the creature's giant, razor-toothed mouth rose out of the water, open wide for the vice-powered bite that ferociously grabbed his left leg above the knee. The gator pulled hard and then spun three times, ripping the limb completely off. It then slunk back into the water. Ray barely had time to scream as a fountain of blood gushed from his wound.

His mind blurred by pain, he watched as an alligator twice as long as Ray was tall came around the side of a tree to his right. He knew it was over twice his size because the entire front of the monster came into his view before the tail even cleared the tree.

"Oh look, Ray!" Ralph screamed with delight. "You get Old Joe himself. What an honor to be eaten by the most famous gator in Florida! And, to think, you were just eatin' at the restaurant named after him."

Gator Joe hissed, arched his back, and then came like a striking snake for Ray's head. In the last seconds of his life from inside the animal's mouth, he saw the top teeth coming downward toward a tongue that looked fifteen inches long, the fading of light, and then heard a thunderous CHOMP, and then the snapping of his neck bones being severed.

28

* **BURKE IS SOUGHT as
LEADER in MASSACRE
ST. VALENTINE'S DAY**
FUGITIVE SLAYER, HIS WIFE,
ARSENAL FOUND IN HOME *

* **DECLARED BY CHICAGO POLICE
TO BE MOST DANGEROUS
CRIMINAL ALIVE**
ACCUSED OF YALE MURDER
$100,000 REWARD
DEAD OR ALIVE *

Without his gat, Fred felt weak. It had been like a third arm through three killings that made headlines and several others that didn't. It was a little troublesome to him that they had not yet linked the Milaflores Apartment Massacre to his gat. He thought about sending them a letter suggesting they check the ballistics on that shooting too.

He shook his head as he read. Who would have thought that he, Fred Burke, would have been responsible for them creating a whole new science that they called ballistics?

Even George Goetz seemed a little envious of Fred's notoriety. The two killers, having just stumbled out of their bedrooms, were enjoying an afternoon breakfast with Gus.

"I heard they avoided sendin' the gat to the laboratory through the Chicago police department," Gus said, ever mindful of the criminal world's effect on politics. "They were afraid Mayor Thompson would bury it rather than let it somehow implicate the corruption of him and his political machine."

"You two might be gettin' a little too well known to the public, don't you think?" George asked, perhaps a little too enviously.

"That's why we're gonna do something about that," Fred said.

After quick withdrawals at banks in Paterson City, New Jersey, and Plano, Illinois, Gus and Fred were ready to get new faces and fingerprints. Gus spent a lot of time on phone calls to Georgette for the next several weeks while the blackness and swelling in his face healed. Thinking it a good joke to not tell his wife about the plastic surgery, he was looking forward to surprising her.

Georgette opened the door to their home to find a handsome man smiling at her. He walked right up to Georgette, grabbed her around the waist, dipped her, and gave her a kiss that would make Rudolph Valentino jealous. She responded by opening her mouth and sticking her tongue in his, something he had never known her to do.

"How did you know it was me?" the new Gus asked when he stood her back up.

"I didn't." Georgette smiled.

***

After robbing a bank with George Goetz in Jefferson, Wisconsin, Fred went on a major three-day bender. He would never remember much about what happened during that drunkfest, but when he woke up sober one morning, a beautiful young girl was lying next to him. He thought he remembered having sex with her, but couldn't remember if she had been willing, drunk, or even if she'd been awake. Though asleep, she still had a dress on. He reached over and ran his hand down her waist. The dress was so thin and silky, stroking it was almost as good as stroking the bare skin beneath it.

"Good morning, tiger," she moaned without opening her eyes.

"How old are you?" Fred asked.

"Seventeen." She giggled. "You asked me that a half dozen times last night."

"Where are we?" Fred looked around the room. Several of his suits, guns, and other miscellaneous clothing were piled onto a chair.

"We're home, silly. Our house in Centerville, Iowa." She reached across him to the dresser, her bare forearm soft and yet firm, brushing his lips. Her hand came back holding a paper. "Don't you remember getting married?"

"Why would a seventeen-year-old girl marry a man my age?"

"There are the haves and the have-nots. I intend to be a have. In case you can't remember, my name's Bonnie, Mrs. Bonnie Burke."

Fred took his new wife, Bonnie, to Chicago and took an apartment a floor below that of the Winkler's. Georgette, never one to judge, accepted Bonnie as part of their crime family, shopping and dining with her daily.

Fred had forgotten what a firm body teenage girls had. That was nice for a while, but it didn't make up for her lack of experience sexually. Over the next several weeks, he taught her many forms of sodomy as best he could but eventually decided he'd rather she be cultivated elsewhere and come back to him when she was better educated.

July 1930

His longing for the sluttiness that he had grown accustomed to brought him one evening to a well-known cat house in Michigan that a wannabe gangster named Thomas Bonner also patronized.

Having recently robbed a bank with Fred, George Goetz was also indulging there, spending his ill-begotten gains in typical gangster fashion by buying drinks and tricks for everyone, which included Bonner, who was sitting nearby.

George didn't even know Fred was there until he descended the stairs with a stout, middle-aged whore of healthy proportions.

"My God, that's Fred Burke," George heard Thomas Bonner say to no one in particular, though a skinny sporting gal was giving him a lap dance as they waited for a room to become available.

"Who, honey?" the girl asked.

"Mr. One Hundred Thousand Dollars." Thomas pushed the girl off him and headed for the door.

Thomas Bonner's wife was just getting ready for bed when her husband came bursting through the front door and raced for the telephone on the wall. Normally, she would say nothing to him when he came home from a night out, but the fact that he was drunk, had lipstick on his face, was reeking of perfume, *and* his fly was unbuttoned was too much.

She grabbed up the frying pan and was set to beam him a good one when the door opened again. Two men rushed in with revolvers drawn just as Thomas was asking the operator to put him through to the Newyago County Sheriff's office. With the telephone line trilling its rings, both men fired headshots into her husband. She screamed, dropped the frying pan, and fainted.

The bloody telephone receiver was hanging by its cord next to her when she recovered a few seconds later.

"This is the Newyago County Sheriff's office," an officer on the phone said. "Is anyone there?"

When the deputy arrived and asked her to describe the shooters, all Mrs. Bonner could remember was that one man was blond-haired and held his gun in his left hand.

Meanwhile, Fred was in Chicago picking up his latest wife, Bonnie, and driving to her parent's home near Green City, Missouri.

***

Flirtation had been a way of life for Fred's seventeen-year-old wife, Bonnie. Therefore, when she found herself back in the rickety old farmhouse of her parents near Green City, Missouri, with no one but her rich husband to flirt with, her demeanor changed and her mysterious smile soon contained a large component of boredom.

The only good thing was that her father, Barney Porter, liked Fred. He liked him mostly because they both enjoyed smoking and drinking until they fell over. Now that his rich new son-in-law was there with his fancy Hudson straight-eight coup, he was having a good old time.

Bonnie still did her wifely duties when summoned, always with moans and movements that she knew her husband desired, but it had begun to become less exciting and she was beginning to tire of Fred's increasingly large belly and his hairy back.

For Fred, the sex had been far from boring, yet he could not entirely banish the consequences from his conscience. Here was a young girl wanting him for his money, so what would she do if she ever found out how much he was worth dead or alive?

The closest Bonnie came to feeling rich was when Fred took her to town in his fancy Hudson to get groceries. She was proud to be seen in the vehicle since most everyone else with any money at all had Model T Fords unless they were upper lower class and could afford a Model A. Regardless of what anyone drove, the roads which were either gravel or just graded dirt quickly turned any vehicle into a dust bowl on wheels. Muddy days made things even worse.

Handyman Joe Hunsaker liked to sit on the bench across from the Green City grocery store sometimes whittling and other times reading *True Detective Mysteries* magazines, when he could afford one. Joe fancied himself a private eye of sorts whenever he didn't work at the Shell gas station.

Joe was whittling the first few times the big Hudson cruised into town and parked in front of the grocery store. While a pretty young girl got out and went inside to shop, the man driving, who looked like he must have been her father, stayed in the car and smoked. When she came out with both arms full of grocery sacks, the man was at least courteous enough to lean across the seat and push open the door for her.

Everyone in town quickly learned that the fellow in the Hudson, when he did venture out of the car, often paid with fifty-dollar bills and always said, "Keep the change." Joe found out while working the filling station that the man always wanted his gas tank topped off until it overflowed, even if it only needed a gallon.

About a month passed before Joe saw the man and woman come shopping again. This time, they drove a brand-new Studebaker President coupe. While the girl did her shopping, the man drove the half block to the filling station.

"I'd like a new set of tires for my car," the man told Joe.

Joe inspected the old tires and saw they were in excellent condition. He didn't have to be Sherlock Holmes to recognize that the vehicle was being kept in top condition for either racing or illicit activities, and the man didn't look like a race car driver.

Joe had changed the tires and was admiring the front end when he saw the strange customer glaring at him. Joe lowered his head and took the fifty-dollar bill followed by the usual, "Keep the change." Joe then returned quickly to the office and opened the brand-new *True Detective Mysteries* magazine he had just bought. He wasn't really looking at the magazine but instead used his peripheral vision to see if the departing customer was still giving him the evil eye, the most hateful and evil eye Joe had ever seen. The man did a U-turn and parked the Studebaker outside the general store.

Joe was still pretending to be reading the magazine when the girl came out, got in the car, and the Studebaker motored away. Joe sighed. It took another minute before he could concentrate again on the magazine. When he finally did, he looked straight away at a picture of a face, a face that would change his life forever.

***

March 26, 1931

Bonnie's father, Barney Porter, was against fornication in his house when he was present. He insisted that Bonnie sleep with her mother and Fred in a separate room with him. Fred didn't mind much since he was going through a worrisome spell and Bonnie tended to toss more than her elderly father.

The next morning, Fred woke to the smell of bacon burning. He was accustomed to his wife burning the bacon, but this time the entire house was rapidly filling with smoke. The sun barely up, a rosy tint showed through the curtains, making the smoke rosy as well. He heard the bed springs heave a sigh as Barney rose and pulled his coveralls up over his long johns. Happy to now own the entire bed, Fred rolled onto his side and fell back to sleep.

Barney's chore in the morning was to stoke the pot-bellied stove and add a coal or two. The cuckoo clock chirped once, telling him it was nearly six thirty. He had overslept again and worried he was slipping. Having a rich son-in-law was most likely the reason for his complacency, but he didn't know what to do about it, nor that he wanted to. Fred was a fine addition to the family, even letting him drive his big, fancy cars now and again, quite a step up from the Allis Chalmers tractor he had to ride into town whenever his Model T quit on him, which was often, it seemed.

Making his way through the smoke, Barney took the frying pan off the burner. The bacon was burnt to a crisp. He pulled a quilt back from the door into Bonnie's room and deduced that his wife had lay back down and fallen asleep next to her daughter after putting the bacon on. Unless it was ghosts that overcooked the bacon. He had seen plenty of ghosts in his nearly sixty years on the farm. Barney doubted they were paying a visit on a Thursday morning, but the shadows moving behind the window curtains were hard to explain. *Folks around these parts don't go window peeping so early in the morning,* he thought. He was contemplating ghosts again when a light tap on the front door made him jump.

Fred Burke lay awake on his back with his eyes closed, listening to the chicken's clucks, the rooster's crows, and songbirds chirping. When he heard a footstep on a loose floorboard, he thought maybe Bonnie was sneaking in for a morning snuggle. He opened his eyes and was so surprised to see four handguns aimed at him that his mustache began to twitch. He glanced at his .38 revolver on the nightstand.

"Well, hello boys," Fred said as he set up and rubbed sleep out of his eyes.

"You'll need to get dressed, sir," one of the men said.

Fred almost laughed when the youngest of the four men bent down and helped him with his shoes while the other three kept him covered with their guns. When they went into the living room, Fred started to pick up his coat.

"Just a minute, sir," the eldest of the men said. He picked up the jacket, felt inside the pockets, and brought out two handguns. Without comment, he held the coat as Fred slid his hands through.

Since they didn't handcuff him, Fred thought he still had a chance if he could make a bolt for his car that he had parked sideways to the porch for just such a quick getaway. These country boys were mighty good with rifles and shotguns, but Fred suspected they had never fired at a man before. He was preparing for his mad dash until they got outside, where he saw two cars had blocked in his Studebaker. They weren't the dumb country bumkins they appeared.

"Hey, Barney," Fred said to his father-in-law when he was in the backseat of the police car. He pulled his wallet out and drew out two one-hundred-dollar bills and two tens. "Take this and get me a lawyer in St. Joe."

"Barney accepted the cash and clipped it in with the two dollars he already had. "I sure don't understand what's goin' on here, do you?"

"Everyone pays the price sooner or later." Fred chuckled, still confident he could get away.

"Yes, sir, I 'spect you strayed a might during your formative years," Barney said. "But I don't hold that against you none."

***

August 5, 1931

Gus woke up in a hospital bed not knowing how he got there. The first thing he noticed was he couldn't raise his left arm. The second thing was he had to turn his head so he could look out his right eye and see that he was handcuffed to the bedpost. The reason he had to turn his head was because his left eye was covered in a bandage. He reached up with his right hand and touched the bandage.

"You lost your left eye in the car crash, Mr. Winkler," a voice told him.

"Where's my wife?"

"She's in the waiting room. We'll let her see you after we have a talk." The man was testing the weight and feel of Gus's revolver by bouncing it in his hand. "Nice piece. Wish I could afford one like this."

"Who are you?" Gus guessed the plastic surgery was wasted since they had already identified him.

"I'm a special agent for the Bureau of Investigation, Mr. Winkler. My name is Melvin Purvis."

***

Gus thought that he was a suspect for enough crimes that the law wouldn't need to try and frame him for one he didn't even do.

"They're trying to stick the Lincoln, Nebraska, bank robbery on me," he told Georgette when she was finally allowed to see him in the hospital room. "Hell, I was in Buffalo at the time, but since I used an alias, I can't prove it. Capone's the only one who knew I was there, and he sure as hell can't testify in court, what with all he's going through with the tax evasion charge."

"How much did they get?" Georgette knew it must have been a large amount for the law to go to such great lengths as to frame her husband.

"Almost three million dollars in bonds," Gus said. "They're going to hold me unless I help them get the bonds back."

"There ya go," Georgette shook her head. "A shakedown from start to finish."

"Go see Capone," Gus said. "He's been out of the pen for a few months and may be able to help. Tell him what's up. If he can bail me out, I'll go talk to Bob Moros. I'm sure he was in on the holdup."

29

Each time Georgette called Capone's office to get help for Gus, Lefty Louie, Frank Rio, or one of the other syndicate thugs would tell her he wasn't in. She finally went to the Circus Café to see if Screwy Maddox could help her get to Capone. Being a former member of the Egan Rats in St. Louis, she hoped she could trust him.

"They're keepin' Capone under wraps while he's goin' through all these tax charges in court," Screwy told her, then leaned across the bar and whispered. "I'm takin' a chance, but you ought to know this. Basically, Frank Nitti's in charge and he don't like us American Boys. His thugs are goin' tonight and try to kidnap Gus out of the hospital. If they can't get him out alive, they'll kill him in his bed. The idea is to get him away from the police, one way or another."

"Who's leading the attempt?" Georgette asked.

"He's right over there." Screwy pointed to a man sitting by himself in the corner booth. "Jack McGurn."

"Give me two of whatever he's drinking," Georgette said.

"Take it on the arches, sister." McGurn told her when she took a seat across from him and placed the drinks on the table.

"Please, Jack," Georgette pleaded. "Tell me what's going on."

"Give me a sawbuck," McGurn smirked. "I'll ditch."

Georgette opened her handbag, pulled out a twenty-dollar bill, and slid it across the table.

"The boys say Gus hasn't been right since the accident and is losin' his mind," McGurn told her. "They say he's been talkin' to the police."

"Don't do it," Georgette begged. "Please don't go. I'll go talk to him myself. I'll take care of every-thing, only don't go."

"You're not goin'," McGurn said with finality. "You're not goin' because we say you're not."

"Jack . . . ." She slid a thick wad of one-hundred-dollar bills across the table. "Give me forty-eight hours. That's all I ask."

McGurn wasn't drunk enough to be callous. "I'll give youse twenty-four hours. That's it."

Georgette rushed to the Lexington Hotel where Capone was staying. She called him from the lobby and was told the Boss was not in.

"The hell I'm not in." Capone's voice suddenly broke in from an extension. "Hello, hello,

Georgette, don't hang up, it's Al. Come right down here, and come right up to the office, and don't let any of these fellows talk you out of it."

"I'm downstairs now," Georgette said. "I'll be right up."

Moments later, the elevator opened on his floor. Georgette was trying to push her way past Frank Rio and Lefty Louie when Capone opened his office door. The two stepped back and Georgette walked in.

"Have a seat, Georgette." Capone moved behind his desk and sat in his big leather chair. "They're gettin' ready to move Gus from the hospital to the jail. I'm gonna fix it for you to get in and see him. The boys all tell me Gus is losin' his mind and talkin' his head off to the cops. They said Gus has refused my help, and if that's true, I don't know what to think about it. On the strength of these reports, I haven't done a thing for him. But what I want is some straight dope. You can get to the truth because I can trust you. I think a lot of Gus, and if the boys are wrong, I'll do what I can to help him."

"The reports are tinged with jealousy," Georgette said. "Order McGurn and the others to hold off until I figure things out."

"We need to know who stole the bonds and where they're being held," Capone said. "I don't sanction robberies. Georgette, I'm going to leave it up to you. You're honest, and you can work out the details to suit yourself. If you can get a good line on those bonds, I'll furnish the hundred-thousand-dollar bail for Gus to get out and get them back. I'll give you all the money you need."

He opened his desk drawer, reached in, pulled out a big roll of bills, and handed it to Georgette.

The Moros Tavern was a dive unlike any Georgette had ever walked into. Every eye turned her way. For a moment, the room became eerily silent. Men were dressed in suits, not expensive ones, but cheap and mostly unkempt.

She had got her lead from the most unlikely of sources, Verne Miller. He had walked up to her in the hotel lobby as she was leaving Capone.

"Did you know Bob Moros was killed last week?" Miller asked without even a hello.

Georgette froze. Was this a threat?

"I'm sure Gus told you Moros was in on the Nebraska job," Miller continued. "Mrs. Moros wants her cut. If you can get her to spill and tell you where the bonds are, I'll make sure Capone bails Gus out, and I'll help him collect."

"What's in it for you?" Georgette asked, knowing that nothing came for free.

"Well . . . ." Miller smiled. "If they are going to give up the bonds, they will want plenty of sugar. And, of course, I'll want a finder's fee."

Miller was standing now at the end of the tavern bar. With his eyes, he guided Georgette to the woman serving drinks at a table. When everyone returned to their conversations, Georgette approached the barmaid.

"Mrs. Moros, my name's Georgette Winkler. My husband and I wanted to give you our condolences on the loss of your husband."

Mrs. Moros studied her visitor for a moment. Georgette hoped her clothing didn't give her away as a snob. She had intentionally dressed down, but after seeing the others in the tavern, she feared she had not dressed down enough.

"You are only the second person to say that," Mrs. Moros finally said. "Thank you, Mrs. Winkler."

"Please call me Georgette. May I buy you a drink? I think we may have much in common." Georgette forced a tear from her eyes. "My husband, Gus, is being held for the Lincoln, Nebraska, holdup."

"Gee, kid, I feel sorry for you. You must be awful lonely."

"I sure am." Georgette put a handkerchief to her nose and sniffed. "I wish you'd come up to my apartment and have dinner with me tonight."

"Why, I sure will, honey. Just let me seat these two customers, and I'll be right with you."

Thirty minutes later, Georgette was serving highballs to her guest—only Mrs. Moros's drink contained three times the liquor as her own. Soon the two women were crying on one another's shoulders, sharing their sorrows over their husbands' misfortunes.

"If I could just buy those bonds from the men who stole them, I could get Gussie out," Georgette lamented. "Surely they know that after the stock market crash, they won't get a fourth of what they are worth."

"He can have my share so far as I'm concerned, if it will do your Gussie any good," Mrs. Moros slurred.

"Thank you, dear, but I'd need to know who has the rest."

"Get a pencil and paper, Georgette, and I'll tell you."

The next morning, Georgette collected every dollar that she and Gus had. Then she went to Al Capone and arranged for him to get Gus released. The next day, Gus Winkler came home.

***

Gus slept a little, but the sleep produced a nightmare. Ray Nugent's loss, he did not lament. Ray was just a criminal, a dumb one at that. Though no body had been found, rumors of Ray's horrifying demise were being leaked into the underworld to serve as a reminder of what could happen to anyone who crossed the Capone brothers.

He and Georgette felt pretty confident in their relations with The Boss. But then, soon after his release and before he was completely recovered, Gus was summoned to Capone's office.

On the day of the meeting, not knowing what was going to happen, Gus and Georgette both chose to lay naked beneath their covers for as long as possible, Gus still with bandages over his lost eye. Though the tide of emotion from the past few days was ebbing, Georgette enjoyed the tranquil moments she could just hold her nakedness next to his.

Gus, not anxious to go find out what fate awaited him, reveled in a little more time next to his wife. "What do you fear?" Gus whispered, then felt sorry he had asked.

"I know there's only a piper's chance." Georgette rolled away from her husband so he wouldn't see her tears. "But Capone's goin' to prison for tax evasion, and Frank Nitti isn't your biggest fan. I fear him more than any other."

He believed, for the most part, that Georgette's reservations were unfounded, though the same thought had briefly crossed his own mind.

She sighed and came back into his arms, wanting to cherish every second they had together. Twenty minutes later, Gus got up, got dressed, and left for his appointment with the biggest crime boss in America.

***

For a man getting his affairs in order before reporting to prison, Al Capone was remarkably gay. He greeted Gus with a warm embrace along with Italian-style kisses on both cheeks.

Instead of going behind his desk to sit, the Boss took a chair next to Gus and sat on the edge leaning into him. "I need someone I can trust to help Ted Newberry run our interests on the North Side," Capone said. "Since he came to us from Moran's gang, Ted's got himself in hock. This stock market crash means we've lost the returns on our laborin' people on the far South Side. We need to beef up our establishments on the North Side where some folks still have money. Ted doesn't have the business sense that you do."

"How does Ted feel about this?" Gus asked. He knew Ted and even liked him, though trust would be too strong a word. "Not so long ago he was a Moran thug, after all."

"Yes, but it is to us he owes money for liquor," Capone, always a businessman rationalized. "He's in no position to say no."

"Okay, but why me?"

"Because you're not officially with the Italian syndicate. Ted will listen to you. I've set up a meetin' for this evening at the Newberry apartment. I want you to take Georgette."

"What about while you're—away?" Using the word *prison* didn't seem right for a man of Capone's stature. "Are the others going to be okay with this?"

"I'll still be runnin' things," Capone said with confidence. "We've worked it all out with the warden. Nitti and Guzik will do as I say."

***

Georgette liked Nelli Newberry the moment she met her. For one, the two had similar tastes in clothes, preferring conservative and comfortable compared to the sheer silk many women of racketeers wore. The two couples spent the evening in the living room of the Newberry apartment, which was on the thirteenth floor of the same building where the Winklers and the Burkes had lived before his arrest.

While the men talked business at a nearby table, the ladies agreed they also enjoyed the same comedic silent stars as well as the new talking pictures—and that handsome new Hollywood star, Clark Gable, was their favorite.

"I just loved him in the movie *The Secret Six*," Nelli said. "And could you believe how beautiful Jean Harlow's platinum blond hair was? I'm thinking of getting it done to mine. Along with a beauty mark on my cheek."

The look Gus gave Georgette from where he and Ted sat confused her. She wondered if he was jealous that she agreed Gable was handsome.

Later that night as they got ready for bed, Gus explained the reason for the strange glance.

"Georgette, I met with the *real* Secret Six after you and Capone got me released." Gus valued her counsel. So quickly did the alliance with the Six form, that hundreds of complicated issues might largely have escaped him.

"Oh, my God. You mean there really is a Secret Six?"

"Sure is. Just like in the movie, they are a committee of big businessmen who are putting their money and resources into cracking down on organized crime. They are the ones who had me arrested for the Nebraska holdup because they knew I had the clout, along with Capone, to get the bonds back.

"They recently hired a lawman named Elliot Ness to go after bootleg liquor. Unlike other Chicago lawmen, he can't be bribed. Ness and his men are part of the reason Capone got charged with tax evasion."

"So, are the Secret Six done with you now?" Georgette was worried. "Charging you with a crime they knew you didn't commit was blackmail."

"Exactly." Gus gave her an honest worried glance. "As part of my release, they're requiring me to check in regularly with a Bureau of Investigation agent."

"Who is that?"

"A lawman named Melvin Purvis."

30

To Rose, the gangsters were mashers. They always grabbed her heart and left her bruised. It had consistently been a problem. In a room full of a hundred men, if there was only one bad one in the lot, she could find him. Every New Year, she resolved this would be the year she would learn from her mistakes. She had often been taken in heat by ugly mobsters who were rough with her and smelled bad. The next guy she spread for would be a gentleman. Maybe an older fellow who only needed sex once or twice a month. But then, in walks Bob Carey, and she's gaga like a toddler in a toy store.

They had been together now for some years, during which Rose seldom saw Bob entirely free of the effects of alcohol.

For Bob, what he felt for Rose wasn't love in any way. He figured it was only educated people who fell in love, and he was far from educated. What he wanted was a fine, sturdy woman, wide at the hips and strong enough to bear him six or eight children. Rose's nose bothered him. He didn't appreciate women with exaggerated anatomical features, other than big breasts, so long as they didn't sag past the belly button, which Rose's didn't.

Bob enjoyed being jealous. In fact, so much so, that he would sometimes set Rose up for a clandestine affair, and then watch their fornication from a closet. She was an attractive woman, despite being a stout lady with a big nose and, if he was completely truthful, somewhat cross-eyed. When Rose finally caught him spying on her liaisons one day, instead of throwing a hissy, she bought him a camera. Bob was so pleased he purchased an enlarger and created his own private darkroom to develop the pictures.

When Rose wasn't around, Bob made good use of the pictures he'd taken with the camera, eventually preferring them and the palm of his hand to actual physicality with a woman.

Ironically, a chance encounter with a local banker led to a new and unique career for the couple. Rose picked up the banker at a local bar and brought him home for some late-night fun. As usual, she rattled the keys and made a lot of noise so Bob would have time to get in position in the closet. The banker was too fat to comfortably sit in a captain's chair, so he opted for the loveseat.

From the closet, Bob watched through the door slats at the banker waiting excitedly for Rose to come out of the bedroom. He imagined the man realized that not many women were willing to couple with him, old and ugly as he was. Or, maybe as the banker waited, he was dreaming of his younger years when he could take a woman four or five times a day with little more than a beer between each frolic. Either way, Bob knew the man had money, a wife, and several young children, though his money was all he and Rose cared about.

Rose came into the room wearing a thin, sheer nightgown. CLICK. Bob snapped his first picture just as the old man's eyes widened.

"Well, don't you look as happy as a rat in a grain bin?" Rose said. "How do you want it, honey?"

The banker stood and removed his clothes, all of them. CLICK, CLICK went Bob's camera.

"Come on, baby, ride me like a horse." The old banker used the arm of the loveseat to ease himself onto the floor and got on all fours. Rose looked toward the closet door and laughed. "Well, sure honey." She went into the bedroom and came back with a handful of Bob's neck ties, tied two together, and looped them into a pair of stirrups which she laid across her john's portly back. Two more she knotted for reins then stuffed the knotted end into his mouth.

The old man whinnied and reared back, then moved his hands in a trotting, then galloping motion. CLICK, CLICK, CLICK. Rose stretched her legs in the stirrups and tugged hard on the reins, pulling her banker-horse's head back so hard he gagged and spit his dentures out onto the floor.

"Don't stop!" he shouted. "Whip me to the finish line!"

SWAT, CLICK, SWAT, CLICK, SWAT, CLICK.

The next day, Rose showed up at the banker's office and made a withdrawal of one thousand dollars—after she showed him an envelope full of photographs.

***

Gus and Georgette, dressed to the nines, walked proudly into the Chez Paree nightclub. Eight long rows of tableclothed tables lead to the end of the room where a large, elevated dance floor stood in front of an even higher bandstand. The Winklers' pride was secretive because few at the establishment knew that Gus was the major stockholder in the nightclub which was much too elegant to be called a speakeasy.

Making their way through the throng of partiers at each table, they shook hands with some and fake-kissed others. Government officials, film and theater stars, and just about everybody who was anybody in Chicagoland said hello or waved.

Carl Shelton, the southern Illinois bootlegger who several years before had stood on a country road smoking a cigar with Gus as they tried to decide if they should shoot one another or negotiate a peace, was there. Gus thought that maybe later that evening he would pull him aside and talk old times.

Shelton's main rival in the roadhouse business, Charlie Birger, was dead, having recently been hanged down in Benton, Illinois. Birger had been too flamboyant for his own good, even making a show of sitting in the jail cell holding a Tommy gun, one of the conditions for his surrendering to the authorities. Like Al Capone, who was now in prison for tax evasion, Birger had enjoyed the notoriety. Now both were out of the picture, but the Shelton brothers, who still maintained their farms and kept a low profile, were thriving.

The Chez Paree was under the direct management of Gus and Georgette. Everything from the food and drinks served to having Willie the Lion perform on this opening night came from their careful decision-making. But, like Carl Shelton, Gus kept his name off as many legal documents as possible, though he was now, with Capone's blessing, virtually in charge of the entire North Side.

When they neared the dance floor, Georgette waived to Willie the Lion and his band, each of whom, without losing a beat, waived back.

Nellie Newberry raced to Georgette, and the two women embraced one another like schoolgirls. Right away they pulled two chairs together and were instantly deep in news and gossip mode. Gus didn't understand why some women felt such a need to give long explanations before saying what they wanted in just a few words.

"The gentlemen will take Manhattans on the rocks," Gus told the waitress when she came to collect drink orders. "But, please, no giggle juice for the ladies."

"Oh, you hush, Gussie," Georgette admonished. "We'll have tequila sunrises. Heavy on the tequila, light on the sunrise."

Gus had forgotten, as love will do, how to feel annoyed at his wife's insolence. The men were silent, watching couples dance and listening to the women jabber. When the drinks arrived, Ted accepted his stiffly. He put a finger in the glass and rolled the ice around in circles.

"What's goin' on, Ted?" Gus finally asked.

"I'm thinkin' a little fuzzy tonight." Ted leaned forward, elbows on the table, head in his hands, grinding his teeth.

Gus himself began to grow fuzzy. Keeping Ted's head above water financially had become a full-time job.

"Why don't you get out of the rackets?" Gus suggested. "Buy a legit business."

"I ain't got the jack," Ted said, his hand shaking a little as he took a swig of his Manhattan. "Besides, Frank Nitti has it in for me unless I get him first."

"What, are you crazy?" Gus, tired of stubbornness, thought it was time for directness. To expect Ted, a man of darkness lately, to produce sensible decisions was asking a lot.

"I'm living on borrowed time," Ted Newberry said. "I'm due for a markdown."

"Why you say that, Ted?"

"Gus, Nitti lets you run your interests any way you want, and I'm happy for you. But he keeps a foothold on everything I do. Even having his thugs watch every move I make in the gamblin' joints."

"Well, he's got them in mine, too," Gus said.

"Not like in mine. He has his men check every dollar comin' and goin'. I have very little say as to operations."

Gus knew he was right. Nitti, in particular, despised Ted. Trust came hard when a man traded loyalty from one gang to another as Ted had.

"Gus, I've made arrangements with Mayor Cermak to have Nitti's office raided. They'll be lookin' for documents that could get him on tax evasion. That will be their excuse."

"Excuse?" Gus wanted to be clear on what Ted was saying. "Excuse for what? Who's the cop?"

"His name is Harry Lang. That's more than I should tell you. I just wanted you to know what's goin' on so you can protect yourself."

The wives turned toward their husbands, obviously ready to dance. Ted raised his glass in a toast. "God willing, we'll all be here at this time next year. Where one is, God grant we may all be."

31

July 29, 1932

The extortion racket was going so well that Bob Carey and Rose decided to take their business to New York City. Their luxurious apartment was a short distance from the Hudson River and not far from Central Park. They were finally living the high life.

When Rose presented herself in the bedroom for weekly amorous service, she found Bob twirling his six-shooter. That was not what caught her attention, though, since he often lay around twirling his six-shooter. This time, he hadn't a stitch of clothing on except for the western-style gun belt he had purchased from someone claiming to be Wyatt Earp. Rose went along with her lover's fantasy by introducing herself as Belle Starr.

Their coupling was intense and short-lived. Short-lived only because when Rose looked over Bob's shoulder in the middle of one of her fake moans, she saw three men standing in the doorway.

"What the hell?" she screamed, pushing Bob so hard that he rolled off the bed and onto the floor.

From that vantage point, Bob looked up into the eyes of Bugs Moran.

"Oh, crap," Bob groaned. "We're in the soup again."

***

"The paper says, 'Police believe Bob Carey took his wife, Rose, into the bathroom and killed her with three bullets,'" Georgette read as her husband finished his breakfast. "'Then he leaned over the bathtub and shot himself in the head.'" She set the paper down. "Do you believe that, Gus?"

"I don't know. Maybe he and Rose were in on the kidnappin' of the Lindbergh kid, after all. Bob told us at the New Year's party he was plannin' a crime that would set the world on its ears. And that maid they suspected in the kidnapping recently killed herself right before they could question her for the fourth time. Now that the Federal Kidnapping Act has passed, the Bureau of Investigation can chase you across state lines, and the punishment is life in prison or even death."

"But it says they found a counterfeit press and plates in Bob's apartment." Georgette shook her head.

"Now *that*, I would say, is suspicious." Gus got up, kissed his wife on the forehead, and put on his coat. "Bob Carey would never have the smarts to be a counterfeiter. But that may take the heat off Bugs Moran. The law thought his gang was doing the counterfeitin' in New York. Gotta get to work. Bye, hon."

Georgette's concern was a sensible reaction, Gus thought as he entered the garage he rented. His concern for how Bob and Rose died vanished, however, when he discovered the two very well-paid mechanics on break and that little progress had been made on the 1929 L-29 Phaeton automobile, the only vehicle in the big room.

"Fellas," Gus said, choosing diplomacy over ass-chewing. "I've decided you boys could use a little extra incentive to finish up this project. If you'll have the car ready by the end of next month, I'll double your pay."

"Bulletproofin' everything includin' the windows will be done by late next week," the older mechanic named Chub promised.

Gus's specially designed getaway car had front-wheel drive, necessary so if chased he could utilize the smoke screen that was produced when a hidden device sprayed oil into the car's hot exhaust manifold. Test runs showed the smoke screen was likely to slow anyone following enough that when Gus took a curve, the pursuing driver would not see the oil slick that was emitted by several shower heads beneath the Phaeton. The car also had one of the new police radios, a siren, gun ports, and both green and red headlights. If all else failed, roofing nails were set to be released beneath the trunk.

"I wanted you to know we have to change out the shower heads after every use," Chub said. "They tend to clog up."

"Well, Chub, I can change shower heads," Gus said. "I've done it at home. Throw a few extras in the trunk in case I'm on the road and need them."

"We'll have it ready on time," Chub assured him. "Even if we have to work nights and weekends."

***

December 19, 1932

George Goetz barged into Gus's office unannounced to tell him some big news.

"Detective Sergeant Harry Lang just shot Frank Nitti three times in the back and neck," George said.

The shock on Gus's face was real, though he had been wondering when Ted Newberry's threat might come to fruition. He had wished that Ted had never shared his plans. If Nitti lived, which George believed was unlikely, the Outfit might decide to take down everyone in operation on the North Side.

"If Nitti dies," George said. "You may have a slim chance of movin' up in the Outfit, what with Tony Accardo wantin' Nitti's job."

Gus recognized George had been developing jealousy toward him. He didn't want to say anything that might fuel that envy, so he said nothing. There was a big meeting of precinct bosses coming up in a couple of weeks. He just hoped Ted lived long enough to be there so he could provide a good explanation as to why he was not the one behind the hit.

*****

January 7, 1933

On the night of the precinct bosses' meeting, Gus asked Georgette to check on Nelli Newberry. He hadn't told her his suspicion that Ted was behind Frank Nitti being shot nor that Ted had not been invited to the meeting. Nitti had lived and was now recovering at home.

When Georgette walked into the Newberry apartment on the thirteenth floor, Ted was not with his wife, which was not unusual for a man in his business, but this time his absence was different. The five men gathered around the kitchen table playing cards were his most trusted aides—two bodyguards, his chauffeur, his accountant, and the pilot who flew syndicate leaders when necessary.

Nellie was a nervous wreck. "Have you seen Gus? I don't know where Ted is."

This was the moment when it all came together for Georgette. She'd assumed Ted would be at the meeting, but his accountant was here at the apartment. Accountants always attended though they often sat in the lobby unless called upon. Since Ted's bodyguards were also here in this room, and Gus had asked her to check on Nelli, it could only mean one thing. It was going to be a long night.

"Why didn't you come home?" Georgette screeched. She just happened to be in their apartment when Gus walked in the door. She had spent the entire night at the Newberry's with hourly trips down to her own apartment to see if Gus had come in, though she had instructed the maid to call upstairs if he did arrive.

"I couldn't," Gus said. "The dagoes wouldn't let me. They practically held me prisoner, and if I had tried to leave, somebody would have found me all shot up this—"

"Ted's missing," Georgette interrupted. "Nellie is beside herself with worry."

"I was afraid of that." Gus reached into his pocket and found his Indianhead nickel. "I tried my best to help him, but maybe it wasn't much use."

The telephone rang, and Gus rushed over to answer. He said hello, listened, and then slowly hung up the phone. Georgette could tell by his face what had happened.

"They just found Ted in Indiana," Gus said as he took her into his arms. "His body was riddled with bullets."

"Oh, Gussie, if they have taken Ted, they will take you next."

"Don't worry. Big Gus can take care of himself, and he isn't afraid of any dago who ever breathed. Stop crying."

But Georgette wanted to cry, and she wanted someone to cry with. Rather than wait on the elevator, she ran all the way up to the thirteenth floor. A dozen syndicate thugs were emptying the apartment of all Ted's belongings, a common thing when the law was expected. Nellie sat on the hallway floor crying.

"What happened?" Georgette asked one of the men carrying a big bundle of papers.

"He must've done something," the man said without stopping. "They don't kill you for nothing."

***

Gus's mind was whirling. With Ted Newberry out of the picture, most of the North Side of Chicago was now in his hands. The first thing he would have to do would be to absorb Ted's night-clubs and protection collections, as well as his legitimate businesses. He spent three days going through the Newberry books, only to discover that Ted was indebted to the Capone syndicate for about twenty-five thousand dollars. Gus immediately made adjustments with cuts and a few sales of unnecessary properties.

The next things Gus did were for his and Georgette's safety as well as their privacy. He had himself removed from the syndicate payroll. The IRS wasn't going to get him if they recovered any documentation with his name on it. He also ordered all business to be conducted through front men in his office with explicit orders that no one was to ever call him or come to his home on Lake Shore Drive.

As far as the citizens of Chicagoland knew, he was a gentleman racketeer who socialized with all kinds of people in the business world and with movie and sports stars, and even government officials, including the police. He expanded into as many legitimate businesses as he could with the hope of soon getting completely out of the rackets.

To make himself even more legitimate, Gus wanted to run straight games in his gambling establishments. Nitti's boys didn't like this idea, since they received a kickback from the wheels of every roulette table in town.

Then news came about the case against Frank Nitti for shooting Detective Harry Lang.

"They dropped the case," George Goetz told Gus after another mad dash to his office. "One of the officers testified that Lang shot an unarmed Nitti, then put a bullet in his own hand to make it look like self-defense."

"You think the cop was bought off?" Gus would rather they believe that than think someone, possibly he, had aided Ted in staging the hit.

"Nope. Looks like Ted offered Lang fifteen K to do the job." George looked right through Gus. "Now that Newberry's bumped off, I guess you figure on moving on the entire North Side?"

"What are your plans?" Gus deflected.

"Bryan and I are heading to St. Paul to do a few jobs with the Barker-Karpis Gang. Alvin Karpis has a pretty nice setup. Then we'll winter with them in Florida. You and Georgette should come down sometime."

"Alvin's smart," Gus said. "He thoroughly plans and executes everything he does. But Fred and Doc Barker are cold-blooded killers. They make sure there are no witnesses left alive to identify them. I'd be careful around that bunch."

By the time George Goetz arrived in St. Paul, he had taken to wearing spats and large diamond rings, fine linen, and even silk underwear. He was admiring himself in the mirror when Irene came into the room, saw him pruning, and laughed.

"What are you laughing at?" George struggled to come up with the right insult. "You're so fat you have to stand at the far end of the room just to get your whole body in the mirror."

He wanted to look at himself a little longer, but now the moment was ruined. Seeing her about to explode, George knew he had hit Irene with the wrong words at the wrong moment, and all he could do was try to maintain the upper hand.

"All I ask is for a woman to sit there and look appealing," George said, then kicked over an end table for good measure. When he saw her about to say something, he added, "If you must talk, keep your sentences short and to the point. I'm going downstairs and have a drink with the boys."

"You'll have to do a lot more than turn a table over if you want to shock me," Irene said. Since she was feeling a little bit forgiving, she went into the bathroom, although she was sure to give the door a good hard slam behind her.

Like most gangsters, the Goetz' and Boltons stayed at the big four-floor apartment at the corner of Summit and Dale. The gang was mulling around in the apartment lounge when George arrived. He found Bryan standing in a corner talking to Fred Barker.

"Creepy wants to talk to you two," Fred said.

"Why do they call Karpis, Old Creepy?" George asked Fred, who had been Alvin's cellmate in prison.

"Because when he's mad at you," Fred said loud enough Alvin could hear from the couch he was lounging on, "he just keeps staring at you until you get creeped out."

"That ain't so," Alvin said, rising and walking over to them. "It's because I'm so good at planning and getting away with crimes, the dicks think I'm creepy good."

George struggled not to look at Alvin's eyes as he approached. They were creepy indeed. The room was filled with gang members and even a few wives or molls. They moved to the far side of the room so the boss could have a private talk with his two new recruits.

"As long as we pay a bribe to Police Chief Tom Brown and promise not to commit crimes in St. Paul, we're safe here," Alvin Karpis told George and Bryan. He took his spectacles off and wiped them with a handkerchief. "Criminals come here from all around the country 'cause Brown has made it a gangster haven. I only have one rule if we let you do a job with us. No shootin' if kids are around. I won't tolerate any kids gettin' shot."

Though the sun was bright and the breeze smelled of wildflowers, Veva Bolton's spirit was not outside. It was stuck instead beneath the covers of her bed, waiting for the bad.

She had been enjoying the trip to the safety of St. Paul despite having to spend more time than she wanted around Irene Goetz. Irene was a little bit of a snob and often crass in her vocabulary. For the most part, Veva was able to overlook it, though it grew wearisome.

Then came word of Rose's death and the bombs of grief began exploding. She had gotten along with Rose better than anyone, except, of course, Georgette Winkler. The ghastly way Bob and Rose died was particularly unsettling. Like almost everyone who knew the Careys, Veva was certain they had been murdered. The news had caused her to even be mean to Bryan, the only person who understood her, and she, him.

Most of the ladies of the gang were laughing and drinking on the big patio outside. Verne Miller's girl, Vi, was sitting alone at the end of the wooden deck happily watching him help her eight-year-old daughter, Betty with her golf swing. Vi was wearing a short white skirt and a top that exposed much of her stomach. Veva found the combination odd, especially for a mother to wear in the presence of her child.

George came out on the lawn to watch Verne and Betty. He stood, a cigarette in one hand, a drink in the other, but it was his eyes that perplexed Veva. They never seemed to leave the young girl, especially when Betty leaned forward to swing the club. She decided not to overthink the observation and turned to Vi.

"Verne is very good with your daughter," Veva said.

"Isn't he?" Vi said proudly. "I've never known a man who does the things he does and can come home and be so loving to Betty and me."

"You know what he does?" Veva asked. Not all gangster molls knew what their men did.

Vi looked at her. "Verne tells me everything. Even when he has to kill."

"Bryan tells me things too, but he's never killed anyone, I don't think." Veva tossed the thought around in her head. Could she stay with a killer? "Do you think we are crazy to love men we should hate?"

When Verne glanced up at her, Vi gave him a little wave. His eyes lit up as he flicked the front brim of his hat.

"Sometimes it's easier to hate someone than to love them," Vi said. "But I could never hate Vernon Miller." She got up and skipped across the lawn toward her man.

***

"Fifty percent of folks in St. Paul are in the moonshine and bootleggin' industry," Verne Miller told George later that afternoon as he sat at a table in the lobby cleaning his weapons. "The other fifty percent are buyin' the liquor."

Verne's rifle was disassembled, its barrel on the couch, the stock and trigger on the table. Verne lifted the parts and quickly fit them together.

"Let's go shootin'," he said to George. Verne carried his Tommy gun and had two sidearms in holsters on either side of his chest.

When it came to Fred Burke, George felt no hesitation that the killer was always ready to kill, but Verne Miller was not someone he could be so sure of. He was scary one minute and cordial the next. Still, it was an honor to go target shooting with the expert marksman.

"Jack McGurn said you reeked of urine after you met with Capone," Verne said bluntly, clearly in a scary mood.

George hoped it was just Verne's way of being a smart ass. He had never heard the killer say a good thing about anyone except that pretty little girl he was helping with her golf swing. George looked back over his shoulder where Betty and her mother were still hitting golf balls. Maybe he'd get a chance to talk to the little girl sometime.

At the bottom of the hill, the gang had set up a dozen cardboard targets and bottles on a fence. Verne no sooner reached the little glen than he whipped his Tommy gun around and blew several boxes away. When his weapon clicked empty, he dropped it, pulled both handguns from shoulder harnesses at once, and knocked off all the bottles.

Several men and women watching from the patio applauded. What was left of the sunset showed yellow through the bluish gray of the gun smoke. George could not help being impressed by Verne Miller's skill with weaponry. Despite much practice, he couldn't come close to matching Verne's ability with a handgun, a rifle, or a Tommy gun.

"Vi, fetch us some more rye," Verne hollered to his woman.

"I can't be gettin' drunk," she shouted back.

"You bring the whiskey," Verne growled. "I'll do the getting drunk."

When Vi returned with the drinks, she wiggled her backend at Verne and ran across the lawn toward the house.

"I'm gonna go upstairs with this gal and get my knob polished," Verne announced.

"Sure, Verne, go get yourself a rim job." George laughed more than he should have when he realized that in his attempt to be nifty he was just embarrassing himself.

Later that evening up in their apartment, Bryan was admiring the way Veva lifted her arms to work on her hair, the feminine curves of her forearm and shoulders accentuated, her hands so delicate. He'd rather be canoodling with his wife than out gallivanting around with members of the Barker-Karpis Gang. But they needed cash.

Most days during this hour, they sat together around the fireplace, united in their silence, yet they were together. Now, however, Veva was standing in her bathrobe and slippers staring at Bryan with a look of woe.

Because of Veva's reaction to the news of the Careys' deaths, she and Bryan had spoken little since the morning before when he had given her the choice to go back to Chicago ahead of him or stay. She was so certain she would not pick the right option that she simply refused to pick.

From the edge of the bed, Bryan looked at her with such a childlike sense of longing, her hardness melted away.

"Sometimes it's easier to hate someone than to love them. I choose to love you, Bryan Bolton," Veva quoted her new friend Vi, then made passionate love to her husband for the first time in several days.

The moon that evening was orange as it rose, but soon became golden, then white. The lights across the city winked on. The entire Barker-Karpis gang rode in a caravan of cars to the Wabasha Street Cave's brand-new nightclub called Castle Royal. The entrance to the caves was a fine-looking brick building on the edge of a hill. Built from nineteenth-century mining expeditions, the caves had been renovated into speakeasies that, since prohibition ended, were now nightclubs catering to the many gangsters who made St. Paul their safe haven.

Veva shivered a little when she left the warm late August night to venture down into the first cavern. The entryway was huge, large enough for an automobile, with walls that arched up from each side to form a beautiful half-circle. While the cavern walls and ceiling were stone, the cave was dry.

They heard music and continued until they came to a chamber branching off to their right. When Veva looked inside, she couldn't believe they were underground. Beautiful chandeliers decorated the arching ceiling. A long bar ran along the left side into another chamber that was as large as a basketball court. All the tables were elegantly set with white tablecloths holding colorful flowers. Beyond the tables, couples swing danced to the fast and hard beat of a big band orchestra.

Many of the single men in the Barker-Karpis gang fanned out, finding stools at the bar or near tables of women, most of whom Veva was certain were girls for hire. She and Bryan joined the other couples at a long table in the center of the room and not far from the dance floor.

"Doesn't look like there's nobody but bad boys here," Bryan commented.

"I'd say most of what they call decent folks stay clear of this area," Verne Miller told him. "We've run off all the regular folks."

"What about the sheriff?" George asked.

"Oh, he's been graftin' off both sides." Alvin laughed.

Veva had a great time dancing with Bryan, Alvin, and even George, though he suffered from two left feet.

"Big fish eat little fish in this place," George told Bryan as they watched his wife Irene dance a little too suggestively with Fred Barker. "They told me the caverns the furthest back are filled with wise guys who couldn't handle their liquor or the bullets donated to them."

"So many people get kilt around here." Alvin laughed again. "The local undertaker has a half dozen men of all sizes and shapes to model for his caskets. Every time a new guy comes to town, he starts building his forever home for him. The only thing you'll find around these parts is death."

It wasn't until the band took a break that Veva was able to just sit next to her husband and enjoy one of the Castle Royal's fine cocktails.

"See those two that Alvin's talking to?" Bryan asked without pointing. "That's Pretty Boy Floyd and Baby Face Nelson. The guy standing behind them is called Machine Gun Kelly. An army of shooters."

"Where's that skirt that dances so good?" Veva heard from behind her.

Bryan stood to face the man. Veva was afraid there was about to be a row, but the man smiled at Bryan.

"May I have a dance with your lady?" he asked, his voice low and friendly. "No mischief intended. I just enjoy hoofing it with someone who knows how."

Bryan looked at Veva, who shrugged. He nodded to the stranger.

The man took Veva by the hand and led her onto the floor. Several other dancing couples looked at them and moved quickly aside. Veva had to admit, the fellow could dance. He moved his feet perfectly to the rhythm of the band. Raising his hands, he swung her back and forth and around and around with such ease she felt she was floating. Even more unusual was that neither his hands nor any part of his body ever touched Veva in any place that might have brought her husband rushing across the dance floor.

While he never laughed or even smiled, there was light in his eyes as if he were lost in the song, the music, and the dance. His lips even appeared to be trying to sing along. Veva sensed he was trying to lose himself in the moment as if when it ended, so too would the fantasy world he was presently escaping into.

When the dance number was over, the man returned Veva to her husband and thanked him for graciously sharing his wife. He shook Bryan's hand and kissed Veva's, then went to the table to sit with Baby Face Nelson, Machine Gun Kelly, and Pretty Boy Floyd.

"Do you know who you were just dancin' with?" Bryan asked.

"No, but he's a gentleman and a fine dancer," Veva said, afraid of what her husband was thinking.

"That was John Dillinger."

33

Two weeks later, Bryan was ready to quit the Barker-Karpis Gang. "Less than eight thousand dollars," he shouted to Veva as he stormed into the apartment. "Can you believe that's all we got out of the hundred K for the Hamm kidnappin'? Hell, you did more than anyone by feedin' and takin' care of Hamm."

Veva let her husband sit in his chair for a bit, squeezing his hands together. She knew better than to talk to him when he was gloomy. He just needed to think and talk his way through the gloom.

"Hell." Bryan rubbed the back of his neck. "The largest amounts went to a St. Paul police chief. He got twenty-five thousand, and the nightclub owner that protected us got ten K."

Veva was also frustrated, but not by the money. "Well, Bryan, I guess you could go back to being a carpenter. You wouldn't make eight thousand in three years, what with this depression going on."

She meant for her words to be less harsh than the ones she was prepared to give. Veva would've been happy if Bryan had stayed a carpenter. She would've been happy to struggle financially month by month, as long as they were together. But her words had come out rough. She wished she could call them back, but her words were history now.

"Take a hike, bitch!" Bryan shouted. Now it was he who immediately wished he had not opened his mouth so quickly. He had every intention of taking his wife away from the world of crime, but he wanted a grub stake. She just didn't seem to understand that being on the lam cost cash, not to mention paying for protection and preparing for each upcoming crime. It took money to pay for the guns and ammunition both for practice and when needed for use, as well as armoring vehicles for fast getaways.

"The St. Paul Chief of Police is helpin' us set up the kidnappings and bank robberies," Bryan said, in a cooler voice. "Alvin has planned two bank robberies for the next month. If we do well enough on those, it's California, here we come."

***

The Packard drove past the St. Paul post office, its white smoke screen hiding the two gunmen who leaped from the car and aimed their weapons at the policeman.

"Stick 'em up!" Doc Barker commanded.

The patrolman threw his hands high in the air. The two postmen he was escorting carried bags and didn't know for sure what to do. Another officer walked around the corner right into the holdup. Startled, Fred Barker fired his Tommy gun, hitting him several times. Not to be outdone, Doc fired his sawed-off shotgun straight into the face of the officer who had his hands up.

The bandits grabbed the bags from the shocked postal workers and threw them into the backseat next to Bryan and George. Fred and Doc both stepped onto the passenger side running board and Verne Miller sped the Packard from the scene while Bryan worked the lever that dusted the street with more smoke.

Then, just as they were nearly in the clear, for a reason Bryan couldn't understand, the Barker brothers started firing their weapons at building windows and streetlamps. Wanting to get in on the action, George shot out the back driver's side window. Verne thought this to be good fun, so he did a U-turn at the end of the block and raced them back down the same street for another go-around.

"Hand me that heater," Doc ordered, tossing his shotgun in the backseat. Bryan passed a Tommy gun out the window to him.

When he'd finished his ammo drum, Fred Barker opened the front car door as it was speeding out of town and was still whooping as he climbed into the seat next to Verne, who, laughing, reached over and rubbed his hair. Doc did the same to get into the backseat, but, as usual, never broke a smile.

With the firing stopped, Bryan immediately realized they had a problem. The back left tire was losing air fast. He told Verne, and he turned down the next country road and made another mile before he had to pull over.

Bryan, being the most mechanically inclined, opened the trunk and extracted a small jack he knew would be ill-fitting.

"Better everyone get out," Bryan suggested. "This old jack may not work so good with the weight of everyone in the car."

Just as the other five bank robbers exited the vehicle, a rusty old flivver pulled up behind the Lincoln. Brakes squeaked, parking brake clicked, and keys jangled as the good Samaritan got out and, smiling broadly, approached the gangsters.

"Need a hand there, fellas?" he asked amicably. "Might want to try a different jack on that big a vehicle."

He retrieved a large jack from the trunk of his car and walked toward Fred, who reached through the open window of the Lincoln and produced his Tommy gun.

"I call this popcorn death by Chicago typewriter," Fred said through teeth that were clinched around his big stogie.

Why Fred was willing to waste an entire fifty-round drum on a guy trying to help him change his tire, Bryan didn't know, but the gleam in Fred's eyes was telling. As three bullets every second struck him, the young man did a jerky type of popcorn dance that brought a wicked smile to Doc's face as he watched.

"Bullets are the best cure for being stupid," Fred said coldly when the weapon finally ran dry. He clicked the hot drum onto the ground and loaded a fresh one. No one seemed willing to pick the empty drum up and bring it along to refill, so after Bryan had used the good Samaritan's jack to change the tire, he bent down, retrieved it, and tossed it into the trunk with their new carjack.

***

June 17, 1933

Those sitting in the Florida sun three months later looked well-cooked. The two-story home on Lake Weir was surrounded by trees with only one road in and swamp all around. It was most famous for a giant alligator called Old Gator Joe.

After several months on the road, Veva had gotten to know the Barker brother's plump and red-haired mother pretty well. Ma Barker went to church every Sunday, did jigsaw puzzles, loved hillbilly music on the radio, and was a simple, uneducated, loving mother. Everyone enjoyed her down-home nature, but not even her boys paid her much attention except to lavish money on their mother for her services.

"Ma's just an old-fashioned homebody from the Ozarks," Alvin Karpis told Bryan and Veva. "She's superstitious, gullible, simple, cantankerous, and, well, generally law-abidin'. We have her travel with us because it makes us appear to be just another respectable family. She rents houses, pays bills, does our shoppin'."

"I've heard that when the old lady gets drunk, she gets nasty-minded and starts talkin' about doing the wild thing," Irene Goetz said out of the blue later as she and Veva were relaxing on the long, screened-in porch. Bryan and George lounged on nearby benches talking to Fred's brother, Doc.

Ma had a gentleman friend, a well-dressed old fellow named Arthur Dunlop. She was just then sitting at the opposite end of the porch holding the old man close, patting his shoulder, and talking quietly to him.

"She's probably whisperin' stories to the old fellow," Irene suggested. "Stories that will remind him of his youth when he could still fornicate without worryin' that his pecker would stay shriveled."

"You're so mean, Irene," Veva said, though she had to admit she was thinking of something similar.

"You need to sit," Ma suddenly shouted at her son, Fred, who was standing behind her. "I don't like the way you loom."

"You'd better tell Arthur to watch his mouth around his friends when he gets drunk," Fred scolded. "I hear he's been talkin' about our business. We don't want anyone to know our business. That way, other gangs get blamed. He's gonna get one of us kilt."

"Ah, what a sign it is of evil life," Arthur recited. "Where death's approach is seen so terrible!"

"What's that mean?" Fred asked.

"Just something I read. Shakespeare, maybe." Arthur had always been adept as a wordsmith, a skill he knew Ma's son deplored, giving him more reason to do so. "Oh, what a troubled web we weave—"

"Said the spider to the fly," Fred interrupted. "You've been known to spin a few webs yourself.

And you'd best keep your trap shut if you know what's good for you."

Having given the warning he wanted, Fred walked to the other end of the porch where the wives and several of the gang were laughing, drinking, and telling tall tales.

"Doc, have you told the boys the story about Verne?" Fred asked. "The one where he's face-to-face with another gunman? That story's right outta a dime novel."

"The legend goes that Verne Miller was in a Mexican standoff with another fella," Doc Barker said. "They were both aimin' their roscoes at the other's head from ten feet away. Verne watched the man's eyes and saw a first-strike chance when the man blinked. He fired right into the barrel of the other fella's gun. Verne's bullet must have met the other guy's bullet as it was about halfway through the barrel because it damned nearly blew the gunman's hand off. His second bullet was right between the eyes. That's enough to give anyone the yips."

"Where is Verne, by the way?" Doc Barker asked.

"Oh," Alvin answered before Fred could let anything slip. "He and Pretty Boy Floyd went down to Kansas City on some business. He said he'd rendezvous back up with us in St. Paul when he's done."

34

Verne and Pretty Boy's business was being called the Kansas City Massacre by newspapers. In their attempt to free gangster Frank Nash, four police officers as well as Nash were killed. Gus was reading the newspaper accounts of the incident when the telephone rang.

Georgette overheard Gus's end of the telephone conversation and took from it that Verne Miller's girlfriend Vivian wanted to have a meeting with him.

"You aren't goin', are you, Gus?" she asked when he hung up.

"I don't know what to do." Gus shook his head and returned to his newspaper.

"Let me go," Georgette said after thinking the problem through. "They aren't gonna do anything to me, and I can deliver whatever message you want."

"I don't want you gettin' involved in this," Gus said. "I'll take care of it."

Fed up with her husband's stubbornness, Georgette got up, retrieved the coffee cups, and headed toward the kitchen. Along the way, she looked down on the table beside the phone and memorized the address her husband had written on a tablet.

***

"This is a bad surprise," Vi said when she saw Georgette at the apartment door instead of Gus. Vi's young daughter, Betty, stood at her side. Three gunmen sat at a table drinking and smoking.

"I'm Gus Winkler's wife," Georgette said, her hand reaching into her purse when the gunmen leaped to their feet. "Who wants him?"

Vi held her palm back toward the three men. "Won't you have a seat, Mrs. Winkler?"

"I'll stand," Georgette said, her eyes remaining on the gunmen. "Well, what is it you want?"

"I've got to have money and a place to hide. That's why I wanted Gus."

"So, that's it," Georgette sneered. "Well, you listen to me, and this is straight from Gus to you. Gus Winkler won't do a thing for you or anyone else connected with the Kansas City Massacre. Gus Winkler does not intend to get mixed up in that mess. He has only advice for Verne Miller, and that is to stay away from him and Chicago."

"Please, Georgette, if Gus won't help Verne, maybe he'll do him a favor."

"What?"

"There's a rooming house just back of the Leland Hotel. There's a man there who knows too much. Verne wants Gus to go up to that room and take him."

"So that's the favor your man wants mine to do?" Georgette asked. She saw a door in the back of the apartment creep open a little. Her intuition was that Verne was standing behind it. She spoke her next words loudly and toward the door. "There's only one answer to that—Verne Miller is insane."

With her hand still in her purse and her eyes on the three gunmen, Georgette stepped backward out the door. She shook with anger all the way to her car and then home. Georgette kept seeing the fear in the eyes of Vi's daughter, Betty. The poor little dear had not chosen to be born into such a mess.

***

The Bureau of Investigation's Chicago office was nothing fancy. Small wooden tables with wooden chairs and lots of files stacked high on every desk. Dozens of bureau agents sifted through papers and answered phones, everyone in shirt sleeves with service revolvers tucked inside their shoulder holsters.

Melvin Purvis had the only office with a door, which was currently shut, shades drawn down.

He and Gus Winkler were alone, so Purvis opened a drawer, extracted two glasses and a bottle, and poured two fingers high into each.

"Why do you John Laws keep bringin' these killers in alive?" Gus asked the conservatively dressed Special Agent as he accepted the glass.

"The law is a shield, not a sword," Purvis said in his gentle southern drawl.

"Well," Gus shook his head. "Now that prohibition's over, they are bringin' heroin and other drugs in. Some of the Barker-Karpis boys are down in Cuba as we speak, arrangin' just that. Those drugs are gonna kill more Americans than you can count, and the only way to stop it is to cut off the head of the snake. Your legal system is more and more workin' in favor of the criminal over the victim."

"So, you want us to just shoot criminals on sight?" Purvis laughed. "How would that have worked out for you ten years ago?"

"You know damned well prohibition was a farce," Gus said, holding up his glass. "And what banks we hit had it comin', plus the public was on our side. We actually did more to protect citizens than your lawmen ever could. Unfortunately, there were always do-gooders like Elliot Ness and J. Edgar Hoover to mess with the peace."

"Yes, until the Valentine's Day thing. The public didn't like you so much then, did they? When are you gonna fess up to what I already know about that day—*American Boy*?"

"One thing at a time." Gus wasn't afraid of Purvis. In fact, he even liked the little guy. "So, tell me why you want the Barkers and Karpis so bad."

"The Barker-Karpis Gang has killed more cops and citizens than Dillinger, Baby Face Nelson, Machine Gun Kelly, and Bonnie and Clyde combined." Purvis picked up a paper from his desk. "Listen to this report by the Minnesota Bureau of Criminal Apprehension: 'After killing one police officer and wounding another, the Barker-Karpis Gang put on a Jesse James exhibition by shooting up and down Concord Street, shooting about a dozen shots into the Postal Building and across the street. These bandits used a Thompson submachine gun and a sawed-off shotgun with which they did their shooting. It's a miracle no one else was shot and wounded. They appeared to be cool and reckless, not giving a damn whom they shot.'"

Gus knew Purvis was right. The Barker-Karpis Gang was a blight on even the criminal code of conduct. The only problem he had with giving information on them was that George Goetz and Bryan Bolton were running with them. For that reason, he decided to throw Purvis a different bone.

"George Kelly is in Memphis," Gus said. "He called me just a few days ago." He lit a cigarette and thought about what else he wanted to share to keep himself on Purvis's good side.

Georgette had told him she suspected Verne Miller had been at Vi's apartment when she visited her, but Gus wasn't prepared to divulge his exact whereabouts when it would be so obvious to the underworld the information had come from him. Besides, Miller was smart enough to have moved on by now.

"Last I heard, Verne Miller was in New Jersey staying with Longy Zwillman. I doubt the relationship will go very well. Then Verne will most probably try to get away to Europe with his girlfriend, Vivian. She has a place here in Chicago you might want to stake out. I doubt he'll leave the country without her and her daughter. Miller still has a few friends here, but a lot of enemies too, so who knows? The mobs are fed up with Verne for the Kansas City botch. I'd love for you to get him, since Frank Nash was one of my friends."

September 26. 1933

A week later, Gus's tip paid off. Machine Gun George Kelly was arrested in Memphis. The Bureau of Investigation Director J. Edgar Hoover saw this as an opportunity to increase the prestige of his department by making up a story that when Kelly saw he was surrounded, he shouted, "I've been expecting you. Don't shoot, G-men!"

***

For their next trip to St. Paul, the Barker-Karpis Gang hit another bank, then successfully kidnapped Edward Bremmer and took his Schmidt Beer family for two hundred thousand dollars. Ma Barker and Arthur Dunlap innocently ran interference for them in setting the gang up in apartments and doing their grunt work.

The problem came when Arthur was drunk, which was most of the time these days. He just couldn't be kept from bragging that he ran with the Barker-Karpis Gang. Lucky for the gang, it was the corrupt St. Paul Police Chief Tom Brown who took the message from a concerned citizen that Arthur had had a snoot full and was talking his head off. Brown immediately called Fred Barker.

Arthur was still drunk a few hours later when Fred put a single bullet into his head and dumped him in the lake. His naked body was found several days later near Webster, Wisconsin. Since he was just another John Doe with no way to identify, Ma Barker never discovered the fate of her sweetheart and believed he'd simply run off.

Word did get out, however, that Chief Brown had tipped the Barkers off about Dunlap, but it couldn't be proven. Still, he was demoted to detective and later fired from the force entirely.

35

October 9, 1933

Gus was propped up on an elbow, admiring his wife's face. The couple liked to sleep naked. On several occasions, always after heavy drinking, they woke in the middle of the night and found themselves in the middle of sex. Neither Gus nor Georgette knew how the dalliance had started, but they always finished, then had a good laugh about it.

Now Gus just lay watching Georgette's soft breaths and thinking how long it had been since they'd had such spontaneous lovemaking.

"We've not woken up in the middle of coitus for quite some time, you know," Gus said when he saw her eyelids flutter open.

Georgette knew that Gus needed her, she liked that about him. He was too naïve to know that if he took up with anyone but her, he was bound to come to great harm, not by her, but by the fact that few others would understand him as well. Her love for Gus Winkler gave him a power over her he didn't even know he had, and she didn't want him to know he had.

She looked at him compassionately. Gus had never had a woman look at him with such compassion. Not even his mother.

"I could please you oftener back then," Gus blushed.

"Oftener, true." Georgette gently rubbed his cheek with the back of her hand. "But with far less satisfaction."

Gus reluctantly pushed the covers off and began getting dressed. She watched him solemnly as he pulled his britches up.

"Are we still going to dinner at the restaurant?" Georgette asked when he was dressed.

"Yes, but I'll be on that side of town, so we will have to meet there." Gus opened the door. Just as he was about to leave, he turned back and blew her a kiss. "I'll be waiting for you." Then he was gone.

***

Gus had his driver let him out at the corner so he wouldn't have to do a turnabout. He wanted to walk a little. He had passed through so much of his life paying only the most casual attention to the natural world, thinking instead of pay-rolls or material wants. Today, he could walk in peace, thinking, being alone. He and Georgette were close to their dream. In another few months, he'd have enough legitimate business interests for them to get out of the rackets. While Nitti and his thugs would object to his walking away, Capone had given Gus his blessing, and Capone, though in prison, still ran things.

In what was essentially his first commune with nature since he was a child, Gus felt he could taste the cool October air. The sound of geese flying overhead brought him a rare feeling of calm, and he wanted it to last.

He started up the steps into the distributing company just as a small, green panel truck cruised slowly down the street toward him, stopping just past him. Gus heard the back door of the truck opening, so he turned toward it. George Goetz and Tony Capezio knelt inside the truck, each holding a shotgun aimed at him.

Gus turned to run. The double blast from each gun hit his back so powerfully it knocked him hard onto the steps. The truck engine roared as it left the scene.

Like the trickles of a warm shower, liquid oozed from his back, then along the concrete and down onto a lower step. He saw the shoes of a man next to his head.

"Roll me over," Gus gasped. "I want to see the sky."

"Who shot you?" the man asked as he helped Gus push himself onto his back.

"Never mind," Gus said.

He had failed in vigilance, and now Georgette would pay the price. It was a failure, a botch. His head was swimming. His breath made a cloud above him. He felt so lightheaded he believed he was floating off the ground into a dark world behind his eyelids. The earth and the sky seemed to be becoming confused.

He felt warm and sleepy. But he didn't feel alarmed, even when he touched his side, raised his hand, and saw the blood, he wasn't alarmed. His bloody hand found its way into his front right trouser pocket and found the Indian head nickel. Everything would be all right. Sleep was all that mattered. He was just so tired. Georgette would be angry if he fell asleep before her. Maybe they would be making love when they woke up. He closed his eyes and felt a great loosening.

***

Georgette got the telephone call at exactly two o'clock that afternoon. Someone said her husband had been killed twenty minutes ago. The person wanted a statement.

Georgette hung up the phone and then pulled the cord loose from the wall. It was true. In her heart just a little while ago, she had felt his soul pass through her. She went to her favorite rocking chair and sat. She calculated that Gus had left the house at one o'clock. One hour ago, he'd said his last words to her, "I'll be waiting for you."

She watched the clock. The maid came, but Georgette waved her away. She wanted to watch the clock.

Seconds ago, Augustus Winkler was with me. "I'll be waiting for you."

The second hand moved slowly, as she wanted it to. When it reached twelve, the minute hand clicked forward one notch. She watched that second hand go around and around, trying to force it with her mind to slow, but it wouldn't.

Now, it was minutes since Gus was with me. Georgette continued to watch every minute—each minute took her further away from her husband, yet she watched the clock as if watching it would somehow keep him close to her longer.

But the clock kept moving. Someone, she knew not who, was talking to her, but she didn't recognize their words. Words didn't matter.

It has been hours now since Gus was with me. I don't want this day to end because it will take me further from the moment he left.

Finally, when it had been twenty-four hours since Gus told her, "I'll be waiting for you,"

Georgette finally allowed herself to fall asleep, but Gus wasn't there, either.

Though it was cold, Georgette insisted on riding in the train luggage compartment next to Gus's coffin all the way to St. Louis.

Photographers snapped pictures of her, of the well-known people who came to the funeral, of the flowers—they even snapped pictures of Gus in his coffin.

Georgette's sister, Blanche, was the only one she allowed to touch her. She turned her head down when hands were offered, forced a weak smile when she had to, and glanced regularly at Gus's body in the coffin until it was closed shut for the final time.

When it was over, Blanche said she wanted to go to Chicago with her. Georgette smiled, kissed her cheek, and said, "No."

She sat by the train window on the way home, thinking it strange she couldn't remember having eaten or drank anything since she received the telephone call. In Chicago, her chauffeur, a nice old Black man named Murphy, waited at the train station. He took her valise in one hand and Georgette's arm in the other. At the apartment building, he did the same as he led her to the elevator and then to her door. She handed him the key, and Murphy opened it. Just as he was about to step aside for her to enter, he glanced into the apartment.

"Stop, Missus Georgette!" Murphy shouted. He blocked the way and tried to shut the door, but she was too strong for the aging chauffeur and pushed past him.

Then she dropped to her knees and cried. The apartment had been ransacked, furniture torn into pieces, and large holes left in the walls.

More and more over the next few days, Georgette was inclined to sulk. Nights were the worst. She'd get so lonely for Gus she'd have to hug the pillow to keep from shaking. The light made her hopeful. As the sun rose, water sprinkled on the grass blades, creating a glow that perked her a little. After that, she sat all day in silence, thinking her thoughts and ignoring attempts to alter her mood. Then, too soon, the darkness came again, and all hope faded. It was a long, rainy dusk, so long it made Georgette gloomy again. She sent the maid home with pay for the next month, telling her she hoped she'd find another job.

Now, alone in the apartment, somehow, she finally slept. Gus was there, waiting for her. She awoke to find it had been a dream, only hopeful thinking. So disappointed was Georgette that she covered her face with her hands and cried. The rest of the night she lay awake trying to bring back the sweetness of the dream. After this, she knew she would always be afraid of the nights. The thought filled her with hopelessness, but hopeless or not, what could she do? Hopelessness was always there, always would be. It's like being a passenger in your own life. She remembered telling Gus that once.

Georgette tried to think of what Gus would want her to do in such a situation. The next morning, lightning flickered as thunderstorms rolled across the prairie all day. She felt her fear rising again. Then, once again, it was dusk, the sun just down. Georgette's spirits fell again. She was in the grip of a terrible indecision. She wished she could learn the trick of dying a quick and honorable death.

October 22, 1933

Shaking the morbid thought away, she rose from her rocker and went into the kitchen. Once there, she stopped and sniffed. The room was hot. She realized she had left the gas oven burning. How long had it been, two, three days? The idea that suddenly came seemed an answer to her prayers. Instead of turning off the oven, she got down on all fours, took a deep inhale, and blew at the pilot light. It took three tries before the flame was gone. The quiet hiss of the gas, though, continued. She laid her head on the cool tile of the floor and shut her eyes, the quiet symphony of Gus's last words in her head, "I'll be waiting for you."

***

Two floors below Georgette's apartment, Bonnie Burke, still wearing her bathrobe and slippers, was sitting at the kitchen table with her head in her arms. She also could only see a vast hole in her life. So many things seemed to happen before she was ready, like people dying or going to prison before she was finished with them.

After Fred was apprehended, she had come to the Chicago apartment to be alone, but the apartment wasn't far enough away from the memories that haunted it. She and Fred had only spent a short time there, but they had been the happiest days of their brief marriage.

Seemingly content to lay on the couch and stay drunk, Fred had seldom left the apartment, so Bonnie had spent many afternoons going shopping or dining with Georgette Winkler. Thanks to Gus, wives and children of syndicate members who were killed or imprisoned received a pension. Now that Gus was dead, Frank Nitti wanted to end that policy. She was afraid—very afraid—if that happened, she would lose everything except her clothes and what little money she had hidden away.

Though he was, at best, looking at a life sentence, Fred thought he would eventually beat the rap on appeal. But he was lying to himself, believing his own lies, as men so often do.

On this day more than most, she felt a sinking of spirits. Since they were in the same building, she thought about going up to Georgette's apartment and seeing if she would go to lunch with her. Even when Georgette was smiling, there was something sad in her look. Maybe the two could somehow bring a little happiness into one another's day.

Bonnie dressed without any concern for how she looked, left her apartment, and took the stairs up to the seventh floor. As she neared Georgette's door, she smelled the gas.

Georgette awoke in Bonnie's bed, too upset to care if she lived or died, recovered, or perished, a doctor hovering over her.

"Georgette," Bonnie said. "Was this an accident or were you trying to kill yourself?"

Bonnie said it without judgment, and even to her own surprise, she took Georgette's hand and pulled her gently into a heartfelt embrace. Bonnie had a habit of simply forgetting people, burning bridges being easier than building them. It was one of the many puzzles of her life. But here was a life she had saved, and it felt good.

Now she needed to find the right words to make her friend want to live, to have something to live for. She did something she hadn't done in a long time. She prayed. Prayed for the wisdom, for the words that Georgette needed, and perhaps she needed also. Then, she opened her mouth, unsure as to what might come out of it.

"Your mission should be to teach others," Bonnie said as she held her friend. "If you could convince only one boy or girl who had dreamed of money, and money alone, that money and power are the least things in life, then these years in your life were spent for a purpose."

36

October 31, 1933

Ever since the Kansas City Massacre in June, Verne Miller felt like a piss ant. He hadn't counted on pissing off so many people, and now he was starting in one direction, then another, then another, avoiding death at every turn, like an ant trying to cross a busy sidewalk full of humans.

Now, here he was driving a black Ford sedan his friend Al Silverman had given him. As he passed along country roads from New York back to Chicago, his situation wore on his nerves. It was hard to remember all the areas he needed to avoid because of previous indiscretions. Even getting gas for his flivver was a chore. Little towns in Pennsylvania, Ohio, and Indiana seemed to look so similar, even their filling stations, grocery stores, and cafeterias might be a place where he had robbed a bank or shot a lawman.

He blamed Gus Winkler for putting the Feds on his tail in New Jersey. Gus got seventy-two buck-shot pellets to his back for such treacheries, but

Verne wished he'd gotten worse. He wished he could have avenged the atrocity precisely in kind by castrating Winkler, then removing fingers, toes, eyes, and ears one at a time. That American Boy's squealing to the Feds had the entire underworld looking over their shoulders, especially after George Kelly was captured in Memphis so soon after calling on Winkler for help.

Verne had thought he was pretty safe at mobster Longy Zwillman's place in Orange, New Jersey. Then when Vernon Miller became a "most wanted," word came that Winkler had sold his location out to the Bureau. The reward money must have caused one of Zwillman's gunmen to have a slip in devotion to his boss, because one day he took a shot at Verne while he was walking out to his car. The bullet grazed Verne's left holster, damaging the gun inside it but giving him time to duck behind the car before the ambusher could get off two more shots toward him.

Verne quickly removed two bullets from his other revolver and then pulled the trigger twice. Hearing the clicks on empty chambers, the gangster jumped out from behind the door and as he attacked, Verne emptied his final four shots into him.

Now, as he crossed the Wabash River into Illinois, Verne contemplated how the attempt to free Frank Nash at the Kansas City Union Station had gone so badly. It should have been a simple affair since both he and Pretty Boy Floyd had the officers outgunned with Tommy guns.

But the idiot police officer sitting in the back-seat behind Nash didn't know how to operate the 16-gauge shotgun, a Winchester Model 97 that had a special feature that allowed it to fire like a machine gun. When Verne yelled, "Put 'em up! Up! Up!" the cop accidentally blew off the top of Nash's head as well as put a hole in the front wind-shield and then into the head of another officer as he moved across the front of the vehicle. As if that wasn't enough, the dumb cop swung the shotgun, which was now in full automatic mode, and killed another officer standing near Verne.

With three people dead before they had even fired a shot, the rescuers unleashed their weapons with fury. Pretty Boy took down one cop, and Verne shot into the car, killing another agent and putting three bullets into the incompetent shotgun fellow before he could inadvertently do more damage to his own officers.

"He's dead!" Verne shouted when he saw Nash minus the back half of his head. He then reached into the car, grabbed the shotgun that had just killed three people, and with great disgust, tossed it on the ground. He and Pretty Boy continued to spray the area with bullets as they raced to their car and made their escape.

Verne had two regrets. One was that the officer who had caused all the mayhem had survived his wounds and was now trying to make himself out to be the hero of the shootout. The other was that J. Edgar Hoover falsely claimed his agents were unarmed and sitting ducks for the ambush. Because of what happened in Kansas City, all of Hoover's agents were now not only armed to the gill, but they had acquired a vast arsenal of Thompson machine guns. The Bureau was also leaning hard on gangsters, especially big-name ones.

Even small-time crooks like Bonnie and Clyde were feeling the heat. Though they mainly robbed gas stations and grocery stores, Bonnie had sent out a letter to newspapers stating they had nothing to do with the massacre at Union Station. Everyone blamed Verne and Pretty Boy Floyd for messing up a perfectly fine harmonious relationship between criminals and the law.

After driving into Illinois, Verne spotted the distant outline of skyscrapers to the north. Winter was coming, but other than his girl, Vi, who still had her apartment in Chicago, he had no place to hide out. His friend Al Silverman had made arrangements at Midway Airport for a flight to

New York and then on to Europe. They would only have a few hours to catch the flight.

Verne could not deny that coming for Vi and her daughter Betty was a major risk. The problem was he loved them both dearly. The thought of living his life without them was inconceivable.

***

What with the July kidnapping of John Factor and then the October crash of United Airlines Trip 23 in which he suspected foul play, Melvin Purvis had his hands full as the Special Agent in Charge at the Bureau of Investigation's Chicago office.

Now Gus Winkler's lead that Verne Miller may be soon coming for his girlfriend had many from his already understaffed office working double time staking out her apartment and listening in on her telephone calls.

He had already figured out that Verne and his girlfriend Vivian were having a ménage à trois relationship with a feisty young girl named Bobbie Moore. Bobbie was definitely a head-turner. Her brief relationships with the law always brought out compassion in those men who arrested her.

The idea the Bureau needed more female agents had crossed Melvin's mind for just that reason. It had even been brought up at meetings, but J. Edgar Hoover would hear nothing of it. It seemed to many that the director was an unabashed woman hater. Of course, this helped feed whispers within the agency that he was homosexual. Melvin, though, doubted this. Hoover just seemed like a man driven to power and glory. He doubted the man could ever love any man or woman as much as he loved himself.

A traffic jam ahead brought much honking from frustrated travelers. Some got out of their cars so they could peer over other vehicles as if anything they could see would clear the street. A mustached man wearing glasses and a brown hat in a black Ford sedan next to him seemed especially upset. The man slammed both hands onto his steering wheel and shouted a dozen swear words in a practiced order Melvin had never heard before. Faces were Melvin's life, having struggled to memorize the features of so many criminals. For a second, a mustached John Dillinger came to mind, though he had just received a report that Dillinger had been spotted yesterday in Tucson, Arizona. When the man turned his head and glared at him, Melvin directed his gaze back to the windshield.

So many men of late were dressing and trying to look like the famous outlaw. He wished they had better pictures of Verne Miller, but the ones they had were years old and very faded. Melvin's secretary, Doris Rogers, one of the only women working in the Bureau office, had grown up in Huron, South Dakota, where Miller had been sheriff until he made off with all the county's money. Doris thought she could identify Miller, so she was staked out at the apartments to watch for him if he came or went.

The jam finally cleared, and Melvin drove on toward the Sherone apartments unaware the black Ford with the impatient Dillinger look-alike also traveled through the heavy traffic in that direction.

***

In their Sherone apartment, Bobbie Moore answered the phone, then quickly looked at Vi, who was lounging on the couch, and gave her a smile and a nod.

"Tell him I've been crying and blue all day," Vi said, then added, "And to come up and see me."

Across the street, a Bureau of Investigation agent with a receiver to his ear heard Bobbie give the message. The line immediately went dead. The agent signaled to his partner to put out a *possible* alert.

In the Sherone apartment lobby, Melvin Purvis' secretary, Doris Rogers, was provided a high stool near the dumbwaiter where she could see the coming and going of people getting on the elevator or taking the stairway. She was a little nervous. It had been years since she had seen Vernon Miller, and even then it was mostly from newspaper clippings. There was also her personal conflict concerning his being a bank robber, a profession she sympathized with. After all, no one liked the banks that charged high-interest rates and foreclosed on innocent farmers every time they had a chance. Still, despite the danger of fingering the most wanted man in America, she was happy that in a man's world, she was given the opportunity to do a man's job.

As always, the apartment building was a busy place with so many people coming and going. Having been sitting on the stool all day, Doris shifted her weight around to lessen the pressure on her stiff back when she saw a mustached man in glasses wearing a brown hat and suit coming through the outside door. He walked close to a woman who appeared much too old to be anything except his mother. The man stepped quickly in front of the lady and pushed the elevator button. She smiled at him, and he tipped his hat. *Not acquainted*, Doris thought.

Doris looked over to the doorway where an agent had just stepped inside to get her signal. She gave him a shrug and a sideways thumb to indicate *maybe*.

As much as Verne was happy to see Vi, intercourse fell under the heading of future pleasures and would have to wait.

"Get packed for a flight," Verne told her when she ran into his arms. He tossed the car keys to Bobbie. "Bobbie, go down the street to the garage and bring the black Ford sedan in number eleven around back. Keep it runnin' and wait."

Bobbie was no sooner out the door than Vi was packing a single suitcase. She looked in her closet. All the beautiful expensive gowns and shoes she took such pride in were once again lost. Every gangster wife or moll she had ever met lamented these losses. Those who did manage to escape the excitement and temporary wealthy lifestyles of criminal life often found the stability of being a small-town housewife much more satisfying. But Vernon Miller was the love of her life. She knew what he did to give her the clothes she was leaving behind. He was always honest with her about the banks he robbed, the men he kidnapped, and even the people he killed. Yet, in the presence of her and her daughter, though Betty wasn't his, he was the kindest, softest human she had ever known.

When she was done filling the valise with necessities, Verne kissed her hard. "Go down to the street in back and wait for me. If there's no trouble,

I'll stop at the corner and pick you up. We'll pick Betty up at her school on the way to Midway."

After another long and passionate kiss, Vi, suitcase in hand, walked out the door. Verne removed his sidearms from their holsters and checked them. Ten minutes later, he opened the door and walked down the hall to the elevator.

When Verne Miller stepped from the elevator, Doris was certain it was him. She nodded to the agent in charge, got up, and headed for the safety of the stairwell in case there was a shooting.

The hair on the back of Verne's head tingled. The sudden movement of the woman and the man on the sidewalk lighting a cigar told him something might be awry. He bolted for the same door the woman had gone out, then on through the door marked exit. Bobbie stood by the Ford, probably having got out to say something to Vi as she passed. A man in a suit stood and smoked along the building wall. Verne tried to walk calmly toward the car, but Bobbie stepped toward him with a smile. The man on the wall ran toward the car, and so did the fugitive.

Bobbie got into the driver's seat while Verne pulled his guns and jumped in beside her. The agent leaped onto the running board. Without aiming, Verne fired a shot over his own shoulder, missing the man but causing him to jump to the ground.

From behind them came machine gun fire that blasted out the back and front window and sent bee-like buzzing past his and Bobbie's heads. Verne leaned out his window and fired both guns.

Before they were two blocks away, Verne heard police sirens.

"Drop me at this corner and keep going as long as you can." He leaned over and kissed Bobbie's cheek. "Tell Vi and Betty I love them." Verne opened the car door and, before it came to a complete stop, got out running.

Bobbie floored the accelerator and raced in and out of traffic. The longer she kept them chasing her, the greater Verne's chance of getting away. Twenty minutes later, a police car rammed the front of her vehicle. She came out of the car laughing as more cars braked to a stop behind hers and agents rushed up.

"One thing for sure about you G-men—" Bobbie laughed. "You never get your man, but you always get your woman."

***

Verne knew the city, and he knew how to lay low. It didn't hurt that he had ten thousand dollars sewn into his suit coat. Still, he was on the lam from everyone. The Kansas City job had been a botch, and now coming for Vi and Betty had also been a mistake. He should've just gone on to Europe from New York and then sent for them. But his longing for the two most important people in his life had been too much to bear.

For twenty days, he stayed in the dark streets of Chicago's south side, never more than one night at each sleaze bag hotel. Days were difficult, trying to find movies he hadn't seen or places to eat where he could hide in the shadows. Then the newspapers came out with the ominous news that the friend who had recently helped him, Al Silverman, had been beaten and stabbed to death, his nude body found on a country road with only a bow tie around his neck.

Silverman had ignored crime bosses who warned the underworld not to protect Verne. His vicious murder was retribution and a warning to anyone who tried to help the man with the bounty on his head, of that he was certain. The description of the killing had the earmarks of Murder Incorporated written all over it. That organization of professional assassins liked to leave their tortuous signature at their killings.

Verne had one hotel he felt safe in, only because it was a flea-bitten place with few amenities and hourly rates. He had spent a few hours there a week ago and had convinced the owner with cash to bring an old hog scalder bathtub up and have some of the ladies fill it. It was an expensive proposition since he had to pay everyone extra to perform this service during what would normally be their daytime sleeping hours.

November 28?, 1933

The big hog scalder bathtub was placed in the middle of the room so that when Verne was in it, he faced the door. As last time, he paid three prostitutes to haul scalding hot water up from the kitchen. When the tub was filled, he locked the door and moved the dresser in front of it. He wedged the window shut by hammering nails into the sides, drew the curtain, and, to be extra certain, draped the quilt from the bed over it. Even with these precautions, he pulled chairs on either side of the tub and placed a revolver on each.

By the time he had the room ready, got his clothes off and hung on a clothesline along the wall, the water had cooled just enough that he could slowly lower his body into the steaming tub. It felt so good. It was the first luxury he had allowed himself since the shootout at Vi's apartment building.

The whole experience of being with Vi and Betty the past few years were the happiest days he'd ever known. Thinking about them felt so relaxing, he drifted off.

Suddenly, a clothesline around his neck pulled him backward so viciously he couldn't reach his guns. He kicked his legs, sending waves of water onto the wooden floor.

"Why?" Verne just had enough air to ask, though he also wanted to know how anyone had got into the room behind him.

"There's a nice price tag hanging on you, Miller."

The killer used the clawed side of the hammer to split Verne's skull.

37

George Goetz was convinced that all women wanted him for his blond hair and wanted him a lot. He blamed his pretty blond hair for getting him in trouble back when he was a twenty-two-year-old lifeguard on the Clarendon Municipal Bathing Beach near Beach Park, Illinois. He had simply been sitting at his lifeguard station when a seven-year-old girl started rubbing her hands along the blond hair on his well-tanned legs. She wasn't the first young child to do this, but George was half asleep at the time and thinking about the body of a particularly well-endowed woman he had met the previous evening.

The next thing he knew, he was following the little girl into an alley and was trying to get her to rub his manhood like she had his calf. She screamed. Before he knew it, George was being hauled down to the police station. At his daunting mother's insistence, his father used some of the family property as collateral on a loan so they could post bail for their son, but once released, rather than face an embarrassing trial, George bolted the state. His parents lost the property and soon after were divorced.

Then to get some dough, George accidentally killed a man in his first criminal attempt. It was supposed to be a simple robbery from a rich doctor, but the damned family chauffeur showed up and got himself in the way of one of George's bullets.

The second man he killed had also been an accident, but he did kill him and most likely would have been convicted if he'd stayed around long enough to explain himself. And if he'd stayed around, there was always seven-year-old Jean Lanbert, whose parents would keep him on the run most of his life.

For that second killing, George was simply trying to get away from an irate husband. If the man hadn't been so jealous, he wouldn't have fallen down the staircase during their struggle and broken his neck. The man lay on his back at the bottom of the steps, glassy-eyed, his long neck at an odd angle, flopping back like a chicken.

George had seen chickens with their heads cut off running across the yard for several minutes. This man's body was convulsing so violently that George waited around to see if he would get up and start running. He didn't, and was soon quite still. Disappointed, George continued on his way, leaving the attractive wife at the top of the stairway screaming, a silly thing to do since the house was a half mile from any other.

After that, there was no way back to where he needed to be. Maybe that was the way Verne Miller had felt just before he was strangled with a clothesline and beaten to death with a claw hammer, beaten so badly his nude body found in a ditch near Detroit could only be identified by his fingerprints.

George hoped that didn't happen to him. He was so handsome he wanted people to walk by his casket and say, "Doesn't George look handsome?"

George was always exceptional at anything he did, but it was still a limited life. He had never lost his eye for the young girls. Therefore, when he spotted one who was dumping her still-alive infant in a garbage can, he saw no reason not to abuse her. He knocked her on the head and threw her in the trunk of his car. Then he went back and carried the baby to a nearby house, set it on the doorstep, and hammered on the door. It felt satisfying to know he had saved the poor baby's life and wished he could be recognized for his charitable action.

When he got the young girl home, he took her just as she was waking up, then tied her up in case he got horny later. When she tried to scream and moan, he grabbed a dirty sock from his laundry and stuffed it in her mouth, then wrapped some tape around her head to hold it in place.

Since he already had his clothes off, George went to bed. The idea of his clothes catching fire was so horrible that he removed them down to his underpants every night when he slept just in case the house caught fire.

He remembered the girl as soon as he awoke. He thought about her young body as he sat in his robe and drank his coffee. When he had worked himself up enough, he went to the closet where he had locked her. She wasn't moving. She had gagged to death on the sock. Annoyed, he took her again anyway before cold and stiffness got any worse, then when darkness arrived the next night, carried her body down to the beach and set it afloat.

March 21, 1934

George was feeling pretty satisfied with himself later that evening as he walked outside The Minerva Café in the mob-controlled Chicago suburb of Cicero. He could tell the waitress had been flirting with him. He was still incredibly handsome, and his blond hair attracted the ladies as well as it had when he was a star football player at the University of Illinois. If the waitress had been ten years younger, he might have considered following her home. There was just something about girls who had not developed pubic hair that he just couldn't resist.

As he came out of the café, a young woman approached him. Despite her long overcoat, George could see she was young enough and pretty enough to fit his needs. She looked at him, and he smiled. She didn't smile back but instead put her hands beneath her overcoat.

George had a habit of patting the holstered gun he had in his shoulder harness. It was a gesture that reassured him but, in this case, also signaled that he was packing.

The shotgun that emerged from the young girl's coat was so big, George didn't understand how she had concealed it so easily. But hadn't he concealed his own beloved Twelve Iron shotgun on that fateful Valentine's Day?

He saw her cock both barrels and aim them at his handsome face.

George Goetz's body had to be identified by fingerprints.

A few days later, in another part of town, Irene Goetz was combing her hair and wondering if another cup of coffee might wake her up when the telephone rang. She answered the phone only to be so thunderstruck by the coroner coldly telling her that her husband was dead, she almost dropped her coffee cup. She liked her coffee cup more than her husband, so she just set it on the nightstand.

When she had woken that morning, she was indeed not far from the point of serious sorrow. She'd thought it was about time she did just die, but now that George was gone, she didn't need a second cup of coffee but did desperately need a cigarette, which she quickly lit as she began pacing and reflecting on their love life, or whatever it was.

She'd put off doing the wild thing with George for as long as she could get away with it. It was tiresome to have to shave her twat every time before they coupled. Still, she did her wifely duties when summoned, always with lustful moans and movements that she knew he desired, but after that she usually retired to her kitchen to smoke and drink until summoned again.

All she could think about just then was a time when she was young and had not known failure yet. Approaching middle-aged now and a little overweight, not too many compliments came her way anymore. She knew it was a little bit of a sad comment on her life that after losing one gangster, all she could think about was the one who got away. So, Irene Goetz immediately packed her expensive coupe with her favorite outfits and jewelry and drove straight to Florida, where she hoped Fred Barker was still hiding. She thought she might just leave it to luck, her future.

38

After her failed suicide attempt, Bonnie's suggestion weighed on Georgette for days. If she could just convince one boy or girl that the gangster life was a horrible way to live, perhaps her own sordid life would have been of some use.

Writing her story since she met Gus was easy. It really didn't seem so long ago she had opened the door to see his shy face looking down at his shoes. Not so long ago, her Gussie was down on his knees proposing to her on one of the good Valentine's Days in their life.

She would, of course, write about the other St. Valentine's Day, the one they both wished had never happened, the one the entire world was still trying to figure out. She would set the record straight once and for all. It was when she got to that point, she hesitated.

Bob and Rose Carey, Ray Nugent, her Gus, and now George Goetz. Four of Capone's original American Boys died horribly, just a few years after they committed the most violent mass murder in the history of the American crime world.

The final journey of the criminal's spirit was inevitable, for some sooner than others, most always sooner for those in Gus's business. To survive past forty years old was rare, past fifty was almost unheard of. Life seemed nothing more than those coming and those going, the spirits of those going casting doubts as to whether there would ever be a peaceful future for those whose lives they affected.

Since that fateful Valentine's Day in '29, the talking pictures seemed to be making most of their money by glorifying gangsters. Several such movies had been made using the stories of Capone and others as an outline, but none captured the horror of what it was really like. It was not as the films portrayed, a man slumping as if stricken with a heart attack, dropping bloodlessly to the floor. Georgette had seen the horror herself, so horrible she wasn't certain she could bring herself to put in sentences what she had witnessed.

After just a week of writing, she was having trouble finishing that part of her story. The violence that was most personal to her was yet to be written. Like the disappearance of Smitty, the simple-minded, loving boy who could not lie and who she had figured out over the years had almost certainly been killed, maybe even by her own husband.

To write about those bad times would mean reliving them, and the motivation to relive them just wasn't there. The only good thing was that if she didn't finish them, no one would care, since she had never let anyone know she was writing her story. She kept the manuscript well hidden at all times, even from Bonnie, who had given her the idea. For if even Bonnie knew and somehow let it slip, it could mean death for anyone associated with the manuscript. The danger to herself and her friends made her dilemma even more vexing.

What would Gus tell her to do?

Then one day she read about the Harry Houdini seance. The Great Houdini escape artist had died on Halloween 1926. Each year his wife held a séance on October thirty-first to see if her husband, the greatest escape artist the world had ever known, could make the most difficult escape in history—death. It was said she and her husband had a secret word no one else knew, and if during the séance he said the word, then she would know it was really him.

Gus had also died in October. She thought back to experiences they had together that only they would know about. Then she picked up her telephone and asked the operator to put her through to Bess Houdini, the widow of the Great Houdini.

August 28, 1934

The six men and women Georgette chose to sit around the large round table with the medium were almost strangers. She didn't want anyone around who might somehow know of the secrets shared by Gus and herself. She desperately needed assurance this séance was going to be legitimate.

The man serving as a medium between this world and the next had been recommended to Georgette by Bess Houdini. He was the same medium who had tried and failed several times to contact Harry Houdini. While those attempts were unsuccessful he did have many other well-documented successes at contacting the spiritual world.

On the table were several items that were personal to Gus including his and Georgette's wedding rings, his cufflinks and tie clip that he loved so much, and even his favorite coffee cup he drank from at breakfast for ten years whenever he was home. Also on the table was a small bell and a megaphone horn such as the ones used by college sports fans.

No one said a word as the medium lit a single candle in the center of the table, turned off the lights, and took his place across from Georgette. He raised his arms to the heavens, then slowly brought them down, palms up. Everyone joined in the circle of hands.

"Oh, thou disembodied spirits," the medium chanted with eyes closed and church minister reverence. "Those of you who have grown old in the mysterious laws of spirit land, we greet thee. Please, now, make yourself known to us, any of you. Please. Manifest yourself in any way possible. Please let your united strength and knowledge aid Gus Winkler in coming through to our world. It is the spirit of Gus Winkler we wish to contact.

"Gus Winkler, are you here? Are you here, Gus Winkler? Please manifest yourself in any way possible. Take from this earnest gathering anyone necessary for you to use. Take any vital thing from us that you may need to come to us tonight, the horn or the bell on this table.

"And Georgette is here, Gus Winkler, your Georgette, who was part of you for those many years, she is pleading in her heart for a sign from you."

The medium quit talking. For several minutes he said nothing. Those in the circle cracked their eyes open and looked between Georgette and the medium. Both seemed to be totally focused on their mission. Then the medium gasped, stiffened, and dropped his head back on his shoulders, eyes rolling slowly upward. The flame mysteriously extinguished from the candle in the center of the table. Only a faint light from the lamps on the street outside cast an eerie glow through the windows. The medium's mouth opened wide but neither his lips nor tongue moved. A moan, low and lonely was heard, like an echo in a canyon.

"Gus," Georgette whispered. Like a freezing wind, a cold passed through her body, one such as she had never known. She smelled Gus, felt his presence. "Gus, if that is really you, tell me something that no other human being could possibly know."

After a long, eerie pause, the feel and smell of electrical burning filled the room. The medium's mouth emitted a strange thin mist that rose rather than fell; upwards toward the ceiling it floated.

"Keep writing," the voice of Gus Winkler said.

Georgette fainted.

***

No one knew Georgette was writing her memoir, which, after the séance, she had given the title *A Voice from the Grave.* Georgette came home from the séance and wrote all that night and through much of the next day. She believed Gus's spirit was guiding her pen. She wrote the story, however, from her point of view, her personal experience, and not from what Gus may have witnessed.

Describing the horror of the killings was not her goal. She feared there may be some readers who would glorify the murders in their sick minds. Instead, she focused on what effect the life of a criminal's wife had on her and would most assuredly have on any other girl who allowed herself to love such a man. She finished her memoir in just a few days.

Finally, the day came. Holding the purse containing the manuscript close inside her overcoat, Georgette Winkler took it to the one lawman her husband had said he trusted, Melvin Purvis.

39

January 8, 1935

Bryan was nervous. Killed in just over a year were some of the most notorious criminals in the underworld—Gus Winkler, Verne Miller, George Goetz, John Dillinger, Pretty Boy Floyd, and Baby Face Nelson.

What the hell was he doing? He and Veva had enough money now to live out their life comfortably in California. There was really no need to do one last job. But here he was still hanging out with Doc Barker and a newbie named Russell Gibson at a hideaway apartment in Chicago.

"I don't like the way Doc looks at me," Bryan whispered to Veva the third night as they lay in bed. He whispered because the walls were thin and Doc slept in the next room.

"He looks at you the way most of your friends look at me." Veva giggled.

"What does that mean?"

"He was in prison for ten years, wasn't he?" Veva attempted to discretely explain. "A young man can change his fancies when all he has is other men to look at."

"You mean—" Bryan was interrupted by the distant sound of a window breaking. He jumped out of bed and rushed to the window. "Feds!" Bryan whispered. He recognized the agents by their conservative clothing. Every gangster he knew would dress better.

Bryan raced out the door and into Doc Barker's bedroom, where he found him so heavily intoxicated, he couldn't be awakened. Veva was suddenly at his side. "Bryan, I think they fired tear gas into the apartment next to us. Maybe they're after someone else."

He hurried to the living room to find Russell Gibson and his wife, Clara, peeping through the curtain. Just then three police cars came barreling up and blockaded the drive by parking sideways. "Okay, you hoodlums!" a voice on a megaphone said. "Give yourselves up or we open fire."

"We're with the Federal Bureau of Investigation, you idiots!" one of the civilian-dressed agents shouted the Bureau's new name from behind a tree. "This is a raid to get Doc Barker and his gang."

The FBI had fired their tear gas into the wrong apartment, but Bryan wasn't about to correct them. Grabbing up a flower vase on the table, he pulled the roses out and tossed them aside, then raced into Doc's room, where he flung the water onto his face. Doc came up sputtering.

"We're surrounded, Doc!" Bryan told him in a louder voice than he intended.

Doc didn't hesitate. He leaped out of bed in his underwear, grabbed up his Tommy gun, staggered into the living room, and opened fire even before he was close to the window.

"I guess they know which apartment we are in now," Bryan shouted to Russell, who he immediately saw was no longer standing next to him. Russell was donning a bulletproof vest. He raced into Doc's bedroom and worked to pry the window open.

Outside the bedroom, FBI agent James White saw the shades pulled back on a window and a man opening it. White wasn't much good with the bone-handled Colt he carried, but was a deadly shot with a thirty-ought-six rifle. He lifted the rifle to his shoulder.

Russell was halfway out the window when a bullet to his upper torso made his legs do a mule kick behind him. The vest didn't prove to be effective against White's high-powered rifle.

Bryan and Veva grabbed Russell's wife before she could rush into the bedroom. They pulled her down to the floor just as the walls were riddled with bullets.

"Crawl to the door," Bryan screamed to the two women. With bullets buzzing inches above their heads, they got to the door just as Doc's gun jammed. The firing outside also slowed.

"Don't shoot, G-Men!" Bryan shouted, hoping the agents would be flattered by his use of the nickname. "We're coming out!"

Bryan stood and, with the two petrified wives huddled next to him, opened the door and surrendered.

***

Georgette wished she had not worn her heels when she went to visit Melvin Purvis of the newly named Federal Bureau of Investigation. Though she was not tall herself, the man barely came up to her shoulders. He was, however, a very pleasant-looking man, handsome, suave, and well dressed. Hard to believe he killed Pretty Boy Floyd, led the assault that killed John Dillinger, and had an inconsequential shootout with Baby Face Nelson before his men finally put seventeen bullets in him a few weeks later.

Purvis came around his desk to greet Georgette as if she were an old friend. "So sorry about Gus," the G-man said, shaking her hand, his own small and soft. "He talked about you all the time, and I know he was looking forward to retiring from the syndicate and spending more time with you."

"Yes, he almost made it, didn't he?" Georgette lamented.

Purvis offered a chair and then sat next to her instead of behind his desk. "Mrs. Winkler, I want to be completely honest with you." His voice was low. "I'm not in very good graces with Director Hoover and am not certain I will be in the Bureau much longer."

"Is there anyone you can trust with this information if you leave?" Georgette clutched her handbag closer.

"Yes, but then their own jobs would be in danger. J. Edgar Hoover is a very vindictive man when crossed."

"But," Georgette said, beginning to panic a little. "You've just been named among the ten most outstanding personalities in the world by *Literary Digest.*"

"And for that accomplishment, Hoover recently stripped me of my command of the Chicago office. I'm fed up with the Bureau. The truth is, I'm afraid he will never allow your manuscript to be published, or, if he can, even be seen by the public."

"But why?"

"Because Hoover doesn't want to admit there is organized crime in America. It makes him look better if he just keeps putting away individual operators like Floyd, Nelson, and Dillinger."

"Why won't he go after the mafia?"

"Well—" Purvis laughed. "The rumor is the mob has something on him. Something that would embarrass Hoover so bad he would not only have to leave the Bureau but the country."

"What?" Georgette's mind raced. "He's not a homosexual, is he?"

Purvis got up and walked around to his chair behind the desk.

Georgette saw the subject had to be changed, so she changed it in her interest. Pulling her manuscript from her handbag, she held it up. then slapped it on his desk. "How would Hoover like to know that a nightclub owner in St. Paul invited Gus to come there, claiming that gangsters have police protection, or that, yes, Pretty Boy Floyd was with Verne Miller at the Kansas City Massacre and even got a flesh wound."

"You're going to get yourself killed if you—"

"I am not afraid to die," Georgette interrupted stubbornly. Her face turned red. The lawman showed no interest in even looking at the story she had worked so hard to write. "I can also give you information on Frank Nitti and Lefty Louie Campagna that will put them away for life."

"I'll do what I can, Mrs. Winkler." Purvis' desk was small enough he could lean across it and extend his hand. "Hopefully someone will call you in for an interview."

Georgette ignored the hand and turned toward the door.

"Oh, Mrs. Winkler."

She turned back toward him. He reached into his drawer and extracted a pistol that she immediately recognized as having belonged to Gus. Purvis held it out to her.

"I thought you may want to keep your husband's weapon as a memento," Purvis said.

"Keep it." Georgette's voice was cold. "You may have need to blow your brains out someday."

***

Meanwhile, in another part of Chicago, Bryan Bolton was spilling his guts to the Chicago District Attorney and the two FBI agents in the interrogation room. He held back nothing—the St. Valentine's Day massacre, the Hamm and Bremer kidnappings by the Barker-Karpis Gang—even telling exactly where the gangs' Bensenville safe house was.

He thought maybe it was the latter spill that caused one of the Bureau agents to leave the room. He returned just a few minutes later.

"Director Hoover wants to know where Fred Barker is hiding."

"I don't know for sure. He might be down in Florida."

"Where in Florida?"

"All I can remember about the place—" Bryan knew if he didn't give them something, he was going to be leaned on hard. "It had a big alligator named Old Joe."

40

"When you boys goin' hunting Old Joe again?" Ma Barker asked her son Fred.

"Shut up about that damned Gator Joe, Ma," Fred shouted. "Don't you care that Doc just got nabbed? We need to break him out."

Ma went out onto *her* end of the porch to sulk. How she wished Arthur was here. She couldn't understand why he ran off the way he did. Arthur was the only one close to her age, and she believed it would take someone close to her age to understand how she felt.

She had raised her boys through the good and the bad, and yet nowadays she couldn't recognize her hand in anything they did. Though they had once been a part of her, now they were part of something else, something she had no say in. Yes, they spoiled her with minks and jewelry, as she wished she could have spoiled them during their youth, but back then, there was nothing to spoil them with.

Ma knew what her boys did, how could she not? They were constantly talked about for the crimes they committed on the radio and on the news reels almost every time she went to a picture show. She had never been much at looking at newspapers, but now she avoided them completely.

Her sons were called killers, and that hurt her more than anything else. She could tolerate bank robberies and even the kidnapping of those rich snobs, but her boys promised her they had never murdered anyone. Yes, they had wounded a few, but only in self-defense. Ma looked down at the table and tried to focus on the jigsaw puzzle she had been working on for a week.

On the youthful end of the porch, Irene sulked with a much different feminine dilemma.

"George and I were always loyal to you, Fred," Irene said. "I came all the way down here to be with you."

"To hell with George Goetz," Fred said coldly. "And to hell with you. Alvin, take this bitch with you when you go. I don't ever want to see her again."

The next morning, everyone except Fred and Ma got in the vehicles and left. Ma looked up from her jigsaw puzzle as the cars pulled away. No one had kissed her goodbye or even waved. But then, she was happy to say, they were not miserable, as was she.

***

January 16, 1935

"I think I'd rather run into Alvin Karpis or a Barker than Old Gator Joe," FBI Agent Charlie Winstead whispered as he tried to raise his foot out of the murky swamp without losing his boot. Unlike the other agents who wore fedoras or straw boaters and brogans, being from Texas, Charlie fancied his dirty Stetson hat, a blue serge suit, and cowboy boots.

"That's cowardly talk for the man who killed John Dillinger," Agent Thomas McDade said and chuckled. Thomas, no slouch to shootouts after his car chase battle with Baby Face Nelson three months before, also kept his eyes peeled for gators.

The two men finally made their way out of the wetland, so they stopped to take their footwear off and wring green water from their socks. Through the trees, they could just make out the two-story house with its long screened-in porch that ran the length of the front.

"Why do you suppose Connelley made us dredge through this muck while all the others stayed on high ground?" Charlie asked.

"I find Connelley to be a competent leader," Thomas said. "He don't risk men to unnecessary gunfire. I guess he ain't so particular about gators. Director Hoover, on the other hand, probably could never imagine a G-man being tasty to a mere reptile. You ever meet Hoover?"

"Well, yes I have." Charlie chuckled. "And if Hoover ever calls you in, dress like a dandy, carry a notebook, and write in it furiously every time he opens his mouth. You can throw the notes away afterward, if you like. And flatter him. Everyone at headquarters knows Hoover is an egomaniac, and they all flatter him constantly. If you don't, you'll be noticed."

"Do you think that this is the right house?" Thomas put his socks and shoes back on, cringing at the uncomfortableness of how wet they still were.

"It fits Bryan Bolton's description, plus they found a map of this area in Doc Barker's stuff. I'm guessin' it's the house."

"Looks like we'll know in a minute. Here comes Connelley now."

All his agents now in place, E.J. Connelley stepped out from behind a tree.

"This is the FBI," Connelley shouted. "We have the house completely surrounded. Throw your weapons out and come out with your hands up."

"He's a braver man than me," Charlie said. He aimed his Tommy gun toward one of the front windows.

Agent James White was not feeling brave, even though there were fourteen agents stationed behind trees around the house. He wasn't sure whether to raise his Tommy gun or the thirty ought six that he'd killed Russell Gibson with. They were both propped against the tree beside him. He opted for the gat, and raising it to his shoulder, aimed it at the doorway.

Silence. Connelly, still standing in the open, shouted the surrender instructions again. He gave it sixty seconds, which felt like much longer to James. Then Connelley took his fedora off and waved it. Several agents popped out from behind trees and shot tear gas canisters at the windows. One didn't make it through a window and bounced off, exploding the gas onto the lawn.

No sooner had the other canisters exploded than from inside the house, Tommy gun fire erupted through the glass of a window, spraying bullets toward Connelley. While other agents opened up with their weapons toward the house, James White raced from the protection of the trees toward Connelley, firing his gat at the window as he ran. He didn't stop shooting until he had Connelley standing safely behind the tree.

Not knowing how many gang members were in the house, all fourteen agents continued firing through every window in the house. Occasional gunfire came from inside, first from one downstairs window, then another.

"How many you think are in there?" Charlie shouted to Thomas when they both leaned against a tree to reload.

"At least two, I think," Thomas said. "I'm pretty sure I saw gunfire coming from a window upstairs and downstairs at the same time."

Inside the house, Ma Barker crawled on the floor toward the staircase. Bullets struck the walls, destroying pictures, lamps, and anything else they happened upon, raining down plaster and glass on top of her. She screamed and shouted for Fred to help her, but he couldn't hear her. With a rag over his mouth to dimmish the gas he raced up the stairs to the second floor. She could hardly blame him since she could barely hear her own cries above the explosions nor see through the tears caused by the gas bombs. The stairwell formed an L, and when a brief pause came, she stood and, crouching as low as she could, scampered on all fours up the steps.

Fred sat in a wooden chair as he fired his Tommy gun out an upstairs window, his white shirt covered with blood stains. The bed to his right was also bloody and littered with debris. Another Tommy gun was on the floor near her as well as a revolver.

She sat on the floor just inside the doorway and screamed at her son to stop.

"Shut up, old woman!" he shouted back at her. "You want to be of help, then reload those ammunition drums."

This was what her boys had become. And what had she done to stop it, to protect them from themselves? She had been trying to live two lives, that of a loving mother and that of a wealthy matriarch of gangsters. If she could only do it over again, to live a life of respect and grace. She started mumbling the Lord's Prayer. She said it through twice, then she reached out to the handgun.

***

Outside, Charlie's guns had become so hot from firing, he stood up behind the tree and peed on the barrels to cool them down. His ears rang despite the plugs he'd put in them. It was during this moment he saw people about one hundred yards away approaching the property. They carried lawn chairs and were setting them up behind trees. Their appearance was so surreal Charlie wondered if he had been shot and died. Maybe a hundred years had passed since his demise and the property was now a picnic area. Then he saw that Thomas must also be dead, because he was still shooting at the house.

"How long you figure we been in this gunfight?" he shouted to Thomas.

Thomas laid his weapon down and sat with his back to his tree. He pulled a railroad watch from his pocket, wiped the carbide from his eyes, and inspected it. "Been two or three hours, I'd say."

"Have you seen any gunfire comin' from inside the house?" Charlie asked.

"I've just been firin' at curtains whenever they move." A faint breeze caused the brim of his hat to wave a little.

Charlie buttoned his pants back up and walked right out in the open toward the trees where Connelley was himself taking a break.

"Chief," Charlie said, still standing in open view of the house. "You think maybe there's a little overkill happenin' here?"

Connelley glanced around. "I was kind of considerin' that myself. Why don't you walk on in there and see if the Barkers would like to take a sandwich break with us?"

The gunfire had slowed to only an occasional pop after the other agents saw Charlie gadding about. Some of the spectators began walking toward the agents.

"Sir, I'm sorry to bother you when you're busy," a colored man said when he was close enough. He was hunched over a little, not ducking, but rather displaying the customary southern Black man's expected respect for Whites. "My name's Willie Woodberry. If you go into the house and anyone is still alive, my wife asked if you'd ask them for last month's money for the work we did on the property. We surely do need it."

"You know the people who live here?" Connelley asked.

"Well, no, I don't personally, but my wife does some."

Connelley took off his bulletproof vest and handed it to Willie. "Why don't you go on in there and ask them yourself? We'll pay you to do it." He took out his wallet and handed over several big bills.

Willie's eyes lit up. It was more money than he and his wife could make in a year. The vest was tight around his middle, but Willie got it on. He walked slowly up toward the house, looking back over his shoulder at the agents after every few steps.

"H-h-hello, in there!" Willie said with as much volume as he could muster. With no answer, he continued up the porch and through the bullet-ridden entrance. "Hello, anybody home?" A few moments later his hand waved from an upstairs window, and then his face appeared.

"They're both up here, and they're both dead," Willie shouted through the window. "And you shot somebody's grandma."

41

February 14, 1935

"J. Edgar Hoover described Ma Barker as the most vicious, dangerous, and resourceful criminal brain of the last decade," Veva told Bryan during her visit to him in the Cook County Jail.

"He's just sayin' that so the public won't know his men killed an innocent old lady," Bryan said. "Ma Barker wouldn't know which end of a gun to aim unless it was shown to her on a jigsaw puzzle box. They say she had a single gunshot wound to the head. Probably killed herself, poor old thing."

"Bryan, five years ain't so long." Veva couldn't hold back her tears any longer. "I want you to know I'll wait for you."

"Don't, Veva. You go on with your life. You're young and beautiful. Find yourself a nice fella to hook up with. One that ain't a criminal."

Veva saw the guard motioning that her visiting time was up. "I'll write you," she promised. "And I'll be here when you get out."

***

February 15, 1936

Jack McGurn was having a tough winter. The Secret Six had named him one of their Most Wanted Public Enemies and the Capone-Nitti Outfit was shunning him. He had lost his night-clubs, and money was getting tight.

Still, a sportsman at heart, he was young enough to hustle some dough by using his God-given ath-leticism. Between throws at the bowling alley, he reflected on his boxing and his golf careers. He could have been great. Bing Crosby, the famous singer, was one of his golfing buddies.

Three strikes in the third frame made McGurn go into the zone, as he called it. No talking or drinking until he had an open frame. Two-sixty had been his best game, and today might be the day he'd break it.

As he waited for his next throw, Jack thought about the 1933 Western Open Golf Championship at Olympia Fields Country Club. Under an alias, he shot pretty poorly the first day, but was on fire the second day and heading toward making the cut when several cops showed up on the seventh green with a warrant to arrest him.

Remembering the confidence he had that day at the Western Open helped him bring about three more strikes. Jack forced himself not to get jinxed by even thinking that a three-hundred game was possible. He sat down and returned his thoughts to that golf tournament.

"Whose brilliant idea was this?" Jack's wife Louise had protested to the four burly dicks who wanted to handcuff him. She was dressed in a tight little skirt that proved a distraction to several other golfers. "Why don't you let the guy finish the round? He ain't goin' nowhere." Since Jack just shrugged his shoulders and laughed, the cops agreed. He shot birdie on the next two holes and thought he still had a chance.

The memory of that golf match helped elevate his bowling game, and he hit perfectly on the side of the headpin on the next two throws. A perfect game through the eighth frame. One more time, then turkey the tenth frame, and he'd have his first three hundred game.

Again, he sat by himself. Knowing how his golf story would end, he tried to force his mind to any-thing except his last holes in the Western Open. He tried to falsify the memory and imagine he finished the round and made the cut. But he knew he had not.

The constant presence of the cops standing around flirting with Louise had been too great a distraction. He double bogeyed the next three holes, then tossed his clubs into the pond, and turned himself over to the dicks.

Shaking off the memory, Jack lined up his next throw. The bowling ball started off perfectly. Then, for some reason, it didn't break quite right. A seven-ten split.

Jack just stood watching the alley. He couldn't believe it. How could such a great game turn out so bad? He didn't even want to try for the pickup. It seemed his whole life had gone that way since being arrested on the golf course. He had been drummed out of the Outfit by Nitti and his cohorts and lost all his money. How could things get worse?

Then he noticed there was no noise, no balls being thrown. From the corner of his eye, he saw people heading for the exit. He turned. Three men pointed revolvers at him.

"Sorry we missed Valentine's Day, Jack," James Gusenberg said. "But here's a little something for your heart anyway, from my brothers."

The bullets came fast and furious, instantly killing Jack McGurn.

Peter and Frank Gusenburg's brother then dropped a note on Jack's body.

"You've lost your job, you've lost your dough,
Your jewels and cars and handsome houses,
But things could still be worse you know...
At least you haven't lost your trousers!".

1938

Walking the streets of Thayer, Illinois, upon his release from prison was something special to Bryan, like walking through his youth. His brain was unusually tranquil as he strode. It sobered him to see that just by being outside a building where he had once stood, the distant past could so easily be brought back to life in perfect detail. The gazebo where he'd had his first kiss, the pond where he and his friends fished, and the hill they sled down in the winter. Down by the park, he recalled turning a car over on himself once while he was taking Deadman's Curve too fast. That memory was now an exciting adventure instead of the tragedy it had once been.

Strange that his criminal life didn't seem to have been an adventure. Instead, those memories were more like nightmares, as were his days in what was to have been the war to end all wars. Those events now felt like something that had happened to someone else.

All the memories, good and bad, and in the midst of them all, stood Veva, his loving wife, who waited three years for him to earn an early release from prison. Theirs was not the lustful rush into one another's arms as it had once been, but there she was once more, moving steadily down the sidewalk toward him. The car was packed with what little they owned, but he was still young enough and strong enough to make a living as a carpenter. They would drive west until either the car quit or they reached California where, God willing, they would live out the rest of their lives—together.

***

1940

"Why do you want everyone to hate you so much?" Fred Burke's cellmate asked. He was an old con named Clyde who'd outlived three wardens.

"If I can't like myself, then I don't want nobody else to like me either," Fred said from the bunk he'd not gotten out of for several days. A male orderly came in regularly to clean him up and feed him.

"Don't you worry about hell?" Clyde asked.

"I need to burn in hell," Fred replied. "But I haven't punished myself enough in this world, yet."

Fred hung on to life for several more days, but only in contradiction to his wishes. That which he perceived as his *self* wasn't gone. He still breathed the air, and yet he was disappearing from the earth, one sad day at a time. Not a soul cared he was dying.

Clyde only checked to see if Fred was alive when his breaths became short, and only then so he could have them get his body out before it started smelling. That Fred Burke was still alive was wonder enough, but the longer he prevailed, the fewer days Clyde would have to spend tolerating a new and possibly more irritating cellmate.

More and more, things Fred didn't want to remember kept popping into his head. A lifetime of disappointments. A lot of loneliness and want, when sober. His life had contained many frustrations, and he needed something to make him forget them.

Still, there were a few moments, not many, when he didn't see defeat in his visions. Instead, he saw himself as he had been when young, half-naked whores served him martinis.

Following these memories, he wasn't so upset for a while; it was the type of death he was at ease with. It was a moment he'd been waiting for. He would've liked to have died sooner, but his stubborn body wouldn't let him go.

Then, one day, he felt it coming. Even as he sank into the darkness, a warmth spread through his body, and he slept soundlessly without moaning—or, finally, without breathing.

Hearing nothing from his cellmate, Clyde got up and checked the pulse in Fred's neck. The interns had just washed Fred's body that morning. *Maybe I'll wait a day or two before I have them take him away.* Clyde shuffled back to his own bunk to continue reading his magazine.

***

1962

Her memory of her life didn't want to go back further than the day she met Gus.

"What day is it?" Georgette asked.

"It's February 14, 1962," the nurse said. She knew of Georgette Winkler's past. "Were you thinking about the massacre?"

"No. I was thinkin' this was the day Gus proposed to me."

Georgette breathed hoarsely, froth foaming at her mouth. She took her last breath and heard Gus's voice saying, "I've been waiting for you."

Georgette Winkler's memoir "A Voice from the Grave" was kept in the FBI Reading Room in Washington D.C. for fifty years before it was rediscovered.

Dec Barker was shot to death while trying to escape with four other inmates from Alcatraz Prison Island in 1939.

On February 29, 1960, **Melvin Purvis** was in his home cleaning a gun. It had a tracer bullet stuck in the chamber. Assuming he should've known how to dislodge it, the FBI investigating his death declared it a suicide, although the official coroner's report did not label the cause of death as such. The gun that killed him was the one he had taken off Gus Winkler during an arrest and had been ceremoniously awarded to him when he resigned from the service. Purvis was fifty-six years old.

Alvin "Creepy" Karpis spent twenty-five years in prison including at Alcatraz, where he became acquainted with Robert Stroud, known as the Birdman of Alcatraz. In the 1960s, he was moved to McNeil Island Penitentiary in Washington State where he taught a young prisoner there how to play the guitar. The young man's name was Charles Manson, future friend of the Beach Boys and leader of the infamous Manson Family of the Tate-LaBianca murders. Alvin Karpis was released on parole in 1969, at which time he collected much of the money he had stored in banks around the country (plus much interest, of course), then was deported to Canada, wrote two books about his criminal life, and comfortably retired in 1973 to Spain, where he died in 1979.

Bryan and Veva Bolton lived out the rest of their lives in Lakewood, California. Bryan worked as a salesman for the Geary Allgrim Furniture Store. In 1977, he became the last of the American Boys and of the participants in the St. Valentine's Day Massacre to die (complications from chronic tuberculosis).

END

CHRONOLOGY OF EVENTS
Not all found in this novel

1920 1/21 Georgette meets Gus Winkler at her boarding house in St. Louis.

1921 12/? Georgette and Gus married.

1922

?/? Fred and Bob Carey run with Shelton Birger Gangs.

?/? Fred gets first gat #2347 originally purchased by Marion County Sheriff Deputy.

?/? Fred runs with Egan Rats leader William "Dinty" Colbrook.

?/? Egan Rats join Hogan Gang under Edward "Jelly Roll" Hogan.

1923

?/? Fred meets Gus Winkler at Sharpshooter's Club Roadhouse.

3/28 Georgette's birthday party for Gus is ruined by part-crashing gangsters.

4/25 Fred, Bob Carey and Ray Nugent rob $80,000 whiskey.

7/? Gus and others take Wesley Smith for a "one-way ride."

7/3 Fred robs $38,000 from United Railways office. Flees to Detroit.

11/? Charlie Birger meets Carl Shelton when Carl visits him at Herrin Hospital.

?/? Birger & Shelton's turn back Egan Rats' invasion of their territory at peaceful ambush.

12/22 Glenn Young's KKK raids bootleggers in "Little Egypt".

1924

4/10 Fred, Bob, Ray rob Kay's Jewelry Store in New York. Fred caught two days later with jewels.

11/10 Frankie Yale kills Dean O'Banion in Flower Shop handshake.

1925

1/10 Fred ATTEMPTED robbery of gambling den & shootout leaves owner and accomplice dead.

1/24 Johnny Torrio ambushed and nearly dies so quits the Outfit and Capone takes over.

4/2 Fred steals $30,000 from Farmers National Bank Louisville, KY.

6/5 Fred & Gus in car chase battle with cops. Fred shot shoulder.

6/29 Fred throws guns over prison fence so fellow Rats can escape but are recaptured.

?/? Fred begins snatch racket of gangsters while Gus in workhouse.

?/? Georgette waitresses while Gus in workhouse9/? First recorded use of Tommy gun in Chicago by Frank McErlane.

1926

5/18 American Boys rob North St. Louis Trust Company $30,000.

9/20 Hymie Weiss leads ambush of Capone at Hawthorne Hotel in Cicero, Illinois.

10/11 Jack McGurn kills Hymie Weisswith gat outside Holy Name Cathedral.

?/? Jack McGurn kills 3 men in separate Tommy gun murders for killing his stepfather.

10/31 Bob and Ray arrested for $40,000 Jewelry home invasion.

11/? Mike Dipisa's brother killed and Mike blames Johnny Reid.

12/25 Johnny Reid killed by Frankie Wright with shotgun blast to back of head.

1927

3/28 Fred uses gat at Milaflores Apartment Massacreto kill 3 including Frankie Wright.

4/? Bugs Moran becomes Chicago North Side Boss when "Schemer" Druccikilled by police.

5/? Gus, Bob & Ray kidnap Mert Wertheimer. Capone asks for sit down meeting.

5/20 Gus, Bob & Ray meet Al Capone. Become his American Boys.

7/21 Fred in drive by shooting of Purples at Chicago's Exchange.

?/? Jack McGurn survives ambush by Frank & Pete Gusenburg.

8/1 Fred and Gus invited to peace meeting w/ Abe Bernstein. Sent Ray Shockler who survives ambush.

9/22 American Boys help Cuckoos kill 3 Green One Gangsters at St Louis Submarine Bar.

11/? Jack McGurn cuts comedian singer Joe E. Lewis' throat and tongue.

12/? Bryan Bolton part of cheating Capone out of bootleg liquor.

?/? Fred has $27,000 price on his head in Detroit so teams with Gus teams in Chicago.

1928

4/10 Capone's Pineapple Primary - pineapple bombs tossed speakeasies, offices and homes.

4/16 American Boys American Express Company robbery of 2 million. George Goetz kills officer.

?/? Fred Burke and Jack McGurn fist fight on golf course7/1 Gus, Fred, George kill Frankie Yale w/ T-guns in Brooklyn.

9/7 Capone's friend Tony Lombardo killed by Aiello/Moran men.

1929

1/6 Capone's friend Pasqualino Lolordo gunned down by Joe Aiello, Frank & Pete Gusenberg.

1/13 Bugs Moran winged by assassination attempt.

2/14 American Boys commit St. Valentine's Day Massacre.

2/22 Bryan Bolton and Tony Capezio injured when Cadillac cruiser explodes.

3/27 Capone legal problems begin and Frank Nitti takes charge of the Outfit.

8/8 Capone in Pennsylvania prison until March 1930.10/18 Gus and Fred steal $93,000 from bank in Peru, Indiana.

12/14 Fred kills Patrolman Charles Skelly in St. Joseph, Michigan.

11/? Fred & George rob $352,000 from bank in Jefferson, Wisconsin.

1930

3/? Ray Nugent arrested for drunk driving with Ralph Capone in car.

5/? Ray goes missing. Fed to alligator by Ralph Capone???

5/31 Verne Miller's friend Red McGlaglin killed by Capone men.

6/1 Verne kills 3 Capone men in revenge for his friend's murder at Fox Lake, IL.

6/17 Fred marries 17-year-old Bonnie Porter.

7/? Fred kills Thomas Bonner for wanting to turn him in, helped by George Goetz.

9/13 Gus and Fred rob $18,000 in New Jersey.

9/17 Gus framed for stealing $2,800,000 in Lincoln Nebraska.

10/? Joe AielloTommy gunned to death with 59 bullets.

12/17 Gus steals $5,000 from bank in Plano, Illinois.

?/? Gus and Fred get plastic surgery in Berwyn, Illinois.

1931

3/? Ness Eliot Ness's Untouchables begin raids on stills and breweries.

3/26 Fred captured by Joe Hunsaker and copsin Green City, Missouri.

3/28 Fred extradited to Michigan because Chicago afraid he would expose the politicians.

4/? Anton Cermak elected Mayor of Chicago.

4/18 Secret Six movie released based on the real secret vigilante organization.

8/5 Gus in car crash looses left eye near St. Joseph, Michigan.

8/17 Ray Nugent killed. Fed to alligators.

8/31 Georgettemeets with Al Caponein Lexington Hotel, Chicago.

9/15 Gus extradited to Lincoln Nebraska for trial on bank robbery.

10/24 Capone convicted of tax evasion?/? Earl Shelton arrested because he couldn't swim to escape.

1932

4/19 Gus gets Mayer Lansky and Lucky Luciano arrested.

5/1 Bob Carey suspected of kidnapping Charles Lindbergh's 22-month-old child.

7/29 Bob Carey dies with Rose in "apparent" murder-suicide Bug's Moran takes credit.

12/16 Barker-Karpis bank robbery. Fred kills good Samaritan and 2 officers.

12/19 Officer Harry Lang wounds Frank Nitti then shoots his own hand. Nitti blames Newberry & Mayor Cernak.

12/31 Gus and Georgette toasts of loyalty with Ted Newberry.

1933

1/7 Ted Newberry murdered by Nitti's men for assassination attempt.

2/? Frank Nitti acquitted of attempted murder of Harry Lang. Lang fired in disgrace.

2/15 Chicago Mayor Andrew Cernak killed standing next to FDR by Nitti gang.

3/28 Gus's 33rd Birthday Partyat Ches Paree Nightclub.

4/1 Gus arrested on street for possessing gun. Probably a frame up.

5/22 John Dillinger paroled from prison goes on robbery and killing spree.

5/27 Chicago World Fair opens with booze by Winkler and soda by Ralph Capone.

6/15 Bryan and George join Barker-Karpis kidnapping of William Hamm $100,000.

6/17 Vern Miller in Kansas City Massacre with maybe Pretty Boy Floyd.

8/30 Bryan, George & Barker-Karpis gang $33,000 robbery, kill officer & shoot up St. Paul.

9/22 Bryan & Barker-Karpis rob Chicago bank. Officer dies.

9/26 George Machine Gun Kelly captured on info from Gus Winkler.

10/9 Gus murdered by George Goetz and Tony Capezio. Buried in St. Louis.

10/? Georgette's home robbed during funeral.

10/22 Georgette attempts suicide by gas stove. Saved by Fred's wife, Bonnie. 10/26 Wabasha Street Caves Opens in St. Paul, Minnesota.

10/26 Georgette moves into hiding in northern Indiana.

11/1 Verne Miller shoots his way out of girlfriend Vi's apartment in Chicago.

11/29 Verne Miller tortured by clothesline strangling and claw hammer. Found in ditch outside Detroit.

1934

1/17 Bryan, George & Barker-Karpis Gang kidnap Edward Bremmer $200,000.

1/25 John Dillinger captured in Tuscon, Arizona.

3/3 Dillinger escapes prison using wooden gun.

3/? Dillinger shoots his way out of girlfriend Evelyn Frechette's St. Paul apartment.

3/21-22 George Goetzkilled in Cicero by shotgun to face.

4/9 Dillinger girlfriend, Billie Frechette captured.

4/22 Dillinger & Baby Face Nelson escape BOI raid at Little Bohemia Lodge in St. Paul.

7/22 John Dillinger killed in Chicago.

8/28 GeorgetteSéance & Gus tells her to keep writing her memoir.

10/22 Pretty Boy Floydkilled by Melvin Purvis?

10/31 World Fair ends second run that started in May.

11/27 Baby Face Nelson kills two agents then killed by Agent McCade in Barrington, Illinois.

1935

?/? Bureau of Investigation (BOI) becomes Federal Bureau of Investigation (FBI).

1/8 Bryan captured. Gives FBI hints to Barker hideout in Florida.

1/16 FBI kills Fred and Ma Barker in shootout in Florida.

11/7 Alvin Karpis in on last robbery of a train $75.000 in Garretsville, Ohio.

?/? Melvin Purvis resigns from FBI because Hoover jealous.

1936

2/15 Jack McGurn murdered in bowling alley.

5/1 Alvin Karpis captured by FBI near New Orleans. J. Edgar Hoover takes credit.

1939

1/13 Dock Barker shot to death attempting Alcatraz escape.

1940

7/10 Fred dies of heart attack while in prison cell sleeping.

1943

3/19 Frank Nitti commits suicide.

1947

1/25 Al Capone dies from complications with syphilis.

1952

Gator Joekilled by hunter Vic Skidmore. His foot kept on display.

1954

7/18 Machine Gun Kelly dies in Leavenworth Prison of heart attack.

1960

2/29 Melvin Purvis dies from Gus's gun---accidental or suicide?

1961

Georgette's 2nd husband Walter Marsh dies.

1962

2/14 Georgette dies in Indianapolis.

1962

Alvin Karpis teaches guitar to Charlie Manson while in prison.

1977

Bryan Bolton dies of tuberculosis in California.

ABOUT THE AUTHOR

After retiring from a career as an educator, Kevin Corley turned to his love of writing as a way to retell the stories he had shared with history students in his classroom. After Tim Sheard of Hardball Press published his first novels that tell of the dark, dirty and dangerous history of central Illinois coal mining, Corley authored three more fact-based novels on the 1920s southern Illinois bootlegging gangs of Charlie Birger and Carl Shelton.

Corley retired to his hometown in Shelbyville, Illinois, in 2017. E-mail him at sixteentons@yahoo.com

Inspiration
for Writers, Inc.

For all your writing and editing needs

<table>
<tr>
<td valign="top">

WE PROVIDE:
Editing
Critiquing
Ghostwriting
Layout and Design
Typesetting
Ebook Design
Coaching
Consulting
Cover Design
Workshops

</td>
<td valign="top">

MISSION STATEMENT:

At Inspiration for Writers, Inc., our mission is to assist writers of all skill levels in achieving their writing and publishing goals. We accomplish this by teaching the craft of writing, by identifying issues that may prevent publication, by encouraging writers to bring their writing to the next level, and by supporting writers throughout the process. We believe in treating our clients with integrity and compassion.

</td>
</tr>
</table>

www.InspirationForWriters.com

IFWeditors@gmail.com

SPECIAL OFFERS:
FREE SAMPLE EDIT: Visit our website today to submit your manuscript for a complimentary edit.
FREE CONSULTATION: Email IFWeditors@gmail.com to schedule a personal consultation about your writing or publishing questions.
NOTE: Offers limited to one per person and valid only for manuscripts over 20,000 words.

Franklin County Historic Jail Museum

Styled in "Georgian Revival" and listed on the National Register as a rare surviving design of renowned architect Joseph W. Royer, the 1905 Franklin County Jail would most likely not have been preserved, if not for its historical significance as the site where the notorious gangster Charlie Birger dropped into history in 1928 as the last public hanging in Illinois.

In addition to having a spectacular collection of related weapons and artifacts relating to the Southern Illinois gang era, the museum explores the rich historical inventory of Franklin County Illinois. Displays feature Benton's Civil War Major General John A. Logan, Benton's historic 1963 "before he was fab" visit by Beatle George Harrison, as well as tributes to Benton native's actor John Malkovich and NBA basketball star Doug Collins. The museum is located at 209 West Main Street Benton, Illinois with hours Tuesday-Saturday 10:00am until 3:00pm. Call 618 435 5777 or visit our website at Historicjail.com